MW00941413

THE LUCKIEST GIRLS

A NOVEL BY

NATHALIE VAN WALSUM FUSON

Copyright © 2019 by Nathalie van Walsum Fuson

All rights reserved.

ISBN-13: 978-1-7337-173-0-4

The Luckiest Girls is a work of fiction. Names, characters, businesses, places, events and incidents are either the products of the author's imagination or used in a fictitious manner. Any resemblance to actual persons, living or dead, or actual events is purely coincidental.

No part of this book may be reproduced in any form or by any electronic or mechanical means, including information storage and retrieval systems, without written permission from the author, except for the use of brief quotations in a book review.

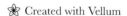 Created with Vellum

For Sasha and Katia

ACKNOWLEDGMENTS

Special thanks to my fellow writers and beta readers, especially Natasha Boyd, for her astute feedback and invaluable advice about everything to do with publishing, and Mimi Thompson, for accompanying me to writing conferences and joining me for long writing sessions at our favorite coffee shops. Many thanks to Laura Bonner of WME for her enthusiastic support and for guiding me through multiple rewrites of the manuscript. My thanks also to Sarah Hall, who was there with me in the beginning when I was one of the Luckiest Girls, for her positivity and encouragement. My thanks to the many brilliant and talented photographers, models, designers and artists whom I had the great fortune of meeting and working with when I modeled in my teens and twenties, all of whom in some way have provided me with material for this book. Many thanks to the extremely talented Micaela Alcaido for her beautiful cover design. (You can see more of her stunning work on her website at https://www.micaelaalcaino.com.) Most of all, my deepest thanks to my family: to my parents for their unwavering encouragement, to my husband, Brad, for standing by me through all-night writing benders and bouts of despair as I waited for replies from publishers, and especially to my most honest and insightful critics, my wonderful daughters Sasha and Katia.

1

JANE

I've read the *Vanity Fair* article about Gigi Towers so many times that the pages of my decade-old copy have come loose at the spine. It describes how Gigi made the Towers Agency the most famous modeling agency in the world, and how, of the thousands of girls who apply to join the agency every year, less than one percent make the cut. Of these, Gigi selects a handful of girls — the very luckiest — to live in her house as she grooms them for stardom. The article calls Gigi "the young models' fairy godmother," and it tells how she just *loves* these girls that she takes under her wings so much, they're like her babies or something and she would do *anything* for them. That's the best part of the article, the absolute punch-line, because there is only one teenage girl who can claim her as a grandmother and whom she should have some personal interest in, and that's me. And Gigi is more interested in her cat than she is in me. But then her cat is actually pretty.

Making a Graceful Entrance
   Do not rush into an event but enter gracefully, carrying yourself with poise and confidence. Smile, and introduce yourself with the firm knowledge that, no matter where you are, you have the right to be there and you are exactly where you belong. — Living a Model Life: Beauty and Style Tips from Gigi Towers by Gigi Towers.

It's pouring with icy rain when the taxi cab drops me in front of the brownstone house in Greenwich Village, and by the time I drag my suitcase up the front steps I'm sopping wet, my hair plastered across my face. I ring the doorbell several times before a tall and totally stunning blonde opens it. She stares at me with open-mouthed bewilderment, blinks her saucer-like blue eyes and says, "I think you're at the wrong place. This is Gigi Towers' house."

"I know," I reply, shivering.

She looks at my suitcase in disbelief. "Are you one of Gigi's girls?"

"Yup. I'm Jane." She's obviously not going to invite me in so I haul my suitcase into the foyer, no help from her.

"Campbell, who's that?" A pair of long legs descend the stairs, topped by a small-waisted torso and an exquisite face under a curtain of silky straight jet-black hair.

"This is Jane. She's one of the new models."

There's a short pause. "Are you sure about that?" the other girl whispers to Campbell out of the side of her mouth.

"That's what she said," Campbell hisses back.

"No, I didn't," I interject. "I said I was one of Gigi's girls. I am. I'm her granddaughter."

I can read their little minds: How did Gigi produce that? Then the second girl laughs and extends her hand. "Hi, Jane.

I'm Ling Wei. Please excuse Campbell, she's an idiot, it's very sad."

I'm not sure if Ling's joking or not. Campbell just keeps smiling, so maybe Ling's right. I wriggle out of my jacket and shake rainwater from my hair like a shaggy dog, and the girls take a step back.

"Gigi said you wouldn't be here until next week, though. Sorry about your dad," Ling adds, wiping water droplets from her shirt.

"What about her dad?" Campbell asks.

Ling rolls her eyes and gives Campbell an exasperated look.

"You know, Steven Archer? The artist who was married to Gigi's daughter? He DIED, Campbell. Remember when Gigi went to the funeral in Colorado? It was even in *The New York Times*. Like you ever read *The New York Times*."

"Oh, yeah, he was in a helicopter accident. It crashed into the side of a mountain, right?" Campbell catches my eye. "Oh…sorry. Welp, I'm late. Hey, did you let your car go? Damn. Now I have to call one."

It takes me a second to find my voice.

"Maybe you know where I'm supposed to take my suitcase," I say to Ling, who seems like the smarter one of the pair.

"I don't know. I guess the single room on the third floor," Ling shrugs. "Margo would know. She's the housekeeper but she's out. Campbell and Maya are in the third floor double, and Brigitte and Isabel and I are on the fourth floor."

I proceed to drag my bag upstairs. I was hoping one of them would give me a hand but I wouldn't want them to break a nail or something. Although Campbell does offer some helpful advice in the form of "Be careful not to scuff the walls or Gigi will kill you."

On the third floor there's a small room to the left, decorated in white and pale blue. I kick off my wet boots and pull some dry clothes out of my suitcase. But right after I've changed into a pair of jeans and a sweatshirt I hear the front door slam all the way downstairs and a very agitated voice rising from the stairwell. Stomp stomp stomp, up the stairs come heavy footsteps.

"*Ah mon Dieu!*" shrieks a stocky middle-aged woman whom I assume is Margo, and who stands in the doorway staring at me with, I kid you not, terror, clutching her chest. "You are TOO EARLY! It is not possible!"

Of course it's possible because here I am but I am not about to argue with this woman who is now clapping her hands at my suitcase like it's a misbehaving dog or something.

"*Non*. Do not unpack. This room is for Sophia Thompson," she snaps.

Even I know who Sophia Thompson is. She's on the cover of this month's *Seventeen Magazine* with a story about her career's meteoric rise. I hate that expression, "meteoric rise." Meteors fall. Everybody knows that.

As I shove things back into my suitcase she starts jabbing at her cell phone. "Oh, what to tell Gigi?" She turns away, speaking in rapid French, then silence as she listens. "*Oui*, one moment," she says, and thrusts the phone toward me.

"Hello?" I say.

"You are a week early," says a cold, clearly pissed-off voice. "The house is full, Sophia is arriving on Friday, and Isabel doesn't leave until next week. I don't know why you aren't in Denver where you're supposed to be, but as it turns out Brigitte just got a booking in Miami so there's a bed available. We'll put you there for now."

It takes me a full minute to realize who I'm speaking with.

"Is this Gigi?"

"Of course this is Gigi. I wasn't expecting you until next week or I would have sent a car for you at the airport."

A car. How thoughtful. I thought a living breathing grandmother meeting me at the airport would have been nice, but now I realize maybe not.

"Oh, hey, Gigi, it's so nice to hear your voice," I say, giving myself huge props for keeping my sarcasm in check. "I've really been looking forward to this. The last time was a little uncomfortable, what with the funeral and all…"

"I don't have time for this, Jane. Three of my models are double-booked, two of my bookers have the flu, I'm leaving for Los Angeles tomorrow night, and New York Fashion Week is right around the corner. You couldn't have arrived at a worse time. I thought you were staying with your father's girlfriend until next week."

Gigi doesn't even refer to Dad's girlfriend by name, which is Melissa. Melissa is a dancer. Actually, she's a waitress who teaches belly-dancing on the side. She and I were never close, but we tolerated each other for Dad's sake. I think we resented each other because we always competed for Dad's attention. Well, we both lost that battle. Dad only loved one thing in the world, and that was painting. He painted obsessively, gripped by painting binges that lasted for days from which he emerged so physically and emotionally drained that he slept like the dead afterward, leaving me and Melissa to tiptoe around each other like a pair of territorial cats. After the funeral, when I overheard Melissa on the phone saying that she couldn't wait till I was gone so she could "get on with healing her life," I decided to split. I didn't warn Gigi that I was coming earlier because I was terrified that she would tell me not to, so I changed my ticket myself and got on the next plane to New York. I desperately want to tell Gigi all these things, but when the realization hits me that I'm speaking with my only living relative left in the world, a huge lump forms in my throat and I don't trust myself to answer without my voice breaking. I hand the phone back to Margo.

"*Oui, oui,* hokay," says Margo. She gets off the phone. "The fourth floor," she says, pointing to the stairs. She tries to help me with my suitcase, but I block her with my body and keep my back to her. I am not going to let these bitches see me cry.

I stash my suitcase in a corner of the small single bedroom decorated with yellow chintz curtains and matching bedspread, while navigating around Brigitte, this six-foot-tall blonde Viking who just emerged from the shower and stands totally naked rummaging through the closet and moaning that she doesn't know what to pack for Miami since she only has winter clothes.

"All you need is a toothbrush," Ling says. "You won't be dressed half the time anyway."

No kidding. Brigitte walks around the fourth floor hall naked, she brushes her teeth naked, and when I try to put my clothes in one of the drawers she stands naked, one hand propped on the dresser, blocking me.

"Are you looking at my boobs?" she asks me. Her breasts are at my eye level so it's a bit hard not to look at them, especially because the view anywhere else is no less awkward.

"Do you want me to?" I answer.

"Aren't they nice? Do you want to touch them?"

"Not at all, thank you."

"GOD, Brigitte," yells Isabel, a dark-haired Brazilian girl with bottle-green eyes. "SHUT UP about your damn BOOBS already!"

"Seriously," adds Ling from Isabel's room. "Nobody cares! Ignore her, Jane."

Brigitte smiles at me and moves aside. I roll my eyes to show her I'm not impressed. She flops naked on her bed, which is now technically my bed. I take my toiletries to the bathroom where I root through the cabinet, pushing aside a mountain of beauty products to find a small corner for my own toothbrush and zit cream. Then I peek into the double room where Ling and Isabel are. Like my room, the decor is feminine and luxurious while at the same time eerily impersonal, kind of like the inside of a dollhouse. The walls are apple-green and the curtains and bedspreads have a green-and-pink floral motif, and the rug in the center of the room is pink. Ling and Isabel lie on their stomachs on the floor, watching videos on a laptop.

Brigitte, finally dressed, is ready to leave for the airport.

"I'll move my clothes out myself when I get back," she says, touching up her lipstick in the hallway mirror. "Don't touch my stuff." She punctuates by capping the tube, then throws it into her bag. With a little wave she flounces down the stairs.

Brigitte is kind of terrifying, but I'm not about to let some psycho model intimidate me, and I don't want to live out of a suitcase so I remove all her clothes from the dresser, stack them on the floor of the closet and unpack my things. Not that I brought very much. Almost everything from Dad's house, including most of my clothes and books, is in storage in Denver.

I NEVER GAVE much thought to my looks, in the same way that I never gave much thought to the fact that I don't play the zydeco or speak Vietnamese. But in the couple of hours since I've been here I feel like one of those little plastic troll dolls in a display case full of Barbie dolls. If I ever make it past 5'2" that would be nice, but I read somewhere that by the time girls are fifteen they've reached their full height so I'm not counting on it. I don't have a curve to speak of and last summer I cut my hair really short, which I regretted after about a week so now I'm trying to grow it out and it's at some weird in-between stage where it sticks out all over my head. It's the color of wet sand or tree bark, neither brown nor blond nor beige. In sixth grade a boy told me I look like E.T. so I guess that's what I look like: E.T. with hair the color of nothing.

After I've unpacked I find Isabel, Ling and Campbell (back from her appointment) in the TV room on the third floor, looking like the mermaids in an illustration from a vintage edition of Peter Pan I once owned. I wonder how much they know about my relationship with Gigi. I don't know if they realize that I've only seen Gigi a handful of times in my life, and that Gigi had no contact with my dad after the car accident that killed my mom when I was four. I don't know if they're aware that Gigi and my mom weren't even speaking by then, a rift that dated back to Mom getting pregnant by an art school punk and then dropping out of Barnard College, and probably a lot earlier. I *do* know that they have no idea that I've saved every article about Gigi ever written, that I've seen every interview she's ever given, that I've bought and read all her books. They have no idea that I've gazed at photographs of Gigi with her perfect girls lounging at her feet and wished them all gone, myself in their place, with Gigi at my side, literally and figuratively. But from the reception I'm getting from the girls, it looks like Gigi hasn't talked about me at all.

Campbell sits on the sofa with her legs tucked under her, stroking Gigi's white Persian cat, Dovima, who glares at me through half-closed green eyes. "Make sure you keep your room and the bathroom super clean, because sometimes Gigi checks," Campbell advises me. "And Margo reports back to Gigi about everything she sees and hears so watch your step when she's around."

"And stay out of the kitchen when Betty's there," Isabel adds, lying in a yoga pose with her legs straight up against the wall. "She's the cook, and she doesn't like any of us."

Just then Maya arrives from a photoshoot, in full makeup, looking like an extragalactic princess. She walks like a dancer, and her luminescent makeup makes her brown skin shine like bronze. I don't think I've ever seen anyone so striking up close in my life. Maya goes upstairs to shower, and when she comes back twenty minutes later, her face clean and her hair damp and curly, she looks so young and natural that it takes me a moment to realize she's the same person. As she sits on the floor and massages lotion into her hands and feet she tells us about her shoot.

"So they had this security guy there to guard the jewelry because we were shooting these beautiful diamonds from Bulgari —have you ever seen a pink diamond? I wore one in a ring and it was *this* big — and this guy, he was *such* a little pervert, he kept poking his head into the dressing room while we were changing, even though we'd already given him our jewels back, so this Ukrainian model, Oksana — right, the one who does J. Crew — she's standing there in her underwear and she sees this nasty horn dog watching us from the doorway, and she picks up a shoe and just *clocks* him, right in the forehead, with the heel, so now he's bleeding all over the place from this gash in his head."

I really want to hear the rest of this story because holy cow, but then Margo appears in the doorway.

"Jane, Gigi is on her way," Margo says, motioning me to join her. "Please wait for her in the living room." She brings me to the second floor living room and leaves me there.

The room is something straight out of *Architectural Digest* (literally, I mean it was actually featured in *Architectural Digest* a few years ago) with a thirteen-foot ceiling, dove-grey walls and white plaster moldings. A nineteenth-century French landscape oil painting hangs over the fireplace, and photographs in silver frames adorn the end tables. I wander the room, getting a feel for my new home. There's the photo of Gigi taken by Annie Leibowitz for *Vanity Fair*, and another one of Gigi on the cover of *Vogue*. And there, almost hidden behind another frame, is a black-and-white picture of a young girl on a swing. My mother, Victoria.

I pick up the frame and examine the picture closely. I've

always thought I looked like Dad, with the same grey-blue eyes and wide mouth. But in this picture I can see how much of my mother there is in me. I have her eyebrows, straight and dark, and her hair, pulled back in a ponytail, reveals the same forehead and hairline as mine.

Just as I lean forward to replace the frame Gigi strides into the room, and with a start I straighten up and drop the picture. With a crash it knocks over the other pictures on the table, and as I scramble to set everything upright again I see that the glass on my mother's picture has cracked.

"Jane," Gigi says. "Well."

She's dressed in a cape and tall black boots, and her hair is snow-white, cut in a chic bob, curling under at the ends and showing off her long neck. You can see immediately why Gigi once used to be a model in her own right, before she left her agency taking a handful of their models with her, and opened up her own agency to become the best agent in the business. I meet her in the center of the room, still clutching my mother's picture. I feel like I should hug Gigi, but we never hugged any of the previous times we met, and now I don't know what to do. When I saw her at Dad's funeral we barely spoke to each other. Gigi places her hands on my upper arms and gives me a small squeeze which doesn't quite pass for a hug and kisses the air above each cheek. She takes the picture out of my hands and places it on a side table without giving it a glance.

"Come, sit down," she says as she removes her cape and places it on the sofa beside her. She wears a pencil skirt and a black cashmere sweater and she sits with her ankles crossed, her back straight. I catch myself doing the same thing, squirming and crossing and uncrossing my ankles until she places a hand firmly on my knee, and I stop instantly.

"Have you found your room? Are you comfortable?" she asks. I assure her I am. "Good. We have a lot of catching up to do, but unfortunately this is a very busy time for me. I have to go right out again after dinner."

If the disappointment shows on my face, Gigi doesn't notice.

"You'll start school on Monday. You're very lucky that they're able to take you. Egleston has a long waiting list, but your grades are excellent and your teachers sent very good recommendations. Fortunately you're a bright girl." *At least there's that.* The unspoken thought hangs in the air.

"I've never transferred to a new school before. I'm a little nervous."

"It's just for a few months, anyway, until the end of the semester."

"You mean I'll go to a different school in the fall?"

Gigi takes a breath.

"We don't need to decide anything right away," she continues. "But everything has happened so fast. I think we should view this as a trial period for both of us."

I feel the floor rock beneath me.

"I thought I was coming to live with you permanently," I say. "I thought that you had custody of me now."

"I do. I am responsible for all the decisions regarding your education and upbringing. One of those decisions is whether you wouldn't be better suited going to boarding school. After all, I'm very busy running the agency and I travel constantly…"

Gigi's words turn into a dull roar in my head. This isn't my new home, I realize. This is a pit stop, on the way to God knows where.

"Now, dinner will be served in twenty minutes so please change," Gigi says with an air of finality.

"Change what?" I say, feebly.

"Your *clothes*, dear," Gigi sighs. "No one wants to look at you in a grubby t-shirt and jeans at the dinner table."

"All I have are T-shirts and jeans."

One of Gigi's eyebrows glides up her forehead.

"Show me your clothes," she says. She marches up the stairs and into my room as I follow. Gigi opens my closet, but there's not much of mine in there, just my fleece jacket and a couple of plaid and denim shirts. Gigi rifles through my dresser and sighs.

"Wear this," she says, taking the denim shirt off the hanger and handing it to me. "Tomorrow you're going shopping."

The Art of Dining

Nowhere else are your upbringing and social intelligence more evident than at the dinner table. An attractive, articulate and well-mannered dinner guest brightens the table like a bouquet of flowers. Be mindful of how you eat, what you eat, how you speak and what you speak about, whether you are at a formal dinner party or a casual lunch for two. — Living a Model Life: Beauty and Style Tips from Gigi Towers by Gigi Towers.

BETTY, the cook, is Irish and large and scowls a lot, and all the girls are scared to death of her. Everything she cooks is from a list of low-fat, low-carb, low-calorie meals, developed by a dietician at a famous spa in California. Gigi is a maniac for good manners. The girls sit at the table with their napkins on their laps and their elbows at their sides, taking tiny careful bites as though we're having dinner at Buckingham Palace. It's a big change from how I typically ate at home, which was usually by myself and in front of the television, and consisted of my own culinary masterpieces like microwave pancakes slathered with Nutella or canned tomato soup with goldfish crackers. Tonight Betty has made a poached salmon with baby potatoes around the sides, and a quivering gelatinous dome with little green flecks floating around in it.

"Herb-infused vegetable aspic," Betty growls as I give her a quizzical look when the dish comes my way. I don't know what kind of herbs are in there but when Betty isn't infusing them in aspic she must be smoking them if she thinks this stuff is food.

I'm a little worried that my table etiquette isn't up to par and that I'll accidentally use the wrong fork or something, but nobody pays me much attention. Gigi sets the tone of conversation, changing the subject if it bores her ("Nobody cares what you dreamed last night, Campbell. Such stories are only interesting to the person telling them," which shuts Campbell up for the rest of dinner). Gigi is just telling the girls about the politics of who sits where at the Fashion Week shows when her eye falls on Campbell's plate. She stops talking in mid-sentence, heaves a big dramatic sigh, and rolls her eyes to the ceiling.

"Tell me that is not a potato on your plate," she says to the ceiling.

Campbell stares wide-eyed at her own plate. The tiny offending potato gleams like a pebble beside her salmon.

Gigi covers her eyes with a slim, manicured hand. "I know that there is no possible way that a potato would be on your plate," she continues, "because *I* know that *you* know that you have five pounds to lose before next week. So, when I look again, I know that potato will be gone."

Campbell quickly picks up the potato and plops it onto Maya's plate, who snatches it and tries to hide it under her napkin, but it rolls away from her across the table, and if there is anything that will make Gigi angrier than an errant potato on a plate it is a potato rolling across a mahogany table. Just before she uncovers her eyes I grab the potato and pop it into my mouth. I feel like a cat with a canary in its mouth, and Gigi rolls her eyes while the girls look anxious.

It's so ridiculous, this panic over a potato the size of a marble, that I can't stifle a burst of laughter. Unfortunately this causes the potato to shoot out of my mouth with an audible POP and land in Ling's aspic. Everyone stares at me.

"I'm sorry," I say, covering my mouth with my hands. I struggle to control my laughter, but the exhaustion, the grief, and the loneliness that I've been carrying for two weeks are finally too much for me, and with a sob my laughter dissolves into tears as I push my chair from the table and rush upstairs to my room.

2

MAYA

W hat, by the gods of all things dorky and pitiful, have we here? What is this, an *orphan*? Not just any orphan, mind you, but one with Gigi's stamp on her sad little forehead. Look at her mirroring Gigi's table manners, all wide-eyed and shy, it's just heartbreaking. I can compete with any one of these girls for Gigi's attention, but a *granddaughter*? Gigi hasn't even said one word to me about my booking for *W Magazine*! It's like I'm invisible. It's like I'm… Campbell or somebody.

Oh hell no, not here, not now. Stop it. Stop stop stop. I thought I had it under control but here we go again, a miasma of panic enveloping me. My breath comes in short gasps and I want to bolt outside into the night, and how can they all sit there talking about bullshit when the bottom has dropped out of the world and I'm free falling. Keep my eyes down — you can see it in my eyes when a panic attack comes on, they're not my own, they're the eyes of a crazy person — and breathe: *in*-two-three-four *out*-two-three-four.

Those pills Dr. Oberhoff gave me aren't doing a damn thing. The only thing that keeps me from spinning off the rails when I have an attack is to go through my win-list in my head, which I've been silently reciting like a malfunctioning robot since I was nine years old: *I'm the best speller in my class, I'm the fastest runner in my grade, I'm the best server on my team*, and so on. The list changes every time there's a new variable, and this week has been full of new variables. With a deep breath (*in*-two-three-four) I begin: *I have more followers than the other girls, I have a better book, I'm skinnier than any of them, I've been booked for more shows.* Even this Jane creature won't matter once the shows start. But then I remember that, when Sophia arrives on Friday, I won't be any of those things. She'll be the best, and I won't be anything.

Then, with a deep, shuddering breath, I remind myself that my pedigree beats all these girls,' even Sophia's, and yes, even Jane's. Don't think that doesn't matter; Gigi eats that stuff up. I've heard her talk about my parents: "Maya's father is the first African-American surgeon to win the Nobel Prize in medicine…be sure and let *Vogue* know so they'll want to do a profile." And, "Salma Robinson's book on women's rights in the developing world got a great review from *Marie Claire*. Do they know we represent her daughter?"

I wonder what Gigi would think if she knew how much my parents despise the modeling industry and everybody in it. A couple of weeks ago, when Mom was in town to speak at the World Conference on Women at the United Nations, she was still fuming at me.

"If I'd known you'd give up on going to college altogether I would never have let you take a semester off," she said over lunch at Bilboquet. "I only let you go to Milan because I thought it would be a unique travel opportunity."

I love this "let" bullshit. I turned eighteen in July, so it's not like I needed anyone's permission. Anyway, we both know the real reason she let me go to Milan, and it had nothing to do with the travel opportunity.

"College isn't going anywhere," I said. "I can take classes part-time at the New School."

"Don't be ridiculous. That's not the same thing at all. You got the highest SAT scores in your class and you have a 3.9 GPA. And now you're surrounding yourself with girls who don't have a thought in their heads and who only care about their looks."

"You don't know what goes on in their heads," I retorted. "And they're not dummies, either. Brigitte speaks four languages and Ling is an award-winning violinist."

"What about college? Do any of them go to college?"

"No, not right now. Campbell is going for her GED…"

"How marvelous. Your new best friend is a high school drop-out."

"I never said she was my best friend."

I didn't want to talk about my friends with Mom. It doesn't matter who they are, she'll find something to criticize. This is a woman who counts Michelle Obama among her best friends. But I had to admit, if only to myself, that she was partly right. Sometimes I feel like I have nothing in common with the other models. Isabel said something so stupid to me the other day: She said, "You're lucky, because black girls are so in fashion now." Really, you idiot? I'm lucky? Have you ever heard a client tell your booker that they don't need to see you because they "already have their black girl," or arrived at a shoot to have a make-up artist say he hopes you brought your own foundation? Yeah, I didn't think so.

"Are you doing this to hurt me?" Mom snipped. That is so

Mom: Me, me, me. "We've given you a lot of slack since your accident, Maya, but that doesn't mean I'm going to let you disgrace us. I don't care what Dr. Oberhoff said."

I couldn't believe she went there! We never talked my "accident." It's like my whole family made an unspoken agreement to pretend that part of my life never existed. Under Mom's pointed gaze, I instinctively placed my hand over the scar on my left wrist and hid my hands under the table.

Early the previous year I temporarily lost the feeling in my right arm, and it was Dr. Oberhoff who figured out that I was carrying so much stress in my upper back that my vertebrae were cutting off my nerve endings.

"A girl your age can't sleep five hours and study eight every day," Dr. Oberhoff said. "You need to flip those numbers around." Whatever, lady. You don't keep a straight-A average while you're having your beauty sleep, and in my family, that's a minimum prerequisite for membership. Dr. Oberhoff made me work with a physical therapist for a while, which helped. But when she suggested that I undergo cognitive therapy, Mom balked.

"Cognitive therapy is a crutch for people who can't solve their own problems," Mom insisted. "There's nothing wrong with you."

Because that's the kind of family we are. We're perfect, and we're especially perfect at hiding our imperfections. We'll even hide them from ourselves. Mom never asked me why she kept finding bloodstained wads of tissue in the wastepaper basket, or where the small cuts around my ankles and on my forearms came from. Perhaps she was afraid I would blame them on a broken glass, a neighbor's kitten or a faulty razor, or worse, that I wouldn't. Nobody ever asked me why there was a box cutter in the bathroom drawer, but I know that someone found it, because one day it was gone.

I don't remember much about my accident. All I know is

what everyone told me after I came home from the hospital: that I reached into the dishwasher and accidentally sliced my wrist on the tip of a knife, and my sister Alexandra found me in the kitchen bleeding from a six-inch cut. You'd think someone would have asked why the bloodstain on the oak-wood floor was on the other side of the kitchen, nowhere near the dishwasher. Or why I would reach into the dishwasher with my left hand if I'm right-handed. Or why I didn't call for help. But people in my family don't ask questions that they don't want to know the answers to.

And that, ultimately, is why they let me go to Milan after a model scout from the Towers Agency spotted me at a volleyball tournament and invited me to spend a month with their agency in Milan. Because Dr. Oberhoff said a change of setting would be good for me. Because having my body scrutinized every day would make it impossible for me to cut myself and keep it a secret. Because my family finds their problems easier to deal with when they're on the other side of the world.

It's been months since I hurt myself, so something is working. I would point that out to Mom, but Mom never accepted that there was anything wrong with me to begin with, so I already know that's a conversation that won't go anywhere.

"It must be uproariously funny to you that your mother is a tenured professor of Women's Studies at Georgetown University, a feminist *icon*, and you're making a career out of objectifying your body," Mom continued.

"Oh my God, Mom! Not everything I do is about you. Listen to me, okay? For once, please *listen*." I pressed my fingers to my forehead, exasperated. "I'm happy doing this. Milan was the most exciting time I've ever had. I felt special, like I was a part of something beautiful and important."

Mom snorts at the word 'important,' but I continue.

"The designers who work for the big fashion houses, they're real artists. So are the top photographers. Fashion isn't just about pretty pictures. It has as much relevance as all important art. It reflects social, cultural, even political values. When a model wears a designer's collection on the runway or in a magazine, then she's a part of creating trends that resonate all over the world. I want to do this, Mom. I know I'm good at it. I've already been booked for my first runway shows, and Gigi wants to send me to Paris in the Spring. *Paris*! Not as a tourist, not like when we went for Dad's conference, but to live and work and meet people on my own."

"You're good at many other things too, Maya. Things that require you to use your brain."

"I don't have to prove to anyone that I'm smart. I know how smart I am. I'll find plenty of ways to use my brain. A lot of models use their success to raise awareness of global issues or to found their own charitable NGOs."

"Nowadays everyone with an Instagram account is an activist," mom scoffed. "No one will take you seriously unless you're one of the best."

"Well, maybe I will be."

Mom was quiet for a moment. Maybe she actually heard me this time. Maybe my little speech got through to her. And just maybe, for once, what I want will matter to her.

"All right," she said finally. "If you insist on doing this, then do it right. Be a model, but be one of the best. Do you understand? If you're going to sacrifice college then you better be getting the high-end work — couture shows, magazine covers, cosmetics campaigns. Don't call me all excited because you're modeling cat litter or something. Be someone I can be proud to call my daughter."

"Of course I want that, all models want that, but it's an incredibly competitive..."

"Are you already making excuses to fail? It's your choice. Either choose to be a success, or be a failure. Like you said, you're a grown-up. There are no participation trophies anymore."

And with the cold finality of her voice, the crushing sensation of panic crept back over me.

I've had a few bookings since I arrived in New York, but mostly for minor catalogs or websites. Those aren't the kind of jobs that do much to boost my followers. Right now I have more than three thousand followers, which isn't too shabby since I'm still kind of a newbie, but Brigitte has almost as many, and when Ling's tear sheets from *Fashion Hong Kong* come out in a couple of weeks she'll pick up thousands of followers overnight. These numbers are laughable, though, when you compare them to Sophia, who has over a million followers. What I really need — what every model really needs — is editorial work. There are only so many magazines to go around, which is why most models spend several months out of the year in Europe — places like Paris, Milan, London, and Madrid — where the magazine market is bigger. I guess you could call my month in Milan a success. I was lucky to rent a room from one of the bookers at Towers Milan, so I didn't have to share a tiny apartment with a dozen other girls. I got some editorial work, but *Grazia* and *Amica* are second-tier magazines. They're not *Vogue* or *Elle*.

It could be worse, though. Take Campbell for instance. Campbell only has a couple of hundred followers, and all she has are test pictures, plus some tacky newspaper inserts for some local department store in Atlanta. Her book isn't even strong enough for Gigi to send her to Europe. So, by comparison, I'm doing okay. But I'm going to need more exposure, lots more. That's why, when I learned this morning that Isabel had a casting for *W* that isn't on my calendar, I called my booker Suzanne and asked her why I'm not being sent on it.

"They're asking for a specific look that is more like Isabel's.

Don't worry, I've got several other castings lined up for you," she said.

I knew what was going on here. Isabel needs editorial work even more than I do, and the agency gave her an extra push at *W*. But if Suzanne thought I'd be placated by her answer then she doesn't know me at all.

Isabel's casting appointment was at eleven. I arrived at the *W Magazine* office (which every model in New York knows is in the Condé Nast building, at One World Trade Center) at eleven twenty, and just as I entered the lobby I saw Isabel exit the elevator bank in the opposite direction, bundled up like a teddy bear in jeans, UGG boots and a puffy down jacket against the February cold.

"Who are you seeing?" the receptionist asked me.

"I forgot her name, I'm sorry. It's for the casting," I answered.

"Lisa, then. Go ahead, third office to your left."

When I entered the office, Lisa, the fashion editor, looked up from a selection of composite cards beside Christophe Malinois, the photographer.

"Hello," she said. "I thought we'd seen our last girl. Are you sure you're scheduled?"

"Yes," I said. "Unless someone at the agency made a mistake. But I'm here now. Can I show you my book?"

Lisa nodded. I put down my bag and took off my Burberry wool coat, unveiling my strongest asset: this five-foot-eleven, former-ballet-dancer, varsity-athlete body of mine. My skin-tight mini dress and low neckline showed off every curve of my body.

"Very nice," Linda said, flipping through my book.

"Yes indeed," Christophe said, looking me up and down. And right at that moment I knew that Isabel was screwed.

When Suzanne called me this afternoon to confirm the booking I bounced around my room with joy. I almost called

Mom, but then I hesitated. What if the booking falls through? What if they decide not to run the pictures? The tightening in my chest was back. I won't do anything until I have the pictures in print, in my book. Then I'll share them with Mom.

Isabel's eyes are red from crying. She thought she had it in the bag. I don't think she knows I stole her casting, but she hasn't looked at me all evening. I almost feel sorry for her, but I have problems of my own. One of which takes the form of this little waif across the table from me — who for some reason just spat out a potato, burst into tears and bolted from the table.

Gigi sighs. "It's been a difficult week for the child. I think I'll have Abby Bernstein take her shopping tomorrow to cheer her up. She's in desperate need of new clothes."

Abby Bernstein is one of New York's top fashion bloggers. There aren't many people in the world who can just beckon Abby Bernstein with a snap of their fingers to take their kid on a shopping spree. Kind of a waste, in my opinion — I bet Jane doesn't even know who Abby Bernstein is. I'm not sure what that kid's problems are, but Gigi is seriously clueless if she thinks they're going to be solved with a shopping trip.

THE NEXT MORNING is cold and damp, and as I enter Christophe's warm, brightly lit studio it's like stepping into another world. The smell of hairspray and coffee fill the air, a combination which for the rest of my life I'll associate with photoshoots. I've checked off a thousand little boxes in my head to make sure everything is perfect today (in keeping with Gigi's three P's that she's always reminding us of: Punctual, Poised, and Prepared). I ran fourteen miles this week, I did five hours of hot yoga, I took a diuretic last night, I used a teeth whitening strip, I brought my vouchers, two working pens, my foundation, eyedrops, toothbrush, I shaved all my bits and pieces, my phone is charged, each fingernail is shaped and polished to perfection.

Ian, the hair and makeup artist, is a freaking genius. He does this exquisite Egyptian cat-eye thing to my eyes that I'll never be able to replicate, and rubs some glossy conditioning stuff in my hair and blows it out. When my hair and makeup are ready, Annie, the stylist, helps me into my outfit.

Which gives me a massive case of the creeps. It's a fur coat, and it probably costs more than your average car, but all I see are hundreds of dead animals hanging off my shoulders. There was a time when I said I would never model fur. But, dammit, I need this job. I need it bad. Like Mom said, if I'm going to model, then I need to do it right. Even if it means selling my soul for a good picture.

"Isn't this a gorgeous coat?" Annie says. "It's silver fox."

Foxes, Jesus. My thoughts scatter like marbles, and totally beyond my control my head fills with images of foxes bleeding in traps, gnawing at cages and writhing in death by electrocution, and my breath starts coming too fast and I think I might pass out.

"Something wrong?" Annie asks.

It must be that look in my eyes again, that one I get when a panic attack comes on. *Chill, Maya. Breathe.*

Here's what I'll do, I tell myself: I'll donate today's paycheck to the World Wildlife Fund. Even better, once I make it big I'll do one of those naked anti-fur billboard campaigns for PETA. That makes it okay, doesn't it? That makes me just a little less of a scumbag excuse for a human being, right?

"I'm fine," I smile, and I take my place in front of the camera. Buried inside the coat, nobody can tell that I'm digging my nails into my arms so hard the pain takes over my anxiety.

"Lean forward just a little, Maya, will you?" Christophe

asks. "Look to your right so the earring catches the light. That's right. Beautiful." Clickclickclick goes the camera.

I relax as the shot progresses. I can tell I'm doing better than the other model, Katie, did in the last shot. I heard Christophe tell her to loosen up, that she looked stiff. Nobody's going to say that about me. I move like a cat and I know it, thanks to a lifetime of ballet.

I thought this was a closed set. Who are those guys hanging out near the door? It seems they're delivering equipment so I guess they're supposed to be here. Still, that bald one needs to put his beady little eyeballs back in their sockets. I wonder if he can tell that I'm only wearing panties under this coat.

"Nice. Lean back on your elbows, and arch your back," says Christophe.

What is my coat doing? I can't tell with my head hanging back but surely they'd tell me if my boobs are falling out of my…oh, look at that, yes they are. Hold on, let me…

"No, don't move a thing, the light on the fur is perfect."

"But my breasts are showing."

"No they're not. I can't see from here. Don't worry about it, you look fine." Clickclickclick.

He's lying, my breasts are definitely out there. But you know what, they look pretty good draped in diamonds. I'm not prudish about showing skin, as long as it's tasteful, and *W* is tasteful. I've always hated the patriarchic notion that women should keep their bodies under wraps for fear of cheapening themselves or some such dictatorial bullshit. Women's bodies are beautiful and powerful, and art has celebrated the female body since prehistory. Every woman should do whatever she damn pleases with her body, as long as it's on her terms. It'll be interesting, though, to hear what Mom, who has written tomes about the empowerment of the female body, will think of her youngest daughter showing boob in a magazine.

Then I realize that bald delivery guy is right behind me,

craning his slimy neck to get a better look, licking his fat filthy lips.

"Wait," I say, and I sit up.

"Don't move!" Christophe yells. "Ah, *merde*, now we have to set it all up again."

"Sorry, but could these guys" — I point right at the creep's face — "please leave? They're making me very uncomfortable."

"You," Christophe says to the guy. "Out of here."

"You want this stuff moved or what?" the guy drawls back.

"Well, either get busy or get lost!"

With an agonizing lack of urgency the men carry supplies through the studio, and Christophe takes a break while Annie readjusts the coat and Ian touches up my makeup.

"All right, *allez*," an irritated Christophe snaps, waving everyone else off the set. But just before the bald guy walks out the door, he snaps a picture of me with his cell phone. I want to leap up, yank the cell phone from his hand and smash it on the ground, but I'm scared of interrupting Christophe again, and if word gets out that I'm hard to work with no one will ever book me again. He might even send me home on the spot. I'm shaken and creeped out and it shows in my expression because Christophe barks at me to relax my eyebrows.

"Lunch break," Christophe finally announces. "Twenty minutes, everyone."

With a sigh I stand up and stretch my stiff, aching limbs.

"Did you see that weirdo staring at you?" asks Katie when I enter the dressing room. "That was just wrong. You should complain to your agency."

Like hell I should. Katie knows as well as I do that if I ever want to work again I won't be complaining about anything to anyone. I change into a robe. They got us sushi for lunch, and I'm so hungry I'm ready to shove that whole tray into my mouth. I reach for one of the tuna rolls, then hesitate. Is that too much? Half a roll, then. Just let me pick out the rice…too many carbs in rice. I'll have some of the seaweed salad, just a small spoonful. Man, if Gigi ever called me out for my weight in front of the other girls, the way she does Campbell, I would never show my face in that house again.

When we finish at three o'clock I feel confident that even Christophe is pleased with me. The samples of pictures that he shows me are some of my best ever. Next I have a fitting at the Jordanne fashion house, one of the designers I'm walking for in the shows.

When I arrive at Jordanne I'm surprised to see little Jane there, in the company of Abby Bernstein. This must be Gigi's idea of an appropriate shopping trip for a fifteen-year-old: a private consultation with one of the top young designers in New York. Abby flutters around in a big floppy hat, a scarf that reaches her ankles and a jacket made of feathers as she and a stylist pull clothes and accessories for Jane to try on. I exchange hellos with Jane, who, by contrast, looks entirely out of place in her own torn jeans, Led Zeppelin T-shirt with a flannel shirt and Converse sneakers.

While I'm being fitted, I watch Abby and the stylist working on Jane.

"Now, remember, she's short," says Abby. "No plaids or horizontal stripes."

"Ugh, take that off at once," says Ethan as Abby zips Jane into a black drop-waisted dress. "Her body's all wrong for it, it looks ghastly."

"No belts," cautions Abby. "She has a waist like a tree trunk so we shouldn't call attention to it."

It's painfully awkward, watching them play with Jane like a defective doll that doesn't fit into the clothes it's supposed to. Not once does anyone ask her if she actually likes the clothes they're selecting, and it's evident that she has nothing to say about it. You'd think a girl being treated to a whole new designer wardrobe would be beaming like a Disney princess, but Jane looks miserable. When I have a short break I ask her what her favorite piece is.

"None of these are things I'd pick out for myself, but I kind of like this one," Jane says of a soft grey asymmetrical tee shirt. "What is it, silk? It feels like…Holy mother of hell, look at the price! It's three hundred dollars!"

"Don't worry about it," Abby interjects. "Everything is on Gigi."

"You sure are lucky," I say, but Jane doesn't look like she thinks she's lucky.

"I don't even know how to wear some of these," Jane says. "I mean look at this. Can I even go to the bathroom in this thing?" She holds up a suede pencil skirt that laces up the back.

"Trust me, you'll get used to it," Abby says. "Ready? We have several other designers to see. Let's go, we have LOTS of work to do."

As Abby and Jane exit I check my emails and read one from Mom.

"I just saw the picture you sent me from your W shoot. You look very nice, although I think the red lips age you, but I suppose you have no say in how they make you up. Tell me, how much of the photos do they photoshop? Alexandra is doing marvelously at Harvard and has just declared her concentration, Molecular Biology (I'm sure you can imagine your father's unbridled delight). She is still dating Douglas Evans, whose parents and younger brother we entertained last week when they came through DC to visit Georgetown U. Such nice people! Do give her a call, she tells me it's been ages since you two spoke. Much love,

Mom."

Why do I even open Mom's emails? The whole thing is dripping with passive-aggression. Not one damn word about how proud she is of me, but plenty of gushing about wonderful Alexandra and her billionaire boyfriend. Nice people my ass, mom wouldn't care if they were pirates as long as they're rolling in money. I do owe Al a call, but I just don't want to deal with her now. If you think I'm competitive, you've never met my sister, the queen of the overachievers. She's so competitive she absorbed her twin in utero. It's a family joke, "Alexandra ate her twin," but when I was really little it seemed perfectly plausible that she'd devour me, too, one way or another, if I infringed in her space.

3

CAMPBELL

I*t's more important for a model to be graceful than sexy. Who cares what men think? Men aren't the ones buying women's clothes. — The Many Faces of Gigi Towers* by L. M. Daly.

THE STREETS ARE ankle-deep in black icy sludge and sky is gray and cold but I don't care, it's the most beautiful, happiest day in the world because I just got off a video call with Sophia!

"I miss you so much. I'm sick of everyone pulling at me in all directions," she said. "I just need some chill time with my bestie." I'm filled with warmth and I feel like I'm walking three feet off the ground. I've been sick with fear that, with everything that's been happening to her, Sophia would forget all about me. But she misses me! I'm still her bestie! And she's coming back on Friday! Seventy-six hours until her flight lands at JFK from Paris.

At a newsstand I buy a pack of gum from an old man with an eye patch. Poor old thing, I hope he has a good day. I hope he goes home to a wife and that they're kind to each other. I hope the darling man selling newspapers for the homeless at the corner has a warm bed waiting for him, and that the dear lady walking the fat pug is in love, and that the dear, dear little fat pug has everything his fat little heart desires. I want everyone in the world to be as happy as I am right now.

I skip into the agency to drop off the voucher from the bridal fitting I did last week. However, as soon as I arrive, Marilyn, the head booker, tells me to come into her office, and poof, the bubble of joy I floated in on bursts like…well, like a bubble. Marilyn scares the crap out of me. There is only one person at the agency who I'm more scared of than Marilyn and that's Gigi.

"We got your pictures back from your test shoot with Petra," she says. "I'd like you to have a look at them with me." She motions me to sit down as she pulls a slideshow up on her computer.

"Look at this one," she says, pointing to the first picture. "What do you see?"

I don't know the answer she's looking for. I mean, I see myself, wearing a pair of cut-off denim shorts and a black tank top, sitting in the sunshine on the floor of the studio. What does she think I see?

"How about here?" she says, as though offering me a clue, pointing to my upper thigh.

"Umm…I see my leg?"

"Cellulite. You see cellulite. See how lumpy the back of your thigh is? And here, do you see that little roll at the top of your hip?"

My heart sinks to the pit of my stomach. I thought these would be some of my best pictures.

"I don't think you'll be able to use any of these," Marilyn sighs.

"I'm shooting another test on Friday," I say, struggling to keep my voice from breaking. "I promise those will be better. I've lost about three pounds since last week."

"Let's hope so," Marilyn says. "We need to start seeing some results from you, Campbell, before we can even think about sending you to any of the magazines or top photographers."

I hold back my tears until I exit the building. Why can't Marilyn get off my ass? The only thing that's keeping me going is that Sophia's coming. I can't talk to any of the other girls about how scared I am about not working. They don't give a damn. I never thought I could be so lonely in a house full of other girls.

It's hard to believe that Sophia and I both started out with the same agency in Atlanta. We met at a fashion show at Saks last year, and I made her laugh so hard with my mimicking of the other girls that she almost peed in her Oscar de la Renta. We hit it off immediately, even though she went to a private school in Atlanta and I went to public school in Fayetteville. Now her face is all over Italian *Vogue*, French *Elle*, and dozens of other magazines, and she even has an international ad campaign for Guess Jeans. I'll admit I've had some major pangs of jealousy when I read her tweets about being dressed by Giorgio Armani and dancing with the crown prince of Dubai while I've been dragging my butt around the city trying to get work, but of course I'm happy for her. But it's time for things to start happening for me too, now. I'm running out of money. Sarah, my booker, told me that I need a new comp card, and it'll cost $500. If I don't start getting some real work, I'm seriously scared that Gigi won't keep me.

One thing's for sure, though. I am not going back home. I

would rather clean bathrooms at McDonald's and sleep in the subway than go home.

I've been sitting in the lobby of *Flair Fashions* catalog for forty minutes now, waiting for the art director, and she still isn't back from her lunch meeting even though I was told to come between one and one-thirty and it's now one-forty five. The receptionist said that she should be here any minute, but that was half an hour ago. Now I have to call the agency and tell them that I'm running late for my casting for a skincare commercial at two o'clock.

"They're only admitting people until two-thirty," says Sarah, "and they want to make a decision today, so you really should try to make it. We can reschedule *Flair*."

The casting is all the way on the other side of town, and when I get outside it's raining and there are no taxis so I walk to the subway and when I finally arrive my clothes are wet, my hair is stringy and my makeup is running down my face in black rivulets. There are a handful of girls ahead of me. When they finally call me in, I hear the casting director murmur, "Oh, great, another blonde," so now I know he's looking for a brunette, so why am I even here?

Next I have a casting for Siren Swimsuits — this one is down in TriBeCa, so it's back into the rain and the subway — and at the studio there's a gaggle of models waiting their turn to try on a bikini. When each girl comes out from the changing area (which is just a small screen in the corner of the room) she stands in front of a panel of people at the front of the room taking notes while all the other girls are right there, in the same room, watching as the clients discuss the girls' bodies among themselves in front of everyone else. Even if the top edge of the bikini wasn't digging into my hips I can tell by the quick, dismissive way they say "okay-thank-you-next" that my body is all wrong for this job.

I try to avoid the smug looks of the other girls as I leave the studio. What a rotten, miserable day, I think while I wait for the elevator, when someone calls, "Excuse me, miss?" and I turn around.

"My name's Luigi," he says, "I saw you at the casting." I don't remember him but there were several people who I didn't meet. "I work with a division of the Siren Swimsuit company called Aqua Bella, a smaller, newer company, and we're looking for models for a campaign, but we can't pay the agency fees so I'm asking girls if they'd be interested in doing some modeling work outside of the agency. Would you be interested? It pays five hundred dollars for two or three hours of shooting."

"I'm not supposed to take any work outside of the agency."

"Lots of girls do it, you know. This way, we don't have to pay the agency fee and you don't have to pay the commission. Everybody wins."

"I don't know," I say. If the agency found out I was taking work on the side, they could kick me out. But meanwhile, I think, five hundred dollars? For a couple of hours of work? "Can I think about it?"

"Here's my number," he says and hands me a card. "We want to shoot tomorrow so let me know soon." I give him one of my composite cards and promise I'll let him know by the end of the day.

I make up my mind on my way home. I really need the money, and it's only a couple of hours of work, and nobody from the agency needs to know anything about it. I call Luigi and tell him I'll do it.

"Great," Luigi says. He gives me the address and tells me to be there at one o'clock tomorrow afternoon.

∾

"A PACKAGE ARRIVED FOR YOU," Margo tells me as I close the front door. "I put it in the kitchen."

I find the package addressed to me on the kitchen counter. At the sight of Mom's handwriting on the address label my heart stops for a second. It's been more than two months since I left home and I haven't heard a word from her all this time. I called her almost every day the first week, and I sent her a dozen texts, but she didn't reply. Finally I decided to wait until she's ready to reach out to me, however long that will take. Maybe she's finally ready.

I run up the stairs to my room, then shut the door behind me. As I tear the package open a jumble of items falls into my lap. The items are trivial, things that only have value to someone who cares about the milestones they represent: A needlepoint sampler I made in fifth grade; my junior prom dress; a photo album my friend Maddie made of us (back when we were still friends); a handful of sports ribbons; and a dozen or so photographs — including one of me at seven dressed for a ballet recital which used to stand in a frame in Mom's room. There's no note, just these artifacts of my life which Mom wants out of her house. The message is clear: Now you have nothing to come home for anymore.

I want to call her, ask her what the hell kind of mother she is, but I know I'll just get a recording in her sing-song drawl telling me to leave a message. She knows the package arrived today. She must be watching her phone, waiting for me to call just so she can let it ring and ring, knowing how much I need to hear her voice, and not pick up. I won't do it. I won't give her the pleasure.

I've known since I was six years old that you don't want to get on Mom's wrong side. When Dad left, he didn't just leave. He disappeared. I mean every trace of him disappeared from the house. Every picture of his, every stitch of clothing, his DVDs, his detective novels, his hunting boots, his tackle box, everything Mom could get hold of she pitched onto the front yard. Then she doused it all with lighter fluid and threw a lit match onto the heap. Flames leaped all over the place while I huddled in the doorway. One of the neighbors called the fire department and the fire truck wailed up to our house right at the same time that Dad's car came tearing up the street.

"Oh my god!" He screamed. "You crazy bitch! You fucking lunatic!" He ranted and flailed and would have probably strangled Mom right there if the firemen hadn't held him back. I think the only reason he didn't press charges against her for arson or destruction of property is because, if Mom went to jail, he would be stuck taking care of a six-year-old daughter.

A year later Dad and his girlfriend moved to Florida, and he promised I could spend my school vacations with them. But the vacation visits never happened.

"You're either on my side or his," Mom said. "You want to spend your vacation with that liar and his whore, that's your choice."

"Daddy said I have to," I protested. "Because of the custody agreement."

"They can't make you. Not if you don't want to, and why would you want to? You don't want to, do you?"

"I don't know." I mean, it was Florida, and I hadn't seen my dad in almost two years, so yeah, kind of.

"You want to be with them, then go! *I'm* not the one who abandoned this family, but go ahead, go live with that cheating bastard. After all the pain your father caused us, by all means, go take their side against me, even though I've always done everything for you."

"It's just Christmas vacation…"

"And what about *my* Christmas? Did you think of that? No, because you only think about yourself."

So I didn't go. And I didn't go the vacation after that, or the next one, until he stopped asking me altogether.

No matter how nuts I knew she was, it didn't make sense to me that Dad would leave Mom for another woman because I thought Mom was the most beautiful woman I'd ever seen. Unlike the mothers of my friends, who wore button-front shirts and cropped chino pants, Mom dressed like a Barbie doll — tight, midriff-baring tops, denim miniskirts, and heels as high as she could walk in. Her hair was big and frosty, she never went anywhere without lipstick, and kept her nails long and polished.

She wasn't alone for long. The first one who moved in with us was Dan, who smelled of sawdust and varnish and who took me to breakfast at Waffle House on mornings when Mom couldn't get out of bed because her head hurt. They smoked cigarettes and listened to music and danced in the living room, and sometimes there was yelling until they'd make up and disappear into the bedroom. Eventually the yelling became more frequent and the making up became less so, and one day Dan and all his things were gone.

Then there was Eddie who we only saw on weekdays, and I learned later that he had a wife and kids in Atlanta whom he spent his weekends with. Eddie was short and didn't have all his hair but he brought us presents every time he came over. He gave me a little yellow chick for Easter which died within a week, because what did I know about taking care of a chick. Mom never told him that it was a stupid and thoughtless gift to give to a child, she just wrapped it in a paper towel and tossed it in the trash. But I cried about it for days.

There was Brian, who was a trainer at a gym and who could lift me over his head like a barbell. He read superhero comics and gave me the ones he was finished with. By the time Mom finally met Jack, my stepfather, there had been half a dozen others whose names and faces I don't remember.

When Jack arrived I knew he was different. For one thing, Mom stopped smoking. It was as though she never had a reason to stop before, but she would do it for Jack. She also became a decent housekeeper almost overnight. Before Jack, Mom would let the dishes pile up in the sink until we ran out of utensils, and I sometimes pulled dirty clothes out of the hamper so I'd have something to wear to school. But when Jack started coming around, Mom cleaned the house like a maniac and kept real food in the house like fresh fruit and chicken instead of frozen dinners and boxes of mac 'n' cheese. She made sure she always had a full face of makeup on from the moment she woke up, just for him. There was no question in my mind: Mom was in love for real this time, and she wasn't going to let anything come between her and Jack. Especially not a teenage daughter.

THE ADDRESS for the Aqua Bella swimsuit shoot is a hotel on the Lower East Side. I arrive in photo-ready makeup as Luigi requested, and when I knock on the door of the room Luigi greets me, invites me in and takes my coat. A camera on a tripod and a studio lamp are aimed at a white paper backdrop hung against the wall. Luigi offers me a glass of wine.

"I'm underage, you know," I say.

"You Americans and your bourgeois prudishness," Luigi laughs. "Here. It's a nice Pinot Grigio." I accept and take a sip.

"Where are the photographer and stylist?" I ask.

"I'm the photographer," Luigi says. "And we won't need a stylist for this job." He shows me the outfits to be shot which include a black string bikini, a beige macrame bathing suit that is almost completely see-through, and a string top and thong bikini bottom which I decide right then and there that I will not allow Luigi to photograph me in from behind.

"We'll start with whichever you feel most comfortable in," Luigi says. In the bathroom I put on the black bikini and examine myself in front of the mirror. (I'm bigger on top than most models, which isn't really an asset in fashion, but I like my breasts. Maybe it's because they came late to the party, when I was sixteen. I was barely a B and wondered whether they'd ever show up, and then I started taking birth control pills and almost overnight they made a dramatic appearance. Suddenly my breasts were a full C and we've been a real team ever since.) The bikini is a bit small on me but when I step out of the bathroom Luigi smiles in approval.

"Beautiful, wonderful, perfect," he says. He has me sit on a stool with one knee up, my arm resting on my knee, touching my lips, my hair falling over one shoulder.

"Lovely," Luigi says from behind the camera. "So beautiful, so sexy."

Luigi guides me into different poses.

"Arch your back a bit more. Open your legs wider. Part your lips, and relax your eyes, that's right."

By the third outfit — the thong bikini— Luigi wants to change up the background.

"Let's move this one to the bed," he says.

It strikes me as odd, since a bikini on a bed with a cheap burgundy quilted spread doesn't make sense, but Luigi is so nonchalant about the request, not even looking at me as he fiddles with the lens of his camera, that I sit on the edge of the bed.

"You look uncomfortable," he says. "Lie down and relax." I lie down on my side, facing him.

"Put your hand on the inside of your leg. More inside. Higher. Touch your lip." Then he says, "The top isn't working for me. Take it off, will you?"

`At first I'm confused. "What should I put on instead?"

"Nothing," he answers.

I sit up. "Are you kidding?"

"Don't worry, you can turn your back to me. It'll be fine."

"I don't want to do that. I'm wearing a thong."

"Don't be a baby, Campbell."

"You never said anything about being topless."

"I thought you were a professional. If you want to stop, then we'll stop, but I'm not paying you for an unfinished job."

"I've worn every outfit for you! That's not fair!"

"What are you going to do?" Luigi shrugs.

That bastard. There's nothing I can do and he knows it. I can't call my booker since I'm not doing this job through the agency, and if I walk out I won't get paid. I decide to do as he says but to kneel and cover my bottom with my feet. I turn my back to him to remove the top, but even as I'm taking it off he's clicking the camera.

"Cooperate, now," he says. "Let me see your face. That's right." Luigi walks around the bed, and no matter how hard I try to cover my breasts or my bottom he's there with his camera, clicking away.

"We're not done until I get my shot, Campbell."

I've never been so uncomfortable, and I'm almost crying. Luigi sighs and puts down the camera.

"You're too stiff," he says. "You need to loosen up. Like this." He reaches around my back and places his hands on the inside of my thighs and pulls them apart, and suddenly his arms tighten around me and his fingers slide up the inside of my thighs and onto my pubic area and he *squeezes*, and I writhe myself out of his arms and leap off the bed.

"We're done," I cry. I run into the bathroom and quickly change back into my clothes.

"Campbell, chill out, will you? You got the wrong idea," Luigi says calmly when I emerge, my coat on and my backpack slung over my shoulder.

"Like hell I do. Just give me my check," I reply.

"You're flattering yourself. Why don't you stay awhile and we'll finish the wine?"

"I don't think so. Where's my check?"

"You don't need to be so hostile. What's the rush? Have another drink." He's already pouring another glass.

"I just want my damn check."

"Here's your check," Luigi says. I reach for the check but he whisks it out of my reach. "Let me have a kiss first. Make up and be friends."

I move in to give him a quick peck on the cheek because I need that check, but he grabs me tight and plants a hard kiss right on my mouth, forcing his tongue between my lips, and, gagging, I twist my head so he leaves a nasty wet trail on my cheek. I snatch the check from him and leave, running down the stairs without looking back.

I get an alert from Chase Manhattan Bank the morning after I deposit the check. The check bounced. It's drawn on a non-existent account. Fake. Worthless. I call the number Luigi gave me but there's no reply, just a recording. I leave a message telling him to call me back right away, but even as I speak I have no hope of ever hearing back from him.

I find the number of the Siren Swimsuit company and, after several attempts, get through to one of their representatives. They tell me they've never heard of a Luigi, there's no division of Siren Swimsuits called Aqua Bella and it's likely that the man I'm referring to was in the building on unrelated business and happened to see me leave the casting. It's a total dead end. I'm crying with frustration and anger when I hang up. Anger at Luigi and everyone else in this sordid business but especially anger at my own stupid, ignorant self for being so naive. Far worse than the money is the knowledge that some of the sleaziest pictures I've ever taken are floating around somewhere. If they ever turn up, I'm as good as finished with the Towers Agency.

Sophia arrives tomorrow night. Hurry, Sophia. I really need a friend right now.

4

JANE

"We have one of the highest college acceptance rates in the city," says the headmaster of Egleston, Mr. Singh, during my tour. "And you'll be pleased to know that we have a very strong art department. Our kids have earned national awards in art, as well as in science, athletics, writing, and music."

See, this happens all the time. As soon as people know who my dad was, they think I must have a great interest in art. But the truth is I suck at drawing and painting. Mr. Singh points out a display of paintings by current students hanging on the wall, and Margo makes little impressed grunting noises. I'm wearing one of my new outfits: a ruffle-sleeved metallic sweater and flared black velvet pants, which Gigi took two seconds to tell me this morning looks "much more adequate." The sweater makes me look like a flightless bird and itches the back of my neck and my pants are sliding off my non-existent hips but, hey, Gigi's happy. As Margo shuffles along beside me dabbing her nose with her handkerchief, I cringe inwardly, and I feel guilty because it's not her fault that I wish she was someone else. It's not her fault she isn't Gigi.

A pair of girls about my age approach us and call out, "Hey, Mr. Singh!"

"Hi girls, come meet our newest student. Jenna, Mikayla — this is Jane Archer."

The girls and I say hello, and Margo extends her hand.

"Hello, Mrs. Archer," Mikayla says.

"She's not my mother," I blurt, too fast and too loud. Right away I'm sorry, but I can't take it back. Mr. Singh clears his throat. "We'd better keep moving if we want to have time to visit the rooftop garden," he says.

For the rest of our tour Margo doesn't make a sound, nor does she look my way. Only when we get home does she inform me that I have another appointment.

"I promised Gigi we'd get your hair done today. Trim, color and highlights. You have an appointment at Bruno's at two o'clock. He does all of Gigi's girls."

Now it's my hair? Is there anything about me that Gigi doesn't want overhauled?

"I'm sure you'd rather go by yourself," Margo says with a haughty air. "It's not far, just on Thirteenth Street. It's already charged to Gigi but here's fifty dollars for tips."

I think I must have misheard, she must have said fifteen dollars, but nope, she hands me fifty dollars in cash. I don't know exactly where I'm going when I leave the house, I just know I want to go the opposite direction from Bruno's salon. I imagine it's chic and luxurious and expensive and everything I'm not, and if one more person tries to force me into a mold that I can't possibly fit into, I'm going to crack. I find myself in

SoHo, and I smile when I stop in front of exactly the place I need.

The tiny salon is manned by a guy with a magenta mohawk and tattoos that cover the length of his arms, and in addition to hair services he also peddles body piercings and an assortment of punk-rock T-shirts and jewelry. I bet this joint is the exact opposite of whatever Bruno's is. This whole place has a grimy feel to it; the vinyl chair feels sticky and the brushes on the counter look kind of gross, with hairballs from previous clients still stuck in the bristles which may be infested with lice for all I know. But after the stylist is done cutting, bleaching, coloring, washing, and drying, my hair has been through its own version of chemical warfare and I'm pretty sure there isn't anything alive in there. It's cut in a wedge and dyed Prussian blue and it looks as unlike one of Gigi's girls as possible. I really, I mean *really*, can't wait to see Gigi's face when she sees this! I may not be as pretty, or as tall, or as graceful as Gigi's girls, but what I will not be is invisible.

When I return home, Margo calls to me as she comes downstairs.

"Jane? Bruno called and said you never..." she sees me and gasps. "*Mais non! Quel horreur*! Are you insane?"

"Fetching, isn't it?" I give my hair a toss.

"Gigi will be furious! WHAT am I going to tell her?"

"Don't tell her anything. She'll see it herself."

When Gigi gets home Margo hauls me before her. Gigi's eyes open very wide and she stares at me for a long while with her lips pressed together. I hold my breath. I'm almost hoping she'll be angry.

"Really, Jane?" she finally says. "You felt this was absolutely necessary?"

"Yup."

"What in the world were you thinking?"

"I was thinking that this was more my own style."

"Are there any other surprises I can look forward to as you cultivate your own style? Will you be getting any tattoos? A couple of facial piercings, perhaps?"

"Maybe later. I saw this cool scorpion tattoo on a girl's neck…"

"I told her you would find her hair in the worst possible taste," Margo interjects.

"Of course I do," Gigi says. Head tilted, she touches my hair, lifting the strands and letting them fall. "But I don't mind *bad* taste nearly as much as I mind *no* taste. At least it's a look." Damn, this woman is chill. There's no question that Gigi hates it, but as much as she hates it, she still hates it less than she hated my natural hair. I don't know whether to be pleased or offended. With that, the subject of my hair is abandoned. Margo breathes a huge sigh of relief and collapses in a chair.

I follow Gigi upstairs.

"Thank you again for my new clothes. But it's far too generous, they're so much more expensive than my old things."

"Of course they are, dear. Your old clothes were hideous," Gigi says. "If you need anything else, just let Carol know."

Carol is Gigi's assistant. She's the one who booked my airplane ticket, requested my school transcripts, ordered my medical records from my pediatrician, and bought my school supplies for Egleston. I haven't met her yet, but I've had more to do with Carol in the past two weeks than I have with Gigi in my entire life.

In my room, I take off the itchy metallic sweater which I have grown to hate intensely in the past few hours. I pull several new items out of the closest and toss them on the bed as I search from something else to put on. I decide on a white asymmetrical top with cut-out shoulders. It's supposed to be a cropped top, but on my stubby body it hits right at the top of my hips. As I pull it on, the other girls poke their heads into my room, probably lured by the brilliance of my hair like moths to a flame. They regard me for the first time with something resembling interest.

"You look amazing. Whatever made you do it?" asks Maya.

"You sure are brave," Campbell says.

"You're lucky," Ling says. "I wish I could do something crazy with my hair. But my booker would be furious."

"Who gives a shit?" I ask. "It's your hair."

"No, it's not. My hair doesn't belong to me. It belongs to the Towers Agency."

"Is this the stuff you bought with Abby?" Campbell asks, exploring the items on the bed. "Can I see? Oh, wow, you lucky dog."

"Hey, is that Stella McCartney?" Ling asks. "That is so cool!" She picks up a crepe-de-chine shirt with tropical birds all over it. I'm pretty sure I told Abby that I hate prints. Ling holds the shirt in front of herself. It looks stunning with her coloring, and right then I know that I'll never wear it myself.

"You can borrow it if you like," I say.

"Seriously? Thanks!"

"By the way, where's Isabel?" I ask.

"Isabel left," Maya answers. "She went to Madrid to try the editorial market, since she's not booked for the Fashion Week shows."

"I didn't know Isabel was leaving today," I say. "I would have said goodbye." It's the first time I realize how easily people come and go around here.

The doorbell rings and Campbell drops the yellow leather jacket she's holding.

"It's Sophia! Sophia's here!" she yells, and goes hurtling down the stairs like a cannonball, bumping into the walls on the landing.

"Ugh, spaz," Maya murmurs.

The rest of us follow, me and my stupid hair completely forgotten, and I descend the stairs to find Campbell and Sophia clutching each other, bouncing around the foyer and squealing like a pair of ten-year-olds.

"Sophia," Gigi cries as she appears from the living room. "Darling!"

Gigi wraps her arms around Sophia in a bear hug, rocking her back and forth so hard that I'm surprised they don't lose their balance and fall on the floor. She gives Sophia a big smoochy kiss on each cheek. Gigi introduces Sophia to the other models, and then Gigi introduces me.

"This is my granddaughter, Jane." (She says it in the same tone with which one might introduce someone to their new potted fern.)

When you're accustomed to seeing someone on a 5,000 square-foot Guess Jeans billboard overlooking Times Square it is to be expected that they should seem smaller in real life, but still I'm surprised that Sophia is this slight, fairy-like girl. Her hair is tied back in a loose bun and she's swimming in a large ivory cashmere sweater from which her skinny forearms poke out.

"I didn't know you had a granddaughter," Sophia says. "How long are you staying for, Jane?"

"Jane is living with me now, Sophia."

"Oh, Gigi, how wonderful for you!"

"Yes, well, Sophia, dear, you must be starving. No? You're certain? Of course, the food in first class on Emirates is actually edible."

Margo comes out of the kitchen and she hugs Sophia to her chest.

"*Ma chére petite*," Margo says. "I have missed you, beautiful one."

Sophia pulls a gift for Margo out of her hand luggage, a box of macarons from the Ladurée pastry shop in Paris. It's very sweet of Sophia, because I don't think the other girls ever remember Margo exists, other than to ask her where the laundry detergent is or whether she remembered to buy their favorite rice crackers.

The models and I follow Gigi and Sophia, their arms linked, into the living room, where Gigi sits and draws Sophia beside her on the sofa. As Sophia talks about her recent work in Paris everyone hangs on her words, especially Gigi. I get it because Sophia is, quite simply, breathtaking. I mean, all these girls are beautiful, but it's hard to take your eyes off Sophia. People often think blondes are the ultimate standard in female beauty, but Sophia's hair is light brown with strands of highlights around her face. Her eyebrows are a shade darker than her hair and perfectly tapered, and her eyes are this weird kaleidoscope of brown with flecks of greenish-blue, like they never made up their minds what color to be. She has the tiniest trace of an overbite and the corners of her mouth tilt up ever so slightly, so she has a serene little smile when her face is relaxed.

I watch Gigi, who gazes at Sophia the way an art collector looks at a priceless painting. Sophia is expected to earn close to a million dollars this year, which is perfectly respectable but it's not nearly as much as some of Gigi's more established models. For example, Evangeline Potter, who models for Victoria's Secret and is the face of Maybelline cosmetics, makes five million a year, and Olivia Knightley who has the Burberry campaign and just landed a part in a movie makes even more than that. And twenty percent of everything these girls earn goes to Gigi.

But I see something special in the way Gigi stares at Sophia. She doesn't look at her the way a businesswoman looks at a commodity. She doesn't even look her in the appraising, satisfied way that she looks at her other girls. She looks at her with complete adoration. Absently, she strokes the back of

Sophia's hand. I wonder what it must be like to have a woman like Gigi, who surrounds herself with beautiful, perfect things, love you more than anything else she owns, and suddenly a hard lump forms in my throat, so hard that it hurts to swallow, and my eyes feel hot and prickly. Nobody notices as I slip into the kitchen to wipe my eyes and blow my nose.

5

CAMPBELL

I just wish everyone would back off and leave Sophia alone so she and I could disappear upstairs and catch up on the last few months, but nope, everyone wants to hover around her. Gigi has a bunch of shoptalk to go over with Sophia, so she waves the rest of us out of the room, and I signal to Sophia that I'll see her upstairs when Gigi lets her go. Gigi keeps Sophia occupied for over an hour. I can hear them chattering and laughing downstairs. I don't think Gigi's ever been as interested in any of the other girls, not even Maya, and she's crazy about Maya. I wonder if Maya is thinking the same thing because she looks very serious and pensive.

Finally Sophia enters the third floor TV room.

"Look what I've got!" She holds a bottle of wine by the neck and five wine glasses, their stems laced between her fingers.

"Where did you get that, you maniac?" I ask.

"From Gigi's wine cellar in the basement."

"We're not supposed to go in the basement," Ling says.

"She'll never miss it. Don't worry, she's gone to bed."

It's one of my favorite things about Sophia, those balls of steel of hers. The rest of us walk on eggshells in Gigi's house, but Sophia totally doesn't give a damn.

"Uh, I don't know, Sophia," says Maya.

"What is this, Montrachet?" I ask, examining the label. "It looks expensive."

"It's pronounced Mon-tra-SHAY, and of course it's expensive, it's Gigi's," says Maya.

"You won't tell, will you?" Sophia looks at Jane and gives her one of those smiles that make people want to wrestle a tiger for her.

"No, of course not," Jane says.

"Want some?" Sophia is handing out glasses. I'm the first one to reach for a glass, and then Maya, and then the others take one.

Sophia sits on the floor with her legs together, her ankles curled under her.

"So guess who I kissed at the Gaultier party in Paris?" She asks. "Jason Cooper!"

Jason Cooper, in case you live at the bottom of a well, is the lead singer of the band 'Viper.' He was recently linked with a starlet named Veronica Parker who nobody ever heard of until she posed nude for *Playboy*, and now she's famous for two things: her breasts, and the fact that she dates Jason Cooper.

"And then he wanted me to go back to his suite at the Crillon with him but of course I said no," Sophia continues.

The girls are all hanging on every word and I feel a nauseating wave of jealousy. Not because I want to go to the Gaultier party and kiss Jason Cooper, but because I want Sophia and her stories for myself. I don't want to be part of her audience. I'm her best friend, not one of her fans.

"Where was whatshername…Veronica?" I ask.

"No idea. Not at the Gaultier party, anyway. Hey, which shows are you guys walking for? Is anyone else doing Zac Posen? Or Tom Ford? Or Marchesa? Or Jason Wu?"

The other girls chime in. Ling is walking in six shows, Maya in nine, and Sophia is walking in sixteen. I am walking in exactly one.

After we finish the bottle of wine and the other girls go to bed Sophia and I stay up in her room until way after midnight, just catching up. I know Maya is dying to join us, because twice she makes up some stupid reason to stick her head in the room about something irrelevant.

"Here, I brought you this," Sophia says and hands me a bundle wrapped in tissue. "For your birthday. It was last month, and I missed it."

I unwrap it and find a sapphire-blue leather Hermes clutch purse.

"For me?" I gasp. "Are you nuts? How much did this cost?"

"None of your beeswax. I bought it at a private sample sale."

"Still. This is way, way too nice." I smother her in a big hug.

"Hey…can you keep a secret?" she asks, her voice low.

"You know I can."

"I did go back to the Crillon with Jason!"

"Sophia! Why didn't you tell me?"

"I wanted to tell you in person. It's not the kind of thing I'd say in a text."

"So did you…"

"Yeah, we did."

"Oh my god. You little slut." I hit her with a pillow. She laughs and hits me back, and we fall over on our sides on the bed.

"Want to know something else?" she says. "He was my first."

"Whoa."

"It's okay. It's what I wanted. There's only one first time, right? For the rest of my life, if I tell someone about my first time, it'll be a good story."

She's probably right. My first time isn't a story worth telling. It involves a pimply sixteen-year-old, a six-pack of beer and the bed of a pick-up truck.

"Are you going to keep seeing each other?"

"We exchanged numbers and he texted me to say they're playing Madison Square Garden in April and that he'd get me backstage passes. Want to go? Might be fun if we're around."

"Of course." Then I ask, "Are you in love with him?"

"No. I don't fall in love with guys who are busy being in love with other girls."

"I bet he's in love with you. Just wait. Veronica is toast."

Sophia shrugs.

"What about you? How have things been with you?" she asks as we lie facing each other. I sigh, my mood suddenly somber.

"It's been kind of a struggle actually. Gigi keeps telling me I need to lose weight. My last test pictures weren't very good, I can't even use them for my book. On top of that, Sarah says I need a new comp card and that it'll cost $500, and I'm afraid to ask Gigi to advance it."

Sophia brushes a strand of hair out of my face. She strokes my head and it feels really nice. Sophia has a smell — a warm, musky, flowery smell, that's a little intoxicating. "Well," she says, "this is a tough time for print work, you know, because of the shows."

"Yeah, I know, but Maya and Ling and Brigitte are all on hold for jobs after the shows, and I'm not."

"Tell you what. I'll lend you the money for the comp card.

No, shut up, you can pay me back when work picks up. After Fashion Week I'm going to introduce you to Theo Wolff. You know who he is, right? He photographed my French *Elle* cover and he shoots the Guess campaign."

My eyes widen. Theo is one of the most influential photographers in fashion. He can turn a model into a mega-star. He totally made Olivia Knightley, and he's doing the same thing with Sophia.

"Seriously? You'd do that?" Even Sarah can't get me a meeting with Theo Wolff.

"Sure. Theo and I are friends. He photographed three of my last covers and he has me booked for two weeks solid after the shows."

"Sophia, you're an angel, you know that?" I say. "Seriously. You're the best."

As the night goes on we fall back into talking about our old plans: we're getting an apartment together, as soon as we're old enough. We plan everything, from the decor (fairy lights and bohemian tapestries and a saltwater aquarium glass coffee table) to the parties we're going to have (everyone in vintage cocktail attire with a chocolate fountain in the center of the room). We even plan to get a cat, preferably a genuine stray that we find lurking behind a dumpster, an orange beast like Holly Golightly's tomcat in *Breakfast at Tiffany's*. I fall asleep with my head on her shoulder, breathing in her warm, sweet smell.

6

MAYA

This is the day I've been dreading since I arrived: Sophia is back. There's been a huge paradigm shift in the house since the minute Sophia walked through the door, and I'm in total recalibrating mode because my whole sense of order has been thrown off its axis. Gigi has completely forgotten that the rest of us exist. The other girls are fawning around Sophia like a bunch of sycophantic groupies, and Campbell is bouncing around like it's Christmas, stupid thing, like she isn't already pathetic enough without Sophia raising the bar for success even higher. And what am I doing? I'm standing against the wall like a coat rack.

I lock myself in the upstairs bathroom and clutch my arms. I try going through my win-list again: I'm smarter than any of the other girls, I've got the best…the best what? Book? Not anymore. Web page? Followers on social media? Not with Sophia around. It's not working. My list is falling apart. I'm not the best anything anymore. And if I'm not the best, then what am I?

My heart flutters frantically, so hard that it physically hurts, and I'm terrified that it'll break like a clockwork toy wound too tightly. There is one thing that I know helps, though it's been months since I resorted to this. I dig into my toiletries bag on the bathroom shelf and find my nail scissors. I hold them almost tenderly, rubbing the smooth, cold steel with my fingertips. I press the sharp points against the skin of my forearm. The pain starts out as a dull throb, and then, as my skin yields to the pressure like a tiny sinkhole, it becomes sharp and searing, spreading out from the point of the scissors, obscuring everything else I feel. I clench my teeth and press harder with the scissors. I want to see how hard I can go, and even though my eyes are damp with tears I am filled with calm because I finally have control over the panic. I've made it stop. All I feel now is the pain of the scissors, this silly little pair of nail scissors that I can control completely, that has no power over me. I press harder, and still harder, until the jarring moment when the pain reaches its apex and I give a little cry as I feel the fiery steel tips burst through my skin.

I watch the small gush of bright red blood pooling from the wound and soak it up carefully with a wad of toilet paper. I make a game of trying to dye the entire paper red with blood, and feel a twinge of satisfaction when every speck of white is gone. When the bleeding stops I patch myself up with a bandaid. I'm much calmer now.

Sophia isn't going away, so I only have one option. I need to make Sophia my friend. My best friend. We need to be a pair, a team, so when people think of her they'll think of me. I don't see why we wouldn't be, we're practically going to be roommates, our looks totally compliment each other and we're booked for most of the same shows.

"Oh, hey, you're fitting for Tom Ford tomorrow morning as

well, aren't you?" I say when we're sprawled on the floor of the TV room, sharing the wine that only someone totally secure of her foothold in Gigi's house would ever have the nerve to steal. "We can share a car in the morning. And do you have Yves Saint Laurent at one? Me too! Maybe we can grab some lunch in between. Do you like sushi?"

I think even Mom might like Sophia.

I COULDN'T GET Sophia to come to lunch with me because she made plans to have lunch with Campbell, and no matter how hard I hinted, those two didn't ask me to join them. I've never seen a more unlikely friendship. I mean, Sophia is a genuine star, and Campbell is just one rejection away from being shipped back to whatever trailer park she came from. It's sad, really. Like watching a lovesick mule trotting after a thoroughbred.

On my way to my third fitting I get a message from Alexandra. I guess Mom told her the same thing she told me about getting in touch with each other.

"Hey sis! I'm coming to NY with Doug tomorrow, spending a couple of days with friends in Brooklyn. Want to get together for lunch? Miss you! XOXO."

We agree to meet for lunch on Sunday in the East Village. When I arrive at the restaurant Alexandra is already there, sitting at the bar. She has her hair pulled back in a ponytail and wears a tight cream-colored sweater and dark jeans. In my opinion she is by far the prettier of us, the feminine, cute one with the curves. I have always been the tall gangly one, the one who towers a head above the boys.

"Sorry I'm late," I say.

"You're not; I was early," she replies as she gives me a brief hug.

"So what brings you and Doug to the city?" I ask once we've placed our orders.

"Doug has an interview at Goldman Sachs for a summer associate position. Wouldn't that be wonderful? It's very competitive, but I think he's got a good chance."

"What will you do while Doug's in New York all summer?"

"Oh, I've applied for a summer research program at Sloane-Kettering. If Doug gets the job, then we'll rent a studio apartment in the city together."

I love how she doesn't even entertain the possibility that she won't get the research position. Doug better not screw up his interview. I wouldn't want to be in his shoes if Al's summer plans fall apart because of him.

"Well," I say. "Looks like you've got everything figured out."

"How about you, Maya? You used to have everything figured out too."

"My plans have changed."

"Mom and Dad are very worried about you, you know," Alexandra says. "They think you're throwing your life away."

"Al, I'm not an idiot. Why does everybody think I don't know what I'm doing?"

"Look, I get it, I really do." Alexandra puts her hand on my arm. "I know how controlling they are. I understand the need to do your own thing."

"Oh please. You've never taken a single step out of line. You're like a perfect doll, Al: wind it up and it goes to college. You're every parent's dream."

I expect Alexandra to get angry and the conversation to end in a fight, but she just sighs.

"It's not like I never thought about it," she says. "I used to want to go to art school, remember? But can you imagine if I told them I wanted to study painting instead of Pre-Med? They'd have lost their minds."

I do remember. Alexandra was a really good artist in high

school. She won several art awards, and one of her paintings was selected to be part of the school's permanent art collection. It hangs in the library and will be there for generations to see. It's strange, though... I don't remember her ever painting anything else after she got accepted at Harvard.

When the waiter takes our plates, he asks us if we want dessert.

"Do you want to share something?" Alexandra asks, looking at the menu. "Ooh, look, they have profiteroles!"

"No, I'm okay."

"You sure? You only had a spinach salad."

A spinach salad full of oil and feta cheese and bacon bits, and it's more than enough for the rest of the day. The last thing I need is a stack of ice-cream filled pastry covered in chocolate sauce.

"I had a big breakfast," I say, which isn't true. I had the same thing for breakfast as always — coffee and a banana — but that's normal for me.

"You sure? You look thin. I mean thinner than usual. You're not going to develop an eating disorder or something, are you?"

"Eating disorders are for stupid white girls," I say.

"That's not true and you know it," Alexandra admonishes. "You look frail. You've got those circles under your eyes that you had when you had the flu."

"I'm tired, that's all. I've been really busy, and I don't think I got a full night's sleep all week." I yawn and cover my mouth.

"I know what that feels like. We just had midterms and I pulled three all-nighters in five days."

"That's insane, Al. How do you function?"

"Everyone does it during exam period. We all run on lots of caffeine, as well as some other stuff."

"You mean drugs?"

"Not *drugs* drugs. Legal drugs, like Adderall, just to give us a little push."

"Do you take it?"

"I have, on occasion," Alexandra shrugs. "It's not a big deal if you're careful."

"I know models who do coke," I say. "Not me, but I know some."

"Don't do coke, okay? That would be unbelievably stupid."

"No. I won't. Duh. But I can see why some girls do. We have to be on, all the time, you know? Especially in front of the camera. If I'm sluggish during a shoot, or I don't project enough energy, they won't hire me again. And then I get anxious about actually being too tired, so then I can't sleep, and it just makes me more tired." I prop my elbow on the table and lean my head in my hand. Just talking about how tired I am is making my head hurt.

"I've got a couple of Adderall left," Alexandra says. "They might help. But only use them if it's really important, and only take half a tablet, ok? Take it in the morning. It'll take about thirty minutes to kick in and you'll have energy for hours." She removes three small blue pills from a pocket in her handbag. Hesitantly, she hands them to me.

"Promise me, okay?" she says. "Only in an emergency."

"I promise. I'll be careful," I say, and I take them from her before she can change her mind.

7

JANE

T*he company you keep will open or close doors for you in all aspects of life. Taste is contagious. At all costs, avoid associating with people of poor taste.* — *Living a Model Life: Beauty and Style Tips from Gigi Towers* by Gigi Towers.

I TAKE the subway to the Egleston School every day. I love the New York subway. You see some crazy things. In my first week I saw a man sitting in the train reading a paperback with a butter-yellow python on his shoulders, and nobody glanced twice at him. I saw a guy come on the train dressed as a giant penis, I saw a foot-long rat running up and down the subway car, and I saw an Olsen twin. In Denver I rode the school bus for eight years and all I saw was the back of someone's head.

In Physics class I sit next to this kid Niko, and I'm pretty sure the reason there's a seat available next to him is because no one else wants to partner with him. He's a big kid, kind of soft all over, with dark hair and glasses and he always wears pleated khaki pants and stiffly ironed oxford shirts like he stumbled out of a Brooks Brothers catalog. He sits with his hands clasped on the desk in front of him, his chin jutting forward, a smug, heavy-lidded expression on his face, and when the teachers call on him he always has the right answer. He has this pompous tone and everything he says is preceded with "Actually." For example — and this to a *teacher* — "Actually, to scan means to scrutinize something carefully, not to give it a quick glance. You said 'scan the article really fast.' You meant 'skim.' Actually, scan and skim are two of the most commonly confused words in the English language." Or, "Actually, Newton's First Law is incorrectly ascribed to Newton. It was actually Galileo who first observed the laws of inertia." You just want to punch him sometimes.

"Actually, you're supposed to use the green marker for deceleration," Niko says as I draw a sloping line on a position-time graph in red marker. "Red is for acceleration."

"Who cares as long as the colors are different?" I answer.

"Because it needs to match the colors in the other graph."

"No, it doesn't. It's a totally different graph." Niko is just trying to be difficult.

"I want it to be consistent."

"You do it, then," I say, dropping the marker.

"It's ruined now. I'll make another one."

"Fine," I say. Niko begins drawing another graph, and since he seems to be doing fine without my help I flip through my binder, organizing my notes.

Ashley, the girl seated on the other side of Niko, leans over and says "Jane, is it true you live at Gigi Towers' house?"

"Yes," I say. "She's my grandmother."

"Really? Gigi Towers is my idol! I read her biography, *The Many Faces of Gigi,* and I've got several of her beauty and style guidebooks."

"Who's Gigi Towers?" asks Connor, a boy with shoulder-length dark hair who's always playing air drums on the edge of the table, which would be irritating if he weren't so darn attractive.

"She's the owner of the Towers Modeling Agency," Ashley says. "They have girls like Sophia Thompson, and Olivia Knightley, and Christy Bennett, right?" Ashley looks at me for confirmation.

"You know those girls?" Connor asks, noticing me for the first time since I started school. I noticed him on day one. He has really nice hazel eyes, although I have my suspicions that he's a moron.

"Some of them. Sophia Thompson lives at our house," I reply.

"Wow! You're, like, roommates!" Ashley gushes. "She's my favorite. I follow all her social media accounts. Is it true that Victoria's Secret wants to book her, but Gigi won't let them have her until she turns eighteen?"

"Um…yeah," I say, but good grief, how the hell would I know? Why do people even know these things?

"What is she, on the cover of *Vogue* or something?" Connor asks.

"No," I answer, "Sophia is still relatively new and *Vogue* only ever uses A-list celebrities for their covers."

"Actually," Niko begins, "the use of celebrities on the covers of *Vogue* was popularized by Anna Wintour, beginning with her using Madonna as a cover model in 1989. The last cover featuring a girl famous only for being a model was a retrospective of Kate Moss, fourteen months ago."

Now, see what I mean about Niko being a pedantic ass-hat?

Why would he know that unless he collects irrelevant factoids just to bore the crap out of everybody?

"Less talking, over there," our physics teacher Mrs. Lowry grumbles in our direction.

"You know some weird stuff, man," whispers Connor to Niko.

I wanted to take theater as an elective at Egleston, but the theater classes are all full. There's no way I'm taking art, and journalism would set me back with a class of freshmen, so I sign up for a documentary film class. We have to work in small groups of two to four people to make a documentary film of our own, and the best films get to compete for a chance at admission to the New York Film School summer program. By the time I arrive everyone has already formed their groups.

"Let's see..." says Mr. Vogels, looking over his notes. "Maybe there's still room for you in one of the smaller groups. Jasmine and Niko, can you accommodate another member?"

Ugh...Niko, again? Niko gives the slightest of nods, and I can tell he's as excited about partnering with me as I am. I don't know Jasmine, a girl with pierced eyebrows and black lipstick who wears a hoodie that hides most of her face. I take my backpack to the empty chair next to Jasmine —or Jazz as she's called -- and sit down.

"So do you guys have a subject yet for a film?" I ask them.

"No," Jazz says, as though it's an idiotic question. "We don't need to submit our final decision until next week."

"Any ideas yet that you're considering?"

"A couple," Jazz says. "Look, if you don't mind, we were in the middle of a conversation." She turns to Niko and they continue talking quietly, ignoring me completely, except to glance at me as Jazz stifles a laugh. Man, what a pair of jerks.

When I get home from school I discover that Brigitte is back from Miami, and now she's rooming with Ling. She removed all her things from my room, but not before taking every one of my clothes and dumping them on the floor, just to make it clear how she feels about being displaced from the single room. While I'm hanging my clothes back up my cell phone rings.

"Hi Jane. This is Niko."

"Oh, hey. What's up?"

"Actually, I have an idea about our documentary film project that I wanted to run by you."

"Yeah?"

"You're Gigi Towers' granddaughter, right? Well, you actually have a unique perspective on the modeling industry. Jazz and I were thinking, you know, we could do a documentary that looks at the inner world of modeling. Kind of a behind-the-scenes story about the lives of these girls."

"I don't know, Niko…"

"You could ask the girls you know if they would let us interview them, and maybe accompany them on a shoot, or something. Sort of follow their progress up the professional ladder."

"When did you guys even come up with this idea?"

"After school today. What do you think?"

"Hmm. Maybe." I'm still a little pissed about their rudeness to me in class.

"And maybe you could actually get Gigi to give us an interview? I mean she's your grandmother, right? She'd do it for you."

I'm not at all sure that Gigi would do it. Gigi has given tons of interviews over the years, but she's famously protective of her privacy. I also don't know if any of the models would deign to help me with a school project, but the more I think about it the more I realize it's not a bad idea.

"Let me talk to Gigi about it," I say. "No promises, though. See you tomorrow."

The next day I find Niko sitting alone on a bench in the courtyard with his laptop sipping a coffee, and I plonk myself beside him, startling him so much he spills his coffee on his shirt.

"Well, it's cool with Gigi if we want to do a film about the models, as long as the girls don't mind," I announce. "She even said she'd give us a quick interview."

"Really? That's great! Hey, will you let me do the interview with Gigi? Please? I'm dying to meet her."

"Sure, whatever."

Jazz approaches us across the courtyard, and she sits next to Niko without a word to me.

"Jazz, we're good to go. Jane is getting us interviews with the models and Gigi," Niko says.

"Joy," answers Jazz.

"Jazz is really good with video editing," Niko says to me. "She knows all about doing the soundtrack and credits."

"Maybe we can get some footage during the fashion week shows," I say. "I wasn't planning on going because it sounds like my idea of hell but..."

At this Niko almost falls off the bench. "*You* have tickets to Fashion Week?"

"Well, yeah. Gigi gets tickets to all the shows but she can only go to some of them. She wants me to go to...let's see, Miu Miu, Stella McCartney and Nicole Miller, because she thinks it'll shape my own nonexistent fashion sense."

Jazz makes a snort of disgust and looks away. Even Niko looks at me skeptically.

"No, seriously," I say. "I usually dress like a total slob. These aren't even mine." I tug at my jacket and sweater. "Well, they are now, but only because Gigi got them for me. She *makes* me wear this stuff."

"You poor thing," Jazz sneers. "Forced to wear those rags." She stands up. "See you in class," she says to Niko, and leaves us.

"Jesus, what is that girl's problem? She really hates me," I say.

"No she doesn't," Niko replies, but he doesn't sound convinced. "She's actually very nice. She's just a little defensive around girls like you."

"Girls like me? What do you mean, girls like me?"

"You know. Rich, privileged, designer clothes…"

Is he kidding? Dad and I lived on rice and beans for a while because his paintings weren't selling enough, and I bought my clothes at Goodwill. But that was then. Now I go to school in a $600 sweater and a $2,000 leather jacket.

"She's wrong about me, you know. I'm not one of those snotty trust-fund kids."

"Okay, but you're the one who's going to Fashion Week. I'm just saying."

"Well, I can't help it that I live in the middle of that world."

"Whatever. It's cool."

"I mean, she's the one being a snob. She doesn't even know me."

"Just give her some time, okay? You don't have to be friends. You just have to work together."

I'm fuming with anger, but Niko gives me a friendly nudge.

"Don't tell anyone, but my parents pick out my clothes too," he says sheepishly.

Later, just before lunch, Ashley and her friends Brooke and Philippa, all of whom are in my English class, approach me in the hall.

"You seem really nice," Ashley says, linking her arm through mine. "You know Philippa and Brooke, don't you?"

"You have such a great sense of style," Philippa says. "I LOVE your jacket."

"Thanks," I say.

"You should totally hang out with us," says Brooke. "I knew

the moment I saw you that you were our type. We totally have the same fashion sense."

"You know, it's really not fair that, as a new student, you have no way of knowing who's who around here before you start making friends," adds Philippa. "But you're lucky, because we're going to help you with that."

By now we're in the cafeteria. Ashley discretely nods in the direction of Niko and Jazz, who sit at a small table, hunched over their food.

"Someone like you really doesn't need to be hanging out with the weirdos," she says. "Those are not the group you want to be identified with."

"I mean, Niko, he's a huge dork," says Brooke. "And Jazz, she's just scary. I heard she got expelled from her old school when she punched a boy in the face because he snapped her bra strap in P.E."

"No, it was a teacher," interjects Philippa. "She punched a P. E. teacher."

"A P. E. teacher snapped her bra strap?" I ask.

"I don't know the details," Philippa answers, "but she's bad news. Nobody likes her."

"Do you want to sit with us?" Ashley asks. "We always sit at that table by the window, with Connor and Jeremy and Portia and those people. I think you'll fit in right in."

I know who "those people" are because we had the exact same table in my old school. They're the quintessential cool kids, and they never paid me a scrap of attention, nor I them. I bet they exist in every cafeteria, in every high school in the world. I look at Niko, in his coffee-stained shirt that his parents picked out for him and his glasses that he keeps pushing back up on his sweaty nose, and at Jazz, almost completely hidden under her hoodie. I have no doubt which group I'll fit in with better.

"Thanks," I say to Ashley, "but I've already got lunch plans with my weirdo friends."

GIGI AGREES to give us fifteen minutes for an interview the next evening. Niko arrives with his camera bag hanging from his shoulder and I introduce him to Gigi.

"So. You're my granddaughter's friend," Gigi says.

"Yes ma'am, and I just want to say that I am so honored to meet you. I've read all about your influence in the fashion and beauty industry. I'm a real fan."

"That's nice to hear. I'm surprised you've connected with my granddaughter. I don't think she has any interest at all in the fashion and beauty industry."

Nice, Gigi. Between Niko's sucking up and Gigi's underhanded jab I'm ready to get this interview behind me.

"Maybe we should get on with it," I say, leading the way into the living room. "Gigi's in a bit of a hurry."

"How about over here?" Niko says, pointing to the chair by the window. It's the exact same spot where Gigi was interviewed for *Sixty Minutes* a few years ago and I bet Niko has seen the interview and knows that. Gigi sits down and I set up the tripod and camera on a table facing her chair.

"All right then," says Gigi, shaping her hair with her hands. "Shall we start?" she says in that clipped voice of hers suggesting she has about a hundred more important things to do.

"Um, okay, let's see…" Niko fumbles with his notecards. "First of all, thank you, Mrs. Towers, for granting us this interview. Oh, are you rolling, Jane?"

"I am now," I say, pressing the record button.

"And thank you for letting us shoot in your beautiful house.

I know how valuable your time is and it's a real privilege to be invited into the privacy of your home and…"

"You're welcome. Now let's get on with the questions," Gigi says.

"Right. Of course." Niko wipes his forehead, which is beaded with tiny drops of sweat. I think he's taking all of this a little too seriously, I mean it's not like Gigi is the leader of the free world, but then Niko takes everything so damn seriously he is probably going to give himself ulcers before he graduates from high school. "Let's see…okay, here's the first one: Mrs. Towers, you have a reputation for being the best agent in the business. What about your role as an agent sets you apart from other agencies?"

"I'm very protective of my girls, and as you know, I take many of the younger girls into my own house. When they live with me I essentially raise them as my own daughters. They must abide by a curfew, use respectful language, eat a responsible diet, and dress appropriately. I allow no boyfriends upstairs and absolutely no drugs, smoking or alcohol. When they live with me I am their mother, their teacher, their mentor, and their boss. In addition to lessons in runway walking and makeup application, I require my girls to take lessons in social media, branding and personal finance. The modeling business is a tough one, and part of my job is to protect my girls by strengthening their characters and judgment."

"Okay, good…Mrs. Towers, how did you become a modeling agent?"

"I was a model myself in the 1970s and 80s, so I knew the industry well, but I always felt that I was better suited for the management side of the business. I lost my husband to cancer when our daughter was still a baby, and I needed to provide for us, so I started managing a handful of models from a tiny office in my apartment, charging less commission and offering more personal attention than the larger agencies, until I built up my own agency."

"What was your childhood like, Mrs. Towers?"

"My childhood, which you will know if you have done any research on your subject, was one of upper-middle-class privilege in suburban Connecticut, after which I attended Vassar College. If you are interested in the factual details of my life, you can find them on Wikipedia. Young man," Gigi says firmly, "when you conduct an interview, do not waste your subject's time by asking questions to which the answers are already public knowledge."

I keep the camera rolling. This is getting good.

"S…sorry," stammers Niko.

"I have been giving interviews for forty years, and the answers to all these questions have been documented by countless interviewers before you. If you're going to take up my time and your own, then ask me questions that go beyond the obvious."

"Okay…I mean, yes ma'am." Niko drops his notecards and picks them up with shaking hands. He clears his throat and presses on.

"Mrs. Towers, is there any truth to the stereotype that the modeling industry is rampant with drug abuse?"

"That's what I mean," Gigi says, nodding with approval. "That's a provocative question. I'll answer with a question of my own. How many teenagers do you think die every year of drug overdoses in America?" Gigi asks.

"I…don't know. Lots."

"And how many of those teenagers happen to be models?"

"Not many, I guess."

"But yet you claim it's the fashion industry where drugs are rampant. Do you think drugs are not rampant in high schools and colleges all over America?'

"No, I just meant…"

"There are a great many places where drug use is a problem, young man. The fashion industry isn't any different. But I know where drug use is not rampant, and that is in my agency, because I don't tolerate it."

'Right. Of course," Niko mumbles.

"I have made it my personal mission to fight drugs. I am on the board of the Coalition for Drug-Free Youth and am a generous donor to various anti-drug organizations. I have been in this business for many years and I have seen the damage drugs can do. I know that these things happen, but they happen all over the world — on the street, in schools, and in workplaces. But not among anyone represented by me, and not among anyone I work with."

Gigi uncrosses her legs. She is ready to wrap things up. "So. Any further questions? Very well then." She stands up, and Niko gets to his feet as well. "Good luck with your project, both of you." Gigi sweeps out of the room as Niko stammers his thanks for the interview.

"Whew," he says after she's gone.

"I told you she was tough. Sorry about that."

"Why sorry?" Niko asks as we clean up our equipment.

"Well, she didn't have to be so mean to you."

"Are you kidding? She was awesome."

"She was rude as hell."

"But she was right. They were stupid questions. She gave us good advice."

As I let him out, he pauses in the doorway.

"Thanks for putting this together," he says. "Wow. What an experience! You're so lucky to have her for a grandmother."

"Trust me, Niko. You don't know anything about what it's like to have her for a grandmother."

"You know, Jane, maybe she was pushing us to do our best because she wants this project to be good. Maybe that's just her personality."

"Nice personality. *I'm* the one who has to live with her."

"All I'm saying is, there are worse families that you could belong to," Niko says, and he turns and walks down the front steps.

I THOUGHT it would be difficult getting interviews with the girls for my film project, but I underestimated how much these girls love being on camera. Each of them is dying to talk about herself.

"Yay, my first interview," squeals Campbell. "What should I wear?"

"Whatever you want," I answer, sitting cross-legged on her bed, adjusting the lens on the camera.

"I'll just brush my hair," she says.

"Okay."

"And put on a little lip gloss."

"Okay."

"Maybe I should change my sweater."

"Okay."

"What do you think…this one, or the blue one?"

"Campbell, you know nobody's going to see this except my classmates, right?"

"I'm ready." Campbell sits on the bed with her back to the headboard, and I start filming.

"Tell me about how you got into modeling."

"It was my friend Maddie's idea. She took a bunch of pictures of me for a school assignment, and then she talked me into letting her show them to an agent in Atlanta. That led to a couple of bookings in Atlanta for some local department stores. That's how I met Sophia, by the way. She was with the same agency. And then, a few months ago, an agent from Towers approached me through my Atlanta agent, and here I am."

"Tell me a little about your transition from Georgia to New York City. Has it been difficult?"

"Not difficult, exactly, because I love it here. There's so much energy, you know? But I've been trying to fit in and it's not always easy. Gigi had me working with an elocution teacher to get rid of my Southern accent before I started going on commercial castings. I spent hours saying phrases like 'I like white rice' before it stopped sounding like 'Aah lak waaht rass.' It's weird, nobody seems to mind Brigitte's Swedish accent or Ling's British accent, but people in New York really *hate* a Southern accent."

"Do you miss your family?"

"Umm...sometimes."

"What about your friends? What does Maddie think of the fact that you're a Towers girl now?"

Absently Campbell traces the pattern of the bedspread with her finger. "Most of my friends...we weren't very close by the time I left."

"Oh? How come?"

Campbell shrugs. "I don't know. People just acted differently when I started modeling. Boys I never spoke to suddenly lied to everyone that we'd fooled around, and girls who were my friends suddenly wanted nothing to do with me."

I'm starting to think that I'm not the only person who is lonely in this house.

"Well, some people are jerks," I say.

And right on cue, Brigitte walks by the room and pops her head in the doorway.

"Oh, you're here," she says to Campbell. "I thought you were out shopping with Maya and Sophia."

"Sophia and Maya went shopping?" Campbell asks.

"I wonder why they didn't tell you. Aren't you supposed to be Sophia's best friend or something? Hey, what are you guys doing?"

"I'm interviewing Campbell for my film project," I answer.

"Do you want to interview me next?"

"Maybe," I say, and turn my back to her. I would love some crazy bitch footage of Brigitte, but right now I don't want to give her the pleasure.

Later that evening when I ask Maya for an interview she does me one better. She invites me to film her during her shoot for a catalog tomorrow.

"Are you sure it'll be ok if I come?"

"You're Gigi's granddaughter, silly, you can do whatever you want."

I have a free study period after lunch, so I leave school right at eleven and arrive at the studio twenty minutes later. Maya is having her makeup touched up when I enter the dressing room.

"I'll introduce you to Marius," she says. Marius, the photographer, looks up and gives me a brusque hello, and after that he ignores me.

I film some scenes of the studio and of Maya being prepared for her shot. The stylist helps her into a yellow chiffon dress which looks luminescent against her dark skin. Maya takes her place on the set and I find a spot out of sight of Marius to set up my own camera.

"Let's see a twirl," Marius says. "Can you do that? Beautiful!" Marius exclaims as Maya does a ballet twirl and then finishes it with a little jump. She looks radiant, and it's not just the dress and the makeup. She really is good at this.

When the shot is finished I accompany Maya back to the dressing room.

"You looked gorgeous out there," I say from behind my camera, still filming. "Did you study ballet?"

"Nine years," Maya answers. "I still go to dance workouts whenever I can."

"Did you ever want to dance professionally?"

"I did want to when I was younger, but I grew too tall. The maximum height for a professional ballet dancer is about five-eight. I was five-ten by the time I was fourteen."

She peels a clementine and opens a bag of almonds.

"I'm famished," she sighs. "I didn't get to break for lunch yet."

"You mean that's lunch?" I ask.

Maya counts a small handful of almonds out of the bag. Then she closes the bag and fastens it with a tight knot, and shoves it into the bottom of her bag. "It's plenty. I'll have a banana or a yogurt at around four, and then dinner at home."

I've seen how Maya eats at dinner. If this is all she's eating, then she's going to starve. I focus my camera on her nibbling on an almond, eating the tiny nut in three bites.

On Saturday I have exciting news for Niko. Carol gave me a couple of extremely coveted press passes for the fashion shows. Niko doesn't answer his phone, and when I look up his address in the school directory I find that he lives only a short walk away from Gigi's house (I wonder if I'll ever start to think of it as my house) on Gramercy Park.

Niko's building is a large and very elegant pre-war with high ceilings and painted murals in the lobby. A doorman sends me upstairs and as I get out on Niko's floor a woman opens the door. She has the same dark hair and eyebrows as Niko but her mouth is thin and tight-lipped.

"Yes?" she asks me. "Who are you?"

"Mama, it's okay, it's my friend Jane," says Niko, appearing behind her.

"I didn't know you were expecting company, Niko," says his mother, staring hard at my hair.

"I wasn't. I mean, I didn't know Jane was coming. Come in, Jane. This is my mother."

Niko's mother stands aside and lets me pass. She gives me a stiff little nod that makes it clear how she feels about people with weird hair showing up at her house uninvited.

"Hey, is this a bad time?" I ask as Niko leads me through the apartment.

"No, no, it's fine." We enter his room which is *pristine*, I mean there's not a wrinkle on the hunter green bedspread and there's none of the clutter of a teenager's room on the walls or the surfaces, the spines of the books are lined up razor-straight and the pencils in the pencil-holder on his desk are sharpened to lethal points.

"I'd offer you something to drink, but I'm not allowed to have any food or drinks in my room," Niko says.

I start to sit on the bed, but Niko blurts, "Don't sit there!"

I take a seat on the leather armchair, cautiously moving the needlepoint pillow on the center of the chair.

"Sorry, it's one of Papa's crazy rules. Once I make my bed in the morning I'm not allowed to sit on it or lie on it again until I go to sleep, unless I'm dying of fever or something. Sometimes he comes in and checks the bedspread."

"Really?"

"Yeah. He also opens my drawers and closets to make sure all my clothes are stacked neatly and facing the same direction."

"Your dad sounds a little psychotic." I look around the room. There is a framed black-and-white photo of three men in English fox-hunting riding habits on horseback in front of a colonial-style estate.

"Where is this?" I ask, pointing at the picture with the horses.

"That's Papa and his brothers in front of their family house in Argentina."

I want to ask him something else about his family in Argentina but I get distracted by Mrs. Aguilar who walks past the room and makes a big show of glaring at us as if she needs to make certain that we're not doing anything scandalous.

"So Carol, Gigi's assistant, got us press passes for the fashion shows," I say. "That means we can film from the press section! We can even go backstage. Isn't that cool?"

"Yeah, that's great."

"You're coming, right? Next week, Wednesday afternoon, at Spring Studios in Tribeca."

"I wouldn't miss it for anything, but don't mention it in front of my parents, okay?"

"Why?"

"It's just…they'll think it's weird that I'm interested in…you know, stuff like that."

"No, I don't know. Tell me."

I can see his mother lurking outside his door again, and she gives a little cough.

"You should probably leave. Come on, I'll walk out with you and we'll get a coffee on the corner."

Fine with me. Niko's house gives me the creeps with his ghoul of a mother and their crazy rules.

At the coffee shop on the corner we sit hunched at a table, our hands around our steaming beverages.

"Sorry," Niko says. "I just have to be so careful around them. Every minute of my life I'm afraid I'll slip up and that they'll guess the truth about me."

"What do you mean?"

"I'm not the kind of son they want. I'm not what they would call normal."

'Why? What's wrong with you?"

"I don't like typical guy things."

"What, like football? Sports cars?"

"Like girls."

"Oh. You mean you're gay." I shrug. "That's okay, isn't it?"

"Not to my parents. They'd throw me out of the house if they knew. They really would."

"Oh, come on. They're your parents. They love you."

Niko shakes his head.

"A couple of years ago, shortly after we moved to New York from Buenos Aires, my father and I were walking down Fifth Avenue in Greenwich Village and this guy in tight leather pants with a cropped tank top and bleached hair passed us in the opposite direction. The guy was looking at a shop window and didn't see us and bumped into me, and he said, 'Sorry, sweetheart,' and he winked at me. And Papa just freaked, he grabbed the guy by the collar and shoved him against a wall, yelling, 'Maricon,' and he spit in his face. The look he gave the man was one of such disgust, such hatred, it scared me."

"Oh, man."

"Another time Mama, Papa and I were watching TV and a thing came on about homosexual teens. My hands started to sweat and I felt this ringing in my ears. I was sure they could tell, that they could hear the roaring in my head. Then Mama goes, 'Those poor people,' about the parents of a teenage boy who'd come out to his parents. 'Can you imagine their suffering?' Papa was silent for a moment. Then he said, 'If that was my child, I'd kill him'."

"Jesus, Niko, do you spend every day of your life in fear of your parents?"

"I'm used to it. I just try to stay under the radar. Right now I'm just trying to make it from one week to the next. At least Fashion Week is something to look forward to. Here, let me show you something." From his backpack, Niko pulls a sketchbook and flips it open. The pages are filled with fashion illustrations: flowing dresses and towering hairstyles; geometric jackets over long, laced-up boots; fabric designs with embroidered tendrils of ivy and flowers; sandals covered with beads, each one drawn in detail; fitted bodices atop billowing skirts, and all over the margins, Niko's notes: *Two-layered chiffon skirt, pink/orange. Hand-painted butterflies on silk. Evening gown hand-sewn feathers on skirt, halter top kidskin lt.green.*

"Are these all your own?"

"Most of them."

"These are beautiful. No wonder you know so much about the fashion world. You're talented, Niko. You could be a fashion designer."

"Hah! My parents would never allow that. They'd disown me first. I'm going to law school or med school. Those are the only options."

I browse through Niko's sketchbook. On one spread of pages he's drawn several versions of a face I know: Connor. Connor in profile staring out the window, Connor looking down with his hair falling in his eyes, Connor with his feet up on the desk, Connor's eyes, Connor's nose, Connor's lips. Of course...Niko has a crush on Connor. Everyone has a crush on Connor. Even I have a crush on Connor. But in Niko's sketches, Connor's features are rendered with such tenderness that I can sense the hopeless intensity of Niko's feelings.

"Is it really up to them what you do with your life?"

"You have no idea what they're like. Everything I do, everything I wear, everywhere I go, has to meet their approval. If I so much as raise my voice then it's total lockdown. I don't think I went anywhere between school and my room for most of freshman year."

"Niko, you can't live like this. You'll go crazy."

"I just have to get out of the house. I've got two years until I graduate."

"And then? Will you come out to them?"

"If I tell them I'm gay they'll cut me off without a dime, and then how will I pay for college? I mean, at least in college I'll be out from under their roof."

"But that's six more years. Six years of living a lie."

"I've been living a lie for sixteen years, Jane. I can keep it up a while longer."

A surge of fury at Niko's parents rises in my chest. What a pair of cruel, inept assholes. I can't help feeling a little angry at Niko, too. I mean, is his parents' financial support really worth this kind of stress? But I realize it's not just about their money. They are the only family he has, and I know a little bit about needing to be accepted by your family, whether or not you like each other.

8

MAYA

There is so much to think about when you're walking on the runway: shoulders back, head up, chin down, arms still but not stiff, hips swaying but not swinging, stride long but not bouncing, feet in line without tripping, all while maintaining an expression of thinking of nothing at all. —*The Supermodel's Handbook* by Gigi Towers.

It's Fashion Week, and if I thought living in a house full of drama queens was irritating before, it was nothing compared to the frenzy of the past few days. We're all up and bickering for the bathroom at five AM and everyone chatters nonstop about who wore the best outfits for each show, and how amazing so-and-so's designs are this season, and how much we hate or love our hair or makeup, and did you see who was sitting next to this actress or that musician, and WHAT was the deal with the outfit the mayor's wife had on, did she think she was at a football game or something? I don't know how Sophia stays so chill. She's walking more shows than any of us, sometimes she literally has to run from one stage to another, and she still has the energy to go to the afterparties and look as perky as a chipmunk the next morning. Meanwhile, we're only on day three of the shows and I'm exhausted.

Early on Wednesday morning we're all crowded in the kitchen eating a hurried breakfast. I take small bites of fat-free yogurt in between gulps of black coffee, while Jane stands beside me smearing peanut butter on a bagel.

Brigitte glares at Jane's bagel. "You're so lucky that nobody cares what you look like," she says to Jane.

"Eat a cookie or something, will you?" Jane, unfazed, says to Brigitte. "It might make you a little sweeter."

Campbell, meanwhile, looks like she's going to throw up.

"Have you seen those heels I'm wearing? What if I trip? What if I miss my cue? Oh, God!" She is actually hyperventilating.

"Campbell, you just have to walk. You've been walking your whole life," I say.

"Could you move?" Brigitte says, trying to reach around Jane for the fruit bowl. Jane slides out of the way and bumps into me, and I spill my coffee on Brigitte's shoes.

"Dammit," Brigitte snaps, as Gigi drifts into the kitchen, adjusting one of her earrings.

"Who's going to Calvin Klein?" Gigi asks. "Sophia and Ling? Your car is here." They scramble out the door. "Jane, I wish you would stay out of the way of the girls when they're getting ready."

"I'm getting ready too," Jane retorts. "I have class in twenty minutes."

"Just for this week, Jane, can't you either get up earlier or come down later? This is a very busy time."

"Fine. I won't be here at all. I'll just get breakfast at the deli. Don't worry about me," Jane retorts sarcastically.

"Thank you," Gigi says. "That would be helpful." Jane grabs her backpack and stomps out of the kitchen.

The car for Campbell, Brigitte and me arrives twenty minutes later to take us to the Spring Studios building in Tribeca. There's a huge throng of people on the sidewalk, scaffolds set up with strobe lights, and camera crews all over the place. We squeeze into the entry line, separated from the throng of hungry onlookers by a metal railing guarded by four burly members of the NYPD. Inside, through a maze of sky-high ceilings and white walls, we reach the showroom, which is as big as a circus tent.

Backstage at the fashion shows reminds me of preparing to go on stage when I used to dance. The energy at the shows is equally exhilarating. It's such a different feel from photography work, where you spend half the day waiting around the set, blind with boredom. The stylists bustle about madly, checking and re-checking each outfit and making last-minute changes to accessories. There are murmurs about which celebrities are in the audience, cries of panic when an accessory goes missing and exclamations of relief when it is found, and a makeup artist howls when a model sneezes and smears her freshly-applied mascara. Sophia arrives at the last minute, the Calvin Klein show already completed, rubbing her makeup off with a wet-wipe so she can have it reapplied all over again.

The makeup artists make us look like ghosts, our faces bland masks and our hair slicked back which isn't exactly flattering but that's the point, our faces mustn't detract attention from the clothes. It doesn't make a difference what you do to Sophia, though. Even with her eyelashes, eyebrows and lips concealed under a sheen of ivory powder, those huge eyes of hers are still mesmerizing.

The dancer in me bursts to come out when I'm on stage

and to put a little jump into my walk and sway down the runway. But that's fatal for a runway model. You need a smooth, steady walk. I'm good at it, but when I saw Sophia walk for the first time I knew who really owns the runway. I don't know what she's doing that I'm not, but she moves like she's floating. They should just have her walk down that runway by herself, because when she's out there nobody is going to be looking at anyone else.

It's time to get into my first outfit. It's a stunning dress with a beaded top and almost completely translucent skirt, and the high-heeled clear lucite platform shoes are works of art. But as my dresser helps me into the dress, the head stylist hurries over with a change of outfit and takes mine from her.

"*Cela n'est pas pour elle, c'est une de nos meilleurs pieces*," he says. "*Vite, mets-la sur une autre fille, une blonde*."

I took four years of French in High School and I got a perfect score on my French SAT Subject Test. So I understood every word of the stylist telling my dresser to put my outfit on a blonde girl instead of me because it's one of their best pieces.

"*Tu sais, je te comprends*," I say. I add under my breath, "*Connard raciste*," If the stylist objects to being called a racist shithead he doesn't let on, and in another minute I'm dressed and ready to go. I look over my shoulder to see who they've given my outfit to. It's Campbell. Are they kidding? My walk is damn near perfect, and Campbell clomps like a stormtrooper. That's who they've put one of their best pieces on? I'm so mad I could scream but I force myself to clear my head and focus. Shake it off. Take the higher road. It's time to go on. I'm ready.

The lights dim and the murmuring of the audience quiets down. Suddenly the air is filled with ethereal, instrumental music, and tiny lights illuminate the runway like the dancing of fairies. The spotlight shines on the top of the runway and the first model steps out. I can see her from the wings. She glides like she's on wheels, her arms barely moving at her sides as her long, full chiffon skirt billows around her. A few paces behind her comes the next girl. The third girl out is Sophia, and a whisper rises from the audience. Her skirt ripples around her ankles like water, and when she walks it looks like her feet aren't even touching the runway. Applause fills the air.

A couple of other girls go out, and then it's my turn. I know I'm killing it — I get one of the loudest applauses, almost as loud as Sophia's, and I don't care about anything else, not even when I complete my turn at the bottom of the runway and make my way back up and I see Campbell coming out in my favorite outfit. As I walk toward her I can see the anxiety in her eyes.

Almost before it happens, I know what's coming. Campbell's eyes go wide in terror a split second before her shoes skid out from under her on the glass surface. Flailing her arms, Campbell comes crashing down like a felled tree. She grasps into the air for something to hold, and her fingers wrap around the skirt of the model in front of her, a girl named Genevieve from another agency. With an audible rip, Genevieve's skirt tears loose from the bodice and the audience gasps as a twenty-thousand dollar dress is destroyed before their eyes. While Campbell attempts to stagger back to her feet, Genevieve pulls her skirt to her waist and, holding it in place, completes her walk with as much poise as it is possible to muster in a tattered dress with your underpants on display to the world, and she even gets a brief applause from the audience. Meanwhile, the models keep coming out and they strut past Campbell like she's roadkill. Finally Campbell is on her feet. By now I'm off the runway, but I can still see Campbell from the wings. She slips into the line, cutting off the model behind her, does her little turn thing at the bottom of the runway and then wobbles back toward the top. She is almost there when she stumbles, her arms flail and — really, Campbell? — down she goes again. The models walk around her without missing a step, and when she finally gets to her feet one of her shoes is dangling from her ankle by its straps as she hobbles off the stage.

"Hurry, hurry, you have another outfit," my dresser whispers frantically, and I rush to my clothes rack and shimmy into my next dress. I don't have time to check on Campbell, and only just make it back into the procession in time. At the end of the show all of us come out for a finale, but I don't see Campbell.

The moment I'm back in my own clothes I try to find her. I squeeze my way past models in various stages of undress, makeup artists packing up their equipment, and dressers sorting the garments onto clothing racks. Everyone is in a hurry to get somewhere else. I find Campbell seated in a corner of the floor, her head in her hands.

"Hey," I say, crouching beside her. When she looks at me her eyes are red from crying.

"Did you see? I ruined everything."

"No, you didn't. It was just one glitch in an otherwise lovely show."

"Bullshit. They didn't even let me go out in my second dress. They put it on another girl."

"Campbell? Are you okay?" says a familiar voice. We both look up, and to our surprise, see Jane.

"What are you doing here?" I ask. I don't mean it as unkindly as it probably sounds. "I mean, shouldn't you be in school?"

"I got a press pass to the show from Carol," Jane says. "I'm here with my friend Niko."

"That was nice of her," Campbell sniffles.

"Campbell, don't worry," I say. "Some of the most famous models in the world have fallen on the runway."

"Not like I did."

"Well, go big or go home, right?" Jane gives a little laugh, but Campbell is so not in the mood.

"Look, people are going to forget all about this by the end of the day," I assure her. But Campbell gives a sob and shakes her head. The three of us walk toward the door together. A pair of models pass us and one of them pretends to trip in an ugly pantomime of Campbell's fall, and they laugh like idiots.

"Why don't you come and do something fun with me and Niko?" Jane says. "We're blowing off class for the rest of the day, and we thought we'd go ice skating at the Chelsea Piers."

"I can't. I have a go-see on Sixth Avenue," Campbell mopes. She murmurs goodbye and leaves.

"Is she going to be alright?" Jane asks.

"I'm not sure. Campbell needs a lucky break soon or she's not going to last another month in this business," I reply.

9

CAMPBELL

I *'m not an unreasonable person. I don't expect more from my girls than I do from myself. Unfortunately for them, I am very, very demanding of myself.* — *The Many Faces of Gigi Towers* by L. M. Daly.

SHITFUCKHELLDAMNCRAP. This was my big chance and I blew it. God, I suck! What will Gigi say? I bet she thinks I'm a big, useless cow. I bet she never sends me on a casting again. I bet she's terminating my contract this minute.

"Somebody posted a video of you falling on youtube," Maya says, seated on the floor and looking at my moment of glory on her laptop. "You've already got eight hundred views. Want to see?"

"No thanks. I was there."

Sophia leans over to take a look, and she scrolls down the

page. I peek over her shoulder, and even though I know nothing good is going to come out of it, I read some of the viewers' comments. I was right, I shouldn't have bothered. Some of them are really mean: *"#Youhadonejob," "What kind of a model doesn't know how to walk in heels"* and *"Who let that Clydesdale on the runway?"* are a few examples. I pull up my knees and bury my face in my arms.

Sophia floats over to me, sits down and puts her arm around my shoulders.

"Never mind," Sophia purrs. "What you need is to get your mind off of it. I'm invited to the *Harper's Bazaar* party at the Turntable Lounge, and I can get you both on the list. Are you in?"

"Oh hell yes," says Maya.

"No. I don't want anyone to look at me," I mumble from under my curtain of hair.

"Oh, come on," Sophia coaxes. "So what if they do? It'll show everyone that you're not curled up in a ball crying."

"I *am* curled up in a ball crying."

"Sophia's right," says Maya. "You'll feel better, really. It'll be fun."

"We have a curfew, remember? Nine o'clock on weeknights," I say.

"Gigi is at a party at the MoMA," Sophia says. "She won't even know we're gone. We can be back by nine. Ten at the latest."

I sigh, but it comes out sounding like a snort.

"Come on," Sophia wheedles. "Please? I don't want to go without you."

"I'll lend you my Alaïa," Maya says.

I wipe my eyes with my sleeve and even though I know I look disgusting and my face is wet with tears and probably snot, Sophia gently kisses my forehead. For a moment I forget that I have just had one of the worst days ever and all I think of is how sweet Sophia is and how soft she feels and that she smells like jasmine. I feel a throb of adoration and gratitude and I know I will do anything for her.

"Okay," I sniffle.

By the time I'm showered and dressed I feel a little better. As we get dressed, Sophia opens a bottle of wine - who knows where she got this one from - and pours us each a glass. Maya lends me a vintage Azzedine Alaïa that she bought from a stylist, a gray-blue sleeveless dress with a low-cut neckline that hugs every curve on my body. Sophia has on a little black dress with a plunging back while Maya wears a short flouncy white thing that makes her legs look like they go up to her rib cage. Sophia helps me with my eye makeup, lining the top eyelids with a smoky black edge.

Outside the Turntable Lounge a horde of people surround the entrance, prepared to wait all night to get in or even just to get a glimpse at some of the VIP guests. Sophia, Maya and I step out of our cab, and the bouncers wave us through the crowd which parts like the Red Sea. Sophia loops her arms through mine and Maya's, and under the bright bursts of flashbulbs we follow the red carpet up the steps and into the club.

Inside, I do my best not to gape like a star-struck imbecile. I recognize other models, and actors, and all the people who are a hundred times more important because they are the ones who make the stars, who cast them and dress them and photograph them and keep them relevant.

"That's the creative director of Armani," says Sophia. "And that's the Editor-in-Chief of French Vogue."

"And there's Frederick, who photographed Kylie Jenner's *Harper's Bazaar* cover," adds Maya. "The naked one with the snake across her boobs."

"Sophia, look this way!" Cameras flash at us from all directions.

"Sophia, over here!"

"Sophia, who's your favorite designer?"

Sophia loops her arms through mine and Maya's, and the three of us pose for the photographers in front of the *Harper's Bazaar* backdrop with Sophia in the middle.

"Can I get your names?" a young woman holding a tablet asks me and Maya. "I know yours, of course," she smiles at Sophia. Maya and I oblige. A passing waiter holds out a tray with an array of drinks.

"What are they?" I ask.

"Chardonnay, Cabernet, Long Island ice tea, and vodka tonic," he explains. I don't really know anything about alcoholic drinks but I know what ice tea is so I take one of those. I sip it, trying to look like I have every right to be here, but the truth is I feel like a big fat fraud and that any minute someone is going to point at me and scream, "Who do you think you're fooling, Campbell Tucker from Fayetteville, Georgia? Until last summer your idea of fashion was sequins on your jeans, and you can't even walk on a runway without busting your ass." Before I know it my glass is empty.

"Let's do a lap and work the room," Sophia says, linking her arm through mine. I don't even know what that means, but I follow her, and I absolutely love the way people just stop talking and stare at Sophia when she walks past. She's not the biggest name in this room, but she is getting the most attention. Dozens of people want to say hello to her and take her picture, and meanwhile I help myself to another drink.

Sophia isn't one to stand around holding up a wall at a party, so as soon as there's a lull in conversation she says "Come on, let's dance," and I put down my drink — is it my third? Not sure — and the three of us take to the dance floor. I'm a decent dancer, and so is Sophia, but neither of us can compare to Maya. She used to be really into ballet, and it shows on the dance floor. I feel dizzy with joy. But soon I realize it's not joy that is making me dizzy. I've got a different kind of dizziness going on, caused by three drinks on an empty stomach. I signal to the other two that I need to sit down, and I stagger off the dance floor.

"You okay?" Sophia asks when she finds me sitting at a table.

"My head feels fuzzy," I say.

"Want me to get you something?" Sophia asks.

"You just need a little energy boost," Maya adds. She leaves us, then returns with a can of Red Bull.

"Here you go," Maya says, popping open the can. "Drink this. It'll make you feel a lot less groggy." I drain the Red Bull. "Better?"

"Yeah, thanks," I say, but no, not really, and when I stand up my stomach flops around like a fish. The room begins to spin very fast and it must show on my face because Sophia holds me by my wrists.

"Uh oh," she says. "Are you going to…?"

"Yes, she is," says Maya. "Quick, this way." The girls take me by the arms and drag me through the crowd, elbowing people out of the way and when I stumble into the restroom I collapse in one of the stalls where I throw up into the toilet.

"That was close," Maya sighs.

"Taken," Sophia snaps as she shoves the door to the restroom shut in someone's face. "Campbell, are you alright? Can you stand up?"

I don't think I can. I think I've been poisoned.

"God, Campbell, can't you even hold your booze?" Maya grumbles as she props me up against the sink. She wets a stack of paper towels and wipes my face and the front of my dress while Sophia stands guard at the door, ignoring the protests of the people outside.

"Uhh, I'm so sorry," I groan.

"We better get out of here," Sophia says. "Hold it together,

Campbell, okay?" She opens the door. With all the composure I can muster, I let them lead me to the exit.

"I've called for a car," Maya says, looking at her phone. "Shit, it's going to be about fifteen minutes."

We lurk in the darkness of the entryway, and I pray that I won't lose my guts again before we get outside, which by some miracle I manage. Finally our car arrives. We bundle into the car and Maya gives the driver Gigi's address.

"God, how'd it get so late?" Maya says.

"What time is it?" I ask.

"Almost midnight."

"What? Oh, crap, that's it, we're dead," I cry.

"No, we're not," says Sophia. "Stop it. Maybe Gigi isn't even home yet. Maybe she came home and went straight to bed. Anyway, what's the worst that can happen?"

Easy for Sophia to say. Gigi would never kick her out of her house. But I bet Gigi's just waiting for an excuse to send me packing.

We arrive home, get out of the car and scamper up the steps as the car drives away. The night is bitter cold and none of us have coats on. We stand on the front stoop shivering while Sophia fumbles with the key in the lock.

"Hurry up, I'm freezing my butt off," Maya says through chattering teeth.

"Uh oh. Shit," Sophia says as she stares at the doorknob. "The deadbolt is locked. I can't open the door!"

"You've got to be kidding," I wail.

"No, seriously. Someone locked it. What should we do?"

"Hang on. I'll call Ling," Maya says, and dials the number on her phone. We wait, huddled together to keep warm. "She's not answering. Dammit. She must have turned her ringer off."

"What about Brigitte?"

"Trying her now...oh, thank god...Brigitte, it's Maya! We're locked outside. Me and Sophia and Campbell. Can you come let us in? Okay, hurry up, will you, we're freezing to death." Maya puts her phone away. "Whew."

We bounce around with relief, then we bounce around for warmth, because Brigitte is taking her precious time getting to the door.

"Where the hell is she?" Sophia chatters.

"Maybe she fell back asleep," I suggest.

"If she did, so help me God, I will slap her in the face with a cactus." Maya calls Brigitte's number again. "Brig…dammit, voice mail." There's a brief pause, then Maya leaves her message: "Brigitte, you useless whore, where the hell are you? If you don't open this damn door in ten seconds I'm going to gouge out your eyeballs and…"

Just then we hear the click of the lock turning over and a sleepy-faced Brigitte opens the door.

"Finally!" Maya hisses in a loud whisper.

"You're welcome," Brigitte whispers back.

"Does Gigi know we were out?"

"Don't know. I didn't see her before I went to bed."

We tiptoe upstairs and I hold my breath as we pass Gigi's floor. I peel off my wet clothes and put on a pair of flannel pajama pants and a T-shirt, then crawl into bed. For the first time I'm actually glad that I'm not booked for anything tomorrow. At least I can sleep in. Gradually I stop shivering and fall asleep.

FROM VERY, very far away, a voice calling my name breaks through the thick fog of sleep. The morning light blinds me like a pair of icepicks jammed through my eye sockets and OH my head, it feels like there's a rabid pit bull trapped inside my brain fighting its way out. I peer outside the covers. Maya is gone already; she had a show this morning. I guess the other girls have left as well. Sunlight is peering through the shades, and according to my phone it is only seven-thirty.

"Campbell, come downstairs, would you?" Is that Gigi? What the hell does she want at this time of the morning?

Somehow I manage to pull on a pair of jeans and a sweater and find my way downstairs, clinging to the railing. My stomach is so queasy that I'm worried the two Advil I swallowed aren't going to stay down. I find Gigi in the dining room, having a slice of wheat toast with smoked salmon and a cup of coffee. Standing upright is a challenge, and I clutch the back of one of the dining chairs for balance.

"There you are," she chirps, laying aside her morning paper. "Good morning, Campbell. I came home so late that I didn't get a chance to see you last night. I hope you girls were able to have a relaxing evening, after how busy you've all been."

"Um, yes, we did, thank you." (Was that croaking sound my voice?)

"I understand things didn't go quite as planned at the show yesterday."

"I'm so sorry, Gigi, I tripped, it was an accident…"

"I want you to work on your walk with our runway coach, Renata. She has time for you at eleven o'clock today. Oh, and I've added several other appointments to your schedule. It looks like you'll have a busy afternoon."

Ugh. At least I don't have to be at Renata's until eleven. Maybe I'll feel a little better by then. I just need to go back to bed and crawl under the covers for a couple more hours, at least until my head stops throbbing with pain.

"Um, okay, good idea, thanks," I say. I make a move to go back upstairs.

"And you know, I have a wonderful idea." Gigi clasps her hands together and smiles. "why don't you take a fitness class this morning? Nothing is better for your coordination than a good aerobic workout."

Impossible. No way. I can't think of anything in the world I want to do less. The blinding pain in my head flares up at the mere thought of exercise, especially in a class with blaring music and a screaming drill sergeant for an instructor. Gigi stands up, folds her newspaper and comes around to my side of the table. Then she drops the paper on the table in front of me. Facing me is a picture from last night's party: a half-page shot of Sophia and me, arms around each other's waists, and I'm holding a drink as we laugh at the camera.

"I'll call Electra at the fitness studio and let her know you're coming. Be prepared to work up a good sweat." Gigi gives me a smug, knowing smile, just *daring* me to protest, and leaves the room.

Somehow I make it through the day, even though I have a major head rush ten minutes into the fitness class and sit down right in the middle of the floor with my head between my knees. It's unbelievably embarrassing getting my ass kicked in a fitness class, especially when most of the other participants are at least twice my age, and when I get home I have just enough time to shower and change and get across town to Renata's, and after two hours of runway boot camp I manage to squeeze six go-sees into the afternoon. I haven't been able to eat anything all day, and when I get home I stumble up the stairs and collapse onto my bed. Point made, Gigi. Message received, loud and freaking clear.

10

_____

MAYA

I was so angry when I left the house this morning that I kicked a dent into the trash can on the corner of Lafayette Street. I should have been in that picture with Campbell and Sophia! There were tons of pictures of us taken last night, including several of me and Sophia without Campbell. Why didn't they use one of those? And that caption! "Campbell Tucker in vintage Alaïa..." That was my damn Alaïa! I only lent it to her because Sophia said she wouldn't take us to the party unless Campbell came along, and I know Campbell loves that dress. And then she throws up in it! I'll have to get it dry cleaned, and I bet she doesn't even have the money to pay me back. I'm losing my grip on this whole situation. Okay, I expect Sophia to take center stage, she's a natural superstar. But I'll be damned if I let that little hick Campbell overshadow me.

I have two shows this morning, and by the time I arrive at

the first one I'm feeling the effects of last night. Fortunately I still have Alexandra's pills. I swallow one while I'm having my hair done, and by the time I'm on the runway I've got my groove back. I feel like a superhero as I walk the runway, and the air is filled with flashbulbs and applause. I'm filled with joy, and I ride that feeling through the next show, high with exhilaration. It's all over far too soon, and backstage the designer pops open a bottle of champagne and we all cheer and sip champagne and take pictures with our arms around each other as though we've all been best friends our whole lives.

The fashion bloggers are just as interested in the models' street fashion as they are in what we wear on the runway, so there are photographers and bloggers all over the place as we leave, eager to catch candid shots of us on our way to our next shows. A young blonde reporter stops me, flags down her cameraman, and sticks her microphone in front of my face.

"Maya, you were magnificent," she says. She knows my name! I'm so excited that she knows my name! Then she continues with, "Don't you just love all the diversity on the runways? *The New York Times* wrote that this is one of the most diverse Fashion Week seasons yet. Isn't it exciting to see racism in fashion finally become a thing of the past?"

She holds the microphone under my mouth, and apparently I'm expected to answer. I'm speechless for a moment, but not because I have nothing to say. There's plenty I can say. I could point out that the Fashion Week shows only take place two weeks out of the year, and the rest of the time models of color have to compete for the very small percentage of advertising, commercial, catalog and editorial jobs available to us. I could suggest that this reporter pick up any fashion magazine and compare the number of pages depicting white models versus pages with black models. I could suggest she look not only at the photographs in the magazines, but also at the masthead, and see how many of the magazine's editors and contributors are women of color. I could point out that girls like me who want to succeed in modeling need to be better and work harder, just to keep up.

"Yes, the diversity on the runways is a start, but we still have a very long way…" I begin. But the reporter cuts me off.

"There's Christy Bennett! Oh, hey, Christy!" she cries, and runs off, cameraman behind her, leaving me hanging in mid-sentence. What an idiot, I think. It's a rude awakening, after feeling like Wonder Woman on the runway, to realize that my opinion is of no interest to anyone, not even to the stupidest reporter who ever held a press pass. I shake off my anger only when Ling bumps into me and pulls me into a playful pose for the cameras. If all these people want me to do is smile, then fine, I'll smile. I'll smile until my face aches.

At home I find Campbell sprawled on her bed. She looks like a train wreck.

"You look like a train wreck," I inform her.

"I feel like one," she grumbles. "How come you don't?"

"I only had one glass of wine at the party, and I didn't finish it. What did you drink, anyway?"

"Just some ice tea or something."

"There's no ice tea in a Long Island ice tea, you half-wit, you know that, don't you?" I tell her. "It's a mixture of vodka and tequila and god knows what else. No wonder you're sick."

Campbell moans as she covers her face with her arm, and then reaches out to me with a small piece of paper in her fist. "Here."

"What is this?"

"Dry cleaning receipt for your dress. So sorry. It's paid, it'll be ready on Monday."

I take the receipt with a twinge of guilt.

Just then Sophia bursts into the room. She is still in full makeup from her last show, and bubbling with excitement.

"Guess what!" She announces. She pauses as though she

actually expects an answer. She's Sophia, so it could be anything: The Metropolitan Museum wants to carve her face on all the statues; she found the lost Faberge Eggs of the Romanovs in a taxicab; The Duke of Cambridge wants to renounce the throne to run away with her. Anything is possible, so nobody answers.

"I just spoke to Theo, and he's invited us to spend the weekend at his house in the Hamptons! All three of us! And Campbell, he saw our picture in the paper today and he said he'll do a test shoot with you!"

Campbell starts screaming with excitement, then clutches her head and grimaces with pain. This is a huge break, especially for Campbell. Theo Wolff doesn't do test shots with new girls. Ever. He only works with the big stars. Even the models who pull in ten thousand dollars a day will work with Theo for nothing. I've met Theo on a go-see but I haven't worked with him, but I guaran-damn-tee you that if he's going to shoot Campbell in the Hamptons he's going to shoot me too.

CAMPBELL, Sophia, me, and, for some reason, Jane, take a Jitney to Bridgehampton. I have no idea why Jane would want to spend a weekend at the beach in midwinter, but here she is. Maybe she asked Gigi if she could come to work on her film project. Or maybe Gigi just wants her out of the house. Anyway, Jane sits a couple of rows behind us, her nose buried in a book, even though the bus is nearly empty. I still don't know what to make of her. Sometimes she seems nice, and other times she acts like she can't stand us.

At the bus station in Bridgehampton, Theo, wearing jeans, work boots and a fisherman's sweater, picks us up in a silver Range Rover. He's probably around forty, of less than medium height and sports a dark blonde ponytail. If you didn't know who he was you'd never imagine the most beautiful girls in the world falling over themselves to meet him. When we pull up to the house, which sits on a small cliff overlooking the beach, the orange glow from the windows is so cozy and warm that it feels like home even though I've never set foot in the place.

Inside, Theo helps Sophia off with her coat, while the rest of us wriggle out of our parkas. "You girls can decide who sleeps where," Theo says. There are three bedrooms: The master is, of course, Theo's, and then there's one room with a queen bed and one with two single beds. Sophia and Campbell immediately snag the queen, which leaves me and Jane with the twin beds. When we're all in the living room in front of the fire Theo brings out a platter of cheeses and crusty french bread.

"Help yourself to whatever you want to drink," Theo says, gesturing to the bar.

"Theo, this is so lovely," Sophia says as she pours herself a glass of white wine. "I would never come back into the city if I had this place. I'd just stay here forever."

"It can get a little dull in winter, but wait until you see the light on the rocks in the late afternoon. That's where we're going to shoot. We have about an hour until the sunlight is at its best."

While Campbell and Sophia are getting ready for their pictures, Jane wanders outside to explore the cliff with her video camera. From the window I watch her filming the grounds and the view. My makeup is done, and I don't need to change clothes until right before my shot, so I follow her outside. She focuses her camera on the house, when suddenly she stops and stares. Over her shoulder I see what she's looking at: Theo and Sophia, framed in the window of one of the downstairs bedrooms, as Theo taps the contents of a little vial onto the top of his hand. He offers a tiny silver tube to Sophia, who snorts the substance off of Theo's hand, then daintily pats her nose while Theo snorts the rest.

"So that's how she keeps it up, then," I say, and Jane, startled, turns to me.

"I didn't know Sophia did coke," Jane says. "What would Gigi do if she knew?"

"You think Gigi doesn't know?"

"Gigi's famous for her anti-drug stance. She said she'd never keep a girl in her agency if she did drugs."

"And you believe that?"

"Well, yes. She says so all the time in interviews and in her books."

"That's her image, but she knows how this business works. Lots of models do cocaine. How do you think Sophia gets through twenty shows and all the parties during fashion week?"

Jane just stares.

"Let me tell you something that happened a few weeks before you arrived," I continue. "There was this girl, Lauren, from Kansas. Pretty girl, but young. She booked a catalog job with this photographer, Daniel, and he and some of the other models were doing coke during the shoot. So Lauren, she gets a little freaked out, and she actually believes Gigi's whole anti-drug spiel, so she tells Gigi all about it, like Gigi's going to make it all better. And you know what Gigi does? She calls Lauren's mother and says Lauren is too young and immature to work in New York and sends her home."

"But why?"

"Because Daniel is a successful photographer who books lots of Towers girls."

"Gosh. Gigi's kind of a bitch."

"Gigi's a businesswoman," I clarify. "As long as we stay thin, our skin is clear and we show up on time, Gigi's happy. But if a girl starts creating problems, she's out of here."

Theo emerges from the house.

"Ready, Maya?" he calls.

As I walk toward him I turn back to Jane and say, "You're lucky, Jane. Gigi doesn't care what you do."

That came out wrong, I realize too late. Sorry, kiddo. At least you don't have to worry about Gigi putting you out on the curb. It's something that I never let myself forget. It's why I won't be running to Gigi saying a photographer was wired out of his skull, or tricked me into letting him photograph my breasts, or copped a feel. Like Theo is doing right now.

"Here, let me adjust this," Theo says as I sit perched on a rock. He tucks a piece of my cashmere shawl between my upper arm and my breast, and then he traces the side of my breast with his fingers. I cock my eyebrow and shake my head ever so slightly, as though he's just a naughty kid and not some old pervert who thinks he owns my body.

"Do you have a boyfriend, Maya?" Theo asks.

"I do," I lie with a sympathetic smile, as though my imaginary boyfriend is the only thing standing between me and a session of torrid lovemaking with Theo. That's one thing I won't do. I'm not sleeping with anyone just to get ahead. Nobody's business, by the way, but I'm still a virgin. Not that I want to wait until marriage or anything archaic like that, but I do want to be in love.

"Does that mean no you and me?" he says, with a sad puppy-dog look. "Well, if you decide to give me a second thought..." Ha. I didn't even give him a first thought. He has graying bristles growing on his upper lip and he smells like cigarettes and stale wine and cologne and the mere idea of sex with Theo makes me stifle a gag. His claw of a hand is still cupping the side of my breast, and now he presses my nipple gently with his thumb. Oh, Theo, if you had any idea. If he wasn't one of the top photographers in the world I would punch him hard enough to split my knuckles on his teeth. I envision myself landing a karate chop to his Adam's apple, grabbing him by his saggy neck and shoving his arrogant ass off the rocks into the sea. Instead, I playfully swat at his hand, when what I'd really like to do is snap it off at the wrist.

We start shooting, the light of the setting sun turning my skin to bronze as the wind blows my hair back in a mane of dark tendrils. He shows me some of the images on his camera in between poses.

"Are you going to post those? They're really beautiful," I say.

"Maybe," he teases, "If you're nice to me."

He thinks he's being cute but I'm dead serious, he'd better. Theo has over two million followers. Everyone in the fashion world follows him, and whenever he tags a model in his pictures her number of followers skyrockets, and so do her jobs.

"Look at this one," he says. "So regal, so untouchable. Maya the Ice-Queen."

When we're done with my pictures I stand to the side and watch as Theo photographs Campbell for a while. I'll say this for Campbell, she's not afraid of being sexy. Sexiness is completely natural to her. She's like a young Marilyn Monroe, all curves and boobs and blonde curls, and she's not at all self-conscious about her body, even though Gigi is always giving her a hard time about her weight. Now I'm worried about my own pictures. I mean I know I'm pretty, but am I sexy? "Maya the Ice-Queen"…is that a good thing? Should I try to be more seductive? I don't even think I know how. Giggling and flirting and carrying on the way Campbell does, that's a foreign language to me. What if Theo trashes all my pictures because he thinks I'm sexually repressed? He's doing that same little move with touching her boob. Campbell doesn't mind at all, she acts like she thinks it's funny. They lean into each other, laughing, and she arches her back and runs her hands through her hair. She's wearing a sheer V-neck sweater which hangs off her shoulders, no bra, and torn, faded jeans which fit her like spandex. If I wore that outfit I'd look like an androgynous nerd. Campbell looks like she belongs on the cover of *Playboy*.

What Campbell does is her own business, but I hope she doesn't give it up for Theo because she thinks he's going to fall in love with her or change her life or something. Even she can't be that naive.

11

CAMPBELL

I*t's not enough to just be beautiful. If you want to distinguish yourself, you must cultivate your own special talent. Find out what you're good at and make it your brand. Don't be shy about sharing your special talent with the world! — The Supermodel's Handbook by* Gigi Towers.

"THIS WAS the most exciting day I've ever had since I started modeling," I say to Theo as we stand in the kitchen. "Working with you, I know we're creating art, something beautiful and lasting." I tilt my head as I gaze at him over the edge of my wine glass. He's not totally repulsive, I decide. He's got the weathered brown skin of an outdoorsman, and his eyes are very blue under his dark eyebrows.

"It's not hard when my subject is as beautiful as you."

Yeah, okay, I know — some of the cheesiest, most absolutely vomitous lines ever uttered. But I know what I'm doing, I'm not as gullible as I sound. Here's the thing: I can't compete with Maya and Sophia with just my looks. I need an edge of my own. And I have that edge. I discovered it when I was fifteen, my very own superpower. Maya has brains, Jane has a family name, and Sophia has...well, everything. Me, I have the ability to make men completely stupid with desire. Some people think that makes me a slut, but I'm not a slut. I enjoy sex, and guys enjoy sex with me, so I don't see what the moral dilemma is. But I only enjoy sex with guys I'm at least halfway in love with. Can I help it that I fall halfway in love so easily?

I had the best teacher in the world in my mom. I watched her reel in countless men by sending the tiniest signals, letting them think it's their idea, that they're the ones doing the chasing. Now, leaning against the kitchen counter, I let my hair cascade over one shoulder and twirl a few strands between my fingertips. From there I absently let my fingers slide down the front of my chest, leading his gaze to the soft, dark spot between my breasts. I bat my eyelashes like a doe, and slowly take a sip of my wine, all the while gazing at Theo like he's the most fascinating thing I've ever seen. He shifts so he's standing so close his knee touches my inner thigh, and I don't move away.

A small smile creeps over Theo's face. He cups my chin in his hand and, with his thumb, gently wipes a drop of wine off my lower lip. Then he leans in and kisses me. He holds the back of my head and his hand slips under my sweater, finds my breast and caresses it. Pretty soon he takes my hand, and I follow him to his bedroom. Just as he closes the door behind us I look over his shoulder, and in the darkness of the hallway I see Jane. She's standing there with that damn video camera, silently filming us.

~

IN THE EARLY DAWN, as Theo gets out of bed, I try not to look too closely. His butt sags and his genitals look gray and shriveled as he makes his way to the bathroom. If I look away, I can pretend he's twenty years younger, and that he didn't make disgusting gurgling sounds in his sleep and that his bristly beard didn't remind me of a goat. I can pretend that we are just two people who find each other attractive and that what we're doing is the most natural thing in the world.

And I almost believe myself. When he returns from the bathroom and doesn't look at me either, I wonder what it is that he's trying to pretend that I'm not.

Without a word to me Theo lies on his side, his back to me, and falls asleep again. But I can't go back to sleep. I remember what it was that I was dreaming before I woke up: I was walking through the halls of my school and no-one would speak to me, everyone went out of their way to avoid me like something disgusting left on the floor, and I started to cry like a little kid but nobody paid any attention, and then my skin started to wrinkle and shrivel, and I was shrinking like an old forgotten dried-up turnip until I woke up gasping.

It's too dark, too quiet, too lonely, even with Theo beside me. *Especially* with Theo beside me.

I have to get out of this room. I get up and use the bathroom in the hall. There's a scale on the floor, and, as though I wasn't miserable enough, I stand on it. I've gained weight again. I'm now easily ten pounds over my target weight, and I don't understand why, other than that this is just my body doing what it's destined to do. Theo seemed to enjoy it enough last night. Disgusted, I step off and walk to the living room.

There are a few glasses and wine bottles lying around, and there's a light left on, but other than that there's no sign of life in the house. Everyone is asleep. I turn on the kitchen light and open the refrigerator door, looking for a diet soda. A rustling noise coming from the bottom drawer of the refrigerator scares the living crap out of me for a second. It's those lobsters that Theo bought us for lunch tomorrow! I didn't realize they were actually alive. Slowly I pull open the drawer, and five brown lobsters, their claws held closed with rubber bands, squirm around inside. They wiggle across one another, clawing at the smooth white plastic sides, trying to climb their way out. Their little black eyes point upward and one of them, I swear to God, looks right into my eyes and spreads his claws in the air, like a small child pleading to be picked up, and the lobster's fear and despair hits me like a truck. In a panic, I yank the drawer out of the refrigerator and place it on the floor. Picking up each lobster I slit through every rubber band with a small carving knife and place the lobsters back in the drawer. I lug the drawer through the back door to the porch and step into the cold night air. The sky is dark navy blue and by the light of the moon I walk through the cold grass, past the still-burning embers of the fire pit, to the edge of the cliff. The water crashes against the rocks below me. Standing on the rocks I fling the refrigerator drawer and its passengers off the cliff. Lobsters fly out of the drawer into the air and splash into the waves below. The white plastic drawer bobs on the waves for a while until it fills with water and sinks.

I imagine the lobsters finding their way to the sandy bottom, then crawling off to go to sleep under rocks and crevices, and slowly my own misery subsides. I think I can try to go back to sleep now. I'll have to think of something to tell the others about why their lunch disappeared during the night. Maybe I'll blame it on an episode of sleepwalking. Or maybe I won't say anything.

_____

12

JANE

Once we're back in the city I start to give some thought to whether I should remind Gigi of my birthday, which is in two weeks. Coming right out and telling her seems childish, as though I'm fishing for presents. After all, I'm not a little kid, I don't need a big production or anything special. But you only turn sixteen once. Perhaps I could just drop a hint when we're talking about something else. The problem is, I haven't really had a chance to talk to Gigi in private. She was out of town all last week, and last night she took Sophia to a party for some designer, and the night before that she took a bunch of other girls from the agency to the opera at Lincoln Center. Early in the evening I stop by Gigi's room to see if I can finally have a word with her, since we've hardly spent any time together since I arrived. But instead I find her in conversation with Sophia who lies curled up on her floor, playing with the cat. They both look at me like I'm interrupting something.

"Yes, Jane, is anything the matter?" Gigi asks.

"Nope," I say. "Everything's peachy." I half expect Gigi to call me back as I leave, to insist I tell her what's wrong. But she doesn't.

Then, at dinner, Gigi makes an announcement.

"In two weeks we'll be celebrating a very special day," she says.

I've just taken a big bite of salad and I stop in mid-chew because I can't believe what I'm about to hear.

"The 23rd is the birthday of a very dear young lady whom you all know, and I would like to celebrate with a party."

Holy mother of miracles, she remembered! I'm so grateful and relieved, I feel like jumping out of my seat and giving her a hug.

"At the Oleander Club," Gigi continues. "We can book the whole top floor."

I'm a little overwhelmed. I think I'm starting to blush. I gulp down my mouthful of salad so I can answer.

"Oh, Gigi, that sounds…"

Gigi interrupts me. "What do you think, darling?" She looks at Sophia. "Is that how you would like to celebrate your eighteenth birthday?"

My heart sinks like a rock. Sophia? Her eighteenth birthday? The 23rd is MY birthday!

"Gigi, thank you!" croons Sophia. "You're much too sweet."

"Carol is already working on a guest list. All of your top clients, of course, and everyone from the Towers Agency. Send her a list of any additional guests you want to include."

They start to discuss menus and musical entertainment, and I'm so disgusted I have to leave.

"May I be excused?" I say. "I think I'm about to become violently ill." Gigi dismisses me with a little wave of her hand. I take my plate to the kitchen where I deposit it on the counter with a clatter. We're supposed to load our own plates in the dishwasher, but I leave it there. Maybe Gigi will call me back downstairs to put it away, I think as I stomp up the stairs. And maybe I'll tell her to put it away herself, and maybe we'll have a good old fight like a normal teenager and parent and she'll have to listen to me. But not at all to my surprise she doesn't even notice.

IN ENGLISH CLASS the next day I am still in a rotten mood. We talk about Jane Austen's *Mansfield Park* and its heroine, Fanny Price. Poor old Fanny Price. She gets dumped with relatives and the whole household treats her like a second-class citizen, forgetting she even exists half the time. Sounds eerily familiar, doesn't it?

"Why is she so spineless?" I ask during the discussion. "She doesn't speak up for herself, she lets her aunt treat her like a doormat, she won't participate in anything. It's her own fault her cousins treat her like she doesn't count."

"Is it, though?" Our teacher, Mr. Bernard asks. "Consider her circumstances. She's a charity case. She knows that if she does anything to offend her relations she could be sent away."

"But why does she have to be such a drip?" Brooke, who sits behind me, interjects. "She even freaks out about her cousins putting on a play in the privacy of their own home. I mean it's just a play for heaven's sake!"

"Well, remember the time period," says Mr. Bernard. "Plays, especially ones with a suggestive theme, were considered morally risky and inappropriate for young people. For the cousins to put on a play in the absence of their parents was similar to someone in today's time throwing a party while their parents are away."

Suddenly I have an absolutely stellar idea.

"I'm having a party," I tell Niko and Jazz after class. "On the 23rd. At my house." I ask a few other kids as well, including Ashley and Connor. I write down Gigi's address on Ashley's spiral notebook. Nothing too big or fancy, but I'm going to celebrate my birthday with my own party, not watching a hundred strangers worshipping Sophia.

"We had the *best* caterer for my sixteenth birthday," Ashley volunteers. "I'll get their name for you. There was a sushi bar and a macaron tower and a chocolate fountain, and my mom hired professional ballerinas in tutus and pointe shoes to pass around hors d'oevres…"

"Yeah, no. I need you to set your expectations a LOT lower," I reply. "I'm just having a small crowd over to hang out. Maybe I'll order some pizzas and get an ice-cream cake…"

"Are you crazy? You can't just serve pizza and ice cream for your birthday. You're turning sixteen, not six."

"Actually, she's right," says Niko. "If you're going to give a party then don't make it a lame one."

"You need at *least* heavy appetizers, and for dessert you could have a cupcake stand, and maybe a sundae bar on the side," Ashley adds.

"What about a DJ? You need a DJ? My brother knows a guy," adds Connor.

"Do you have a theme? Ohmigosh, you *gotta* have a theme," says Ashley. "There are so many themes. Like Arabian Nights, or The Academy Awards, or The Great Gatsby…ohmigosh, I saw the cutest favors at a Bat Mitzvah last year. They were little Tiffany-blue purses, each of them with a pair of Audrey Hepburn sunglasses and a strand of fake pearls and a Star-bucks card inside. You could do something like that…"

"Ohmigosh, you *gotta* shut up," I reply. "You're stressing me out. I'm not going to be able to do any of those things."

"We're just saying that people are going to expect a certain amount of panache, given that it's at Gigi's house and all," says Niko.

They do have a valid point. By the end of class I've decided on a theme that also ensures that my guests' expectations will stay under control.

"It's going to be an Anti-Fashion Party," I announce. "That means you have to wear clothes that are tacky, kitsch, outdated, ugly, and above all totally unfashionable."

"And where am I supposed to get an outfit like that?" Ashley asks.

"You could check out thrift stores, bargain basements, Goodwill, Salvation Army, those kinds of places."

Ashley looks aghast. Niko doesn't look happy either.

"You mean secondhand clothes?" Niko says. "Do you have *any* idea how badly that creeps me out?"

"Don't be such a pair of fops," I say. "Trust me, it'll be fun." They don't look convinced, but I don't care. This is going to be a party on my terms.

Even an ironic party costs money, so I have to find a way to pay for it. Fortunately, I don't have to look farther than my own closet. In my room I separate my new wardrobe into piles on my bed. The Stella McCartney blouse, the suede skirt, the metallic sweater and a color block mini-dress which is cute but clashes with my hair — those I'll give to the girls. I know Ling likes the shirt, and Maya's coloring is perfect for the dress. The leather jacket I'm keeping because it's actually kind of badass, along with the silk T-shirt and cashmere sweater. About a dozen other pieces end up in a third pile, which I shove into my duffel bag.

I drag my duffel bag to a thrift store on Christopher Street. The saleslady practically salivates as she pulls the items out to examine them.

"We pay a flat rate for each category of clothing," she

explains as she taps at a calculator. "You've got four tops, two skirts, two dresses…"

"Not so fast," I say. "These are this season's collections, never worn. I don't expect you to pay me anywhere near their true value, but I also know what you can make from them so let's both leave this negotiation happy."

She doesn't look happy with me, but she is not going to let me and my duffel bag walk away, so she makes a big show of crunching numbers again. Finally she heaves a huge sigh, and shows me her number.

"Three hundred dollars."

"Ha. I could sell one dress for that."

"Perhaps, but where? You won't get more than that even if you sell everything on consignment. Shop owners need to make a profit too, you know."

We exchange scowls, and I turn away from her and look around the store. Then I have an idea.

"How about this," I say. "I'll take three hundred dollars if you throw in that skirt and that top." I point to a lime green tulle skirt and a black knit tank top with skulls all over it. The saleslady looks pained.

"Come on," I persist. "I bet that skirt has been hanging here since the eighties. I'll give it a good home."

In the end, she even throws in some fishnet stockings and a pair of fingerless gloves. I leave satisfied, with both my party costs and outfit taken care of. All I need now are food, beverages and music, and how hard can that be? I don't know why everyone acts like throwing a party is such a colossal production.

13

MAYA

J ane and I are sitting on her bed, her Trigonometry notebook open between us.

"See, for the first part of the equation, you work out y in terms of x," I explain. "Like this. And then you plug this into the second part of the equation to get the tangent. Makes sense?"

"Oh," Jane nods. "Now it does."

"Let's do a few more together. By then you'll be ready to ace your test tomorrow."

"Thanks, Maya. There isn't anyone else in this house who I could have gone to for help." Jane scratches away in her notebook. "Math problems drive me insane."

"Don't think of them as problems," I say. "Think of them as puzzles. That way you can convince yourself that they're sort of fun."

Jane gives a dry laugh. "You're lucky you don't ever have to deal with this stuff again."

But I'm enjoying working with her. I realize, with surprise, that I've missed schoolwork. I miss exercising my mind. I always liked math. It feels like solving a riddle, and I love the satisfaction when, after several calculations, it all falls into place in a perfect solution.

We're interrupted by the ringing of my cell phone. It's Suzanne.

"I'm about to make you very happy," says Suzanne.

"Why? What's up?"

"You just got booked for *Vogue* with Theo Wolff!"

I shriek into the phone, totally losing my marbles. *Vogue*! It's finally happening, everything I've dreamed of! All my other work was peanuts next to this.

"What's going on?" Jane hisses, as I'm jumping around, pumping my fist in the air. I cover my phone with my hand.

"I'm booked for *Vogue*," I whisper.

"He absolutely loved shooting you in the Hamptons," Suzanne continues. "He booked you for a short fashion trend story, the kind of job where they try out new models before they use them for the full-page editorial features. I don't need to tell you what a big break this is. I'll send you the details shortly."

"Congratulations," Jane says, hugging me. "That's great news."

"Oh, man. I don't know if you realize how huge this is."

"I know what *Vogue* is. I do know some things. I'm really happy for you."

And you know, I can tell she really is. The other models, they'll congratulate me, but they're not going to be happy. They're going to hate me. They're going to wish I was dead. I know, because that's exactly how I'd feel if it were one of them.

When I call to tell Mom about the booking, she actually pays attention.

"Are you still depositing your checks into your Money Market account?" she asks. "I think you could be earning a higher interest. I'm going to make an appointment with a financial advisor for you." That, in Mom-speak, is about as warm and fuzzy as it gets, but I'll take it.

I can't wait until Gigi gets home. It'll be like that time she told us all over dinner about Sophia landing the Prada Perfume ad campaign, and she beamed with pride, and we all congratulated Sophia and secretly we were all thinking, why can't it be me? This time, it will be me. Gigi will hug me and say how proud she is, and that I'm going to be one of her biggest stars.

But it turns out there's other big news going on at the house this evening, news that eclipses my *Vogue* booking. And of course it involves Sophia.

Gigi and Sophia arrive home together, because Sophia was at the agency to meet with Gigi and with Tom Dillon, the head of the TV and Film division at the Towers Agency. When the rest of us come downstairs for dinner, Gigi brings us up to speed.

"You've all probably heard of the film director Alan Dvorak," Gigi says. "He's currently working on a movie titled *The Siren of Greenwich Village*."

The Siren of Greenwich Village is based on a book about college students at NYU during the 1980's — the punk rock heyday of Greenwich Village clubs like CBGBs and The Bottom Line. I know this because I read the book. This guy falls in love with a beautiful young singer, Zoey, who draws him into this privileged and hedonistic crowd who seem super cool but they're actually cruel and selfish and almost ruin his life.

"Well, today I received a call from Alan," Gigi continues. "He saw Sophia's current French *Elle* cover, and he says she is exactly what he has in mind for the role of Zoey. He wants her to audition for the part! Isn't that wonderful?"

Let me just explain that there isn't a model in the world who doesn't want to break into acting. Any model who says different is lying. Some girls take acting classes for years and audition everywhere and if they're very lucky they manage to land a part in a TV show. If they're very, *very* lucky they might get a part in a movie, typically in an action flick or an adaptation of a Marvel comic as the chick who runs around in spandex. And if they're Sophia Thompson, then Alan Dvorak just happens to see them on a magazine cover and offer them a role in a movie which, like all his movies, will probably be a huge success and an instant classic.

"Sophia," Campbell cries. "That's fantastic!" She gives Sophia a big hug. The other girls echo her congratulations.

"I don't have the part yet," Sophia says. "I still have to audition."

"Alan told me, 'If she can act, she's got the part.'" Gigi says. "I've hired one of the best acting instructors from the Lee Strasberg School of Theater to work with you on your audition. You'll meet with her tomorrow for private coaching."

Gigi doesn't say one word to me about being booked for *Vogue*. It's all about Sophia. Which wouldn't be so bad if I could be sure that I was in Sophia's inner circle, but right now Sophia is in her room running lines with Campbell, who is almost as excited as Sophia is. I swear, Campbell acts like a demented puppy around Sophia, bouncing and panting and giddy with happiness just to be graced by her attention. I don't know how she doesn't drive Sophia insane. Meanwhile, it's like I don't even exist. Even though my followers have increased to over ten thousand since fashion week, right now I feel like I'm totally and completely invisible.

Anxiety attack coming on again. It's like a lump of ice is wedged in my chest cavity and I'm having trouble breathing.

God, I loathe myself when I get like this, it's so weak and stupid. I squeeze my upper arms so hard that my nails leave little crescent moons of blood on my skin, partly to stop the anxiety and partly out of fury at myself. I've got to get out of here. I need to go for a run. It's going to be dark soon, and dinner is in a little over an hour, but I need to move or I'll go crazy. I can get in five miles before dinner if I leave now. I quickly change into my leggings, sneakers and a hooded sweatshirt and leave the house.

The West Village isn't a very good place to run. There are plenty of so-called runners on the streets, but they are the kind of runners who don't mind starting and stopping, jogging in place while they wait for the light to change at every street corner. When I run, I RUN, hard and fast. I head west to the Hudson River Greenway and break into a fast warm-up, the rhythmic pounding of my feet blocking out the pounding of my heart. I speed up, not pacing myself at all, and I'm at a full clip way too soon because my breath is coming in gasps and I've barely run a mile but I go faster, harder, hearing nothing but the thumping of my sneakers on the pavement beating out my mantra, "harder, better, faster, stronger…harder, better, faster, stronger…" just like I did during track meets at school. I felt like a cheetah when I ran, taking down my prey with every person I passed, and once again I feel a surge of power as I run except this time I'm not overtaking other runners but an imaginary parade of strutting, skinny models, and I'm soaring past them — faster than this one, stronger than the next one, thinner than that one, taller than the next, better than the one after her. I'm better than all of them.

I turn around at Battery Park and give it my all, a full sprint, so I'll have time to cool down for a few minutes before I go home. As I turn into Christopher Street I slow down to a jog, and suddenly my legs quiver and my knees buckle. I stumble and crumple to the sidewalk, my back against a store window. I'll be okay in a minute, I tell myself. I just need to catch my breath. I sit with my forehead resting on my knees, my hoodie pulled up over my head, panting. I'm shaking. I never feel like this after a run. I wonder what's going on? Maybe I'm coming down with something.

Just then there's a loud banging noise above my head. I turn to look behind me, propping my head up with my hand. Through the shop window I see a fat old man waving angrily at me.

"Get lost, junkie!" I hear his muffled shout. "This isn't a homeless shelter."

Is he talking to me? I stagger to my feet, incredulous. I probably don't look like the picture of health, collapsed on the sidewalk, but a junkie, really? I want to argue with him, but I barely have the energy to walk. Instead I push back my hood, salute the fat bastard with my fist and middle finger extended, and walk away. At home, I lock myself in the bathroom with my nail scissors. It takes twenty minutes for me to stop the bleeding from the inside of my thigh when I'm done.

14

CAMPBELL

Even here, in the waiting room of Silverstar Studios, Sophia doesn't betray a glimmer of anxiety. I'm biting my nails out of excitement, but Sophia is as composed as I've ever seen her. She's far too charming to appear blasé, of course, that would just be obnoxious, but she looks like she knows she's on the path she was born to be on. I wish that, for just a day, I could be that confident.

Turns out I'm wrong.

"Campbell, I'm really nervous," Sophia whispers and grabs my hand. I squeeze her hand and she's actually trembling. "I want this so much."

"Don't be. You've as good as got the part already. You just need to read a few lines, and you know them by heart."

"What if they don't like me?"

"Don't be ridiculous." That really is ridiculous. Everybody, and I mean absolutely everybody, loves Sophia.

"What if I can't do the crying part? Remember how much trouble I had?"

"Yes, but you got it, finally. You were really good."

"Only with your help."

"Well, just remember what we did."

"Will you go in with me? If I can look at you while I'm reading, I'll be able to do it again."

"If they'll let me, sure."

The casting director, Monica, appears.

"Sophia! Thank you for coming. We're all so excited about this. Have you been able to learn the lines? Are you ready?" She shakes hands with Sophia, and then looks at me.

"This is my friend Campbell. Would it be okay if she came in with me?"

"Sure! Whatever you like." Monica leads us into the room. Inside the taping room, we meet the others: a production assistant, the camera operator and Alan Dvorak, the director. I recognize him immediately. He's shorter and his hair is thinner than I expected, but he has a huge presence: When he stands up to shake Sophia's hand everyone gets out of his way and when he speaks everyone else is quiet.

"Sophia Thompson, what a pleasure," he says. "Thank you for coming to meet us. I know how busy you are." (Like *she's* the one doing him a favor! How cool is that?)

"Mr. Dvorak," Sophia purrs, "I am so pleased to meet you. I'm such a fan of your films."

Monica gestures to an empty chair and I sit down. I don't expect Alan to notice me, which is good, because he doesn't.

"Sophia, would you like some water?" Monica asks. She signals to the production assistant who runs to bring her a glass, and while she gets comfortable in one of the chairs facing the camera, Alan gives Sophia some background about the character.

"Zoey is a free-spirit with an edge. She projects an attitude of not giving a shit, like none of the rules apply to her, but at the same time, she has to be really likable. People take all kinds of behavior from her because she's charming and affectionate, you know? She makes you feel like you're the most important person in the room even when you know she probably makes everyone feel that way but you don't care, you know what I mean?"

Sophia nods. Does she know what he means? Because I do. I know exactly what kind of person he's describing. This Zoey character sounds just like Sophia.

Monica begins reading the lines of the male lead, Griffin. Sophia replies with Zoey's lines. Her voice is beautiful as always, even though she stammers just a tiny bit.

"Just relax," Alan says. "Let's start over. Take your time, Sophia."

They continue, and Sophia repeats the lines flawlessly, but Alan stops them again.

"Good, but can you give it a little more feeling? Remember, she knows she's setting Griffin up to have his heart broken."

When she stumbles on a line she looks at me. I've run these lines with her so many times I know them by heart. I give her a prompt. She keeps going, but once again she gets stuck, and I feed her the line in a soft voice.

They reach the part where Zoey is supposed to start crying. It's a scene where Zoey breaks down because she blames herself for her younger brother's heroin overdose.

"Tim is the only person Zoey really cares about," Alan says. "She's not just crying from grief, she's also feeling anger and guilt."

Sophia nods. She reads her lines just as she did at Gigi's house, and when she acts as though she's crying her brows wrinkle and she buries her face in her hands, her shoulders shaking with sobs.

"Let us see your face," Alan says.

Sophia drops her hands and tilts her head upwards, her eyebrows furrowed over sad, doe-like eyes.

"Don't be afraid to be ugly, Sophia," Alan urges. "Crying is ugly, it's snotty and sticky and messy. Let yourself go."

Sophia tries, but she's struggling. She looks at me pleadingly. I know what she needs to do, and how to do it. I can feel it so plainly, but how can I convey it to Sophia?

I think of the scene and about Zoey's suffering, her anger at herself and her yearning to undo the past. Sophia's acting coach told her to dredge up her most painful memories, the ones that hurt like hell, the ones we bury because we can't bear to carry them on the surface. And that's the problem. Sophia has no painful memories. Sophia's life is a fairy tale. I wish I could give her mine. I wish I could show her what it looks like to dredge up painful memories. So I try.

I close my eyes. In my memory the house is quiet because Mom is sleeping off a hangover and I'm at the stove making a grilled cheese sandwich. Jack is pacing around the kitchen, poking around the pantry. He is barefoot and he moves silently and catlike, grumbling that there's never anything to eat in the house, and then he's behind me, leaning on one arm against the edge of the stove, standing so close to me that his front touches my back.

"That looks good," he says in his deep, rich voice as he looks over my shoulder. "Will you make me one?"

"You can have this one," I say. "I'll make another."

"You're such a sweet kid."

I smile. I like it when Jack compliments me.

"You're so much sweeter than your mom," he jokes. "Can you imagine what she'd say if I asked her to make me a sandwich?" We both give a little laugh.

I switch off the stove and turn around to get a plate from the cabinet, but Jack doesn't move. We stand face to face. I can't walk around him because his arm is blocking me, and honestly, I don't really try, because he's just playing, right? He's my stepfather, so what's the big deal, right?

"Seriously," he says. "You're an angel, Campbell. You're a very special girl."

I look down, a little embarrassed but pleased as well. Jack brushes a strand of hair out of my face, then traces the side of my face with his finger and gently lifts my chin.

"And you're turning into a real beauty, did you know that?"

"Really?"

"Oh, yeah." He strokes my hair. "Makes me real proud." He kissed me on the forehead. It's a chaste kiss, totally normal for a stepfather, I think, even though he's never done this before. Then he gently kisses me on the lips. I think this can't be wrong, because it's Jack, who's been my stepfather for three years, who loves my mom and is proud of me. This is okay, I think, it has to be. Jack holds my face in his hands and kisses me again, longer, and I don't move. I know I should, but a tiny part of me felt good, as though this is what is feels like to be loved back by someone special. Jack's kiss feels so different from the sloppy, awkward kisses of the boys at school, with their tongues jamming between my teeth and their sweaty hands grappling with my bra straps.

We're jolted apart by the sound of shattering glass above our heads, broken shards spraying off the backsplash of the stove. We turn to stare at Mom in her silk bathrobe, her make-up smudged eyes wild, the glass that she has flung scattered in pieces around our feet. With a feral scream Mom lunges at us, and Jack raises his hands to deflect her, but it is ME, not Jack, that she claws at, screaming.

"You little whore! You filthy little slut!"

I try to protect my face and she pulls at my hair and slaps and punches at my head. Blood smears the floor from her bare feet, cut on the broken glass. Jack pulls her off of me and I run to my room. There's the sound of a struggle followed by footsteps bounding up the stairs and then my door is flung open and Mom bursts into my room and she towers over me as I sit curled up on my bed, cowering.

"Get out. Pack your shit and get out of my house," she says.

"Mom, please. I didn't mean it."

She slaps me again and I cover my head in my arms. It's no good to try to say anything. She's completely crazy.

"He told me what you did, you liar. I see how you look at him, how you jiggle your tits and wiggle your butt every time he's around." She opens my dresser drawers and starts flinging underwear, T-shirts, socks, any clothes she can get her hands on at me. "You think you can have everything, don't you? You think you can take my whole life from me? I've had enough of you. Get out of here."

Her face is contorted in rage. Over her shoulder I see Jack looking through the door, expressionless. He meets my gaze and turns away, the message clear. He's chosen his side. I am totally and completely alone.

I open my eyes, and I am back in the studio. It's the first time I've let myself think of Mom turning on me, really think about it, really remember that day, and it hurts, it hurts so bad, and my throat tightens with an unbearable pain and my eyes fill with tears.

I know my face probably looks grotesque but if Sophia can mimic it then maybe it'll help her. I croak out the lines, and I probably am doing it all wrong because it's hard to talk when you're crying, but miraculously, it works. Sophia watches me, and when she does the scene her face scrunches up as if she's crying, not some pantomime of a Disney princess in tears but genuinely crying, and she sobs her lines.

"Better," says Alan. "Much better."

Sophia gives me a grateful smile.

After taping a few more scenes they're done. Alan and

Monica congratulate Sophia on a terrific job, and Sophia beams with joy and relief.

In the cab on the ride home Sophia looks a bit more relaxed. She was marvelous, she's got this in the bag, and I tell her so.

"Nothing's definite yet," she says. "This is a whole other world. It's Hollywood, not the fashion world. Anything can happen."

"I wouldn't worry. Even Page Six of the *New York Post* wrote that you were getting the part. The final word lies with Alan, right? And he loves you."

"I hope so," Sophia sighs. "God, I really want this. I've never wanted anything so badly."

Gossip in the entertainment industry travels at light speed, and by evening every entertainment news channel has a segment on Alan Dvorak's choice of Sophia as his new protege. There is nobody who I would rather see great things happen to, but a secret feeling of dread lurks inside me, that every minute that Sophia ascends higher into the stratosphere, she drifts further away from me. Every day she is approached by new people who are a thousand times more interesting and exciting than I am, and I'm scared that I can't keep up. Jason Cooper has been calling her again, and he's coming to New York and wants to see her, and Sophia is playing it super cool, she said she won't be seen with him if he's still attached to his girlfriend and he said he's going to break up with her before then and Sophia said she's not promising him anything, and meanwhile I can't even get Theo to call me back.

Damn Theo. I really let myself believe he was falling for me in the Hamptons. And then, today, I saw his picture with some other model draped over him at a New York nightclub. I know I shouldn't let any man make me feel bad about myself, especially a weasel like Theo, but dammit!

15

MAYA

Y*our body is your most prized possession, so don't subject it to anything less than the finest quality. Do not eat, drink, read, watch, wear or purchase garbage.* — *Living a Model Life: Beauty and Style Tips from Gigi Towers* by Gigi Towers.

IT's the day of my *Vogue* booking. If they like me, it could lead to an editorial feature in *Vogue,* and it doesn't get bigger than that. This is the most important job I've ever had. If I screw it up, they'll never book me again and I might as well quit altogether.

I get up before the sun to go for a short run before my booking. I have a quick shower, and then join Brigitte and Campbell downstairs for breakfast, bouncing with every step. Campbell's expression, however, is almost enough to bring me down.

"Theo got you this job, but he hasn't booked me for anything. And I was the one who…I mean he and I…" her voice trails off.

"You know, it's not always up to him," I say. "Just because your look isn't right for a client doesn't mean he doesn't like you."

"He hasn't even spoken to me since the Hamptons. He won't even acknowledge my texts."

"I'm sorry, Campbell."

I think she got a rotten deal out of Theo. I mean I don't know if he promised her anything but if he had any class at all he would have booked her for something. It's just the right thing to do. To me, her story is just further proof that you don't show your soft underbelly to the wolves or you'll get eviscerated. You have to keep a shield up all the time, and never make yourself vulnerable. If that makes me Maya the Ice-Queen, then fine. I know Campbell has been called worse. Not by me, though. I've always hated people who slam women because of their sexuality, especially when those people are women as well. You have to be either a real prude or a real bitch to put someone down because of her own personal sex life, which is why I shut down Brigitte's smug expression with a narrow-eyed glare, turning my back to her as I sip my coffee.

"Good morning girls," Gigi says as she enters the kitchen, fully dressed and made up. (I swear, that woman keeps a tiny stylist hidden in her room who dresses and accessorizes her every day before she shows her face.)

"Maya, come upstairs please. I want you to step on the scale for me."

I almost spit out my coffee. Brigitte and Campbell stare. Whenever Gigi orders someone to step on the scale it means she thinks they've gained weight and she wants to know exactly how much. It doesn't matter if there are other people around,

Gigi will call you out on your weight in front of the whole house if she feels like it.

"Did I hear her right?" I whisper to Campbell. Campbell nods, wide-eyed.

"She must have meant Campbell," Brigitte says.

"Oh, shut up," Campbell replies.

I head up the stairs. She can't be serious. I've been so careful. I haven't gained an ounce, I'm sure of it.

In the second-floor bathroom stands a beam scale, the kind you see in a doctor's office with a height measuring rod attached. Gigi beckons me to get on the scale, and I pull my boots off and step on.

"One hundred and thirteen pounds," she says when she finishes sliding the weights along the beam. "Do you remember what you weighed when you arrived in January?"

"Um, one hundred and twenty?"

"That sounds about right. I'm glad you're watching your weight, but be careful, Maya. There's such a thing as being too thin. Don't lose any more weight, do you hear?"

"Okay."

"Are you still running?"

"Yes."

"Good for you. I wish all my girls were as active as you are. But I want you to make sure you compensate for all the calories you burn off. What are you having for breakfast?"

"Coffee, and a banana, and some yogurt." Okay, the yogurt isn't true, but I'll have some yogurt if it gets Gigi off my back.

"I want you to have a bowl of cereal as well before you leave the house this morning," Gigi says. She pats me on the shoulder and goes to her room.

"What did she say?" Campbell asks when I return to the kitchen.

"She says she doesn't want me to lose any more weight."

"Lucky," Campbell sighs.

I take the smallest bowl I can find from the cabinet and pour about a quarter cup of fat-free cereal into it, then add a splash of skim milk. I take tiny bites, but every bite feels like an enormous mouthful of soggy dough. But when Gigi enters the kitchen she smiles at me with approval. It's alright, I tell myself. I can run it off later. And I can skip lunch.

Gigi doesn't know what she's talking about, I think as I leave the house. Sophia is just as skinny as I am and she eats the exact same things I do. Okay, I'm a little taller, but we wear the same size and that's what really matters. At the entrance of the subway I reconsider; my booking is about fifteen blocks away, less than a mile. I've got twenty minutes to get there. If I walk a little fast I can make it on foot easily. As I march down the street I imagine my breakfast cereal burning away with every step, and I still take an extra three-block detour to help make the lump of food in my stomach disappear.

When I arrive at Theo's address I take a deep breath, shake my hair and walk briskly up the steps. Anyone who sees me will think I know exactly what I'm doing and that I belong right where I am, but the truth is I'm terrified. I pop one of the blue pills Alexandra gave me. I know I said I would only use them if it was really important, but if my first *Vogue* booking isn't important then nothing is.

The elevator opens into a huge bright loft on the second floor.

"Maya, darling. You look fabulous," Theo greets me as I enter his studio.

This is the biggest of the big leagues, I realize as I look around at his framed magazine covers. Some of the most famous photos in the world were taken by Theo, like the one of Olivia Knightley with the cheetah, which hangs on the wall above a sofa. Claire, the fashion editor of *Vogue* is here, and as she greets me she looks me over like a hawk and I know I'm still being appraised, that everything comes down to how today goes.

I wish I felt as fabulous as Theo says I look. Henry, the makeup artist, gently dabs concealer under my eyes.

"You have gorgeous eyes," he says. But he must see how dark the circles under my eyes are.

Part of the reason why they booked me for this job is because of my background in ballet, since the story has a ballet theme. The first shot features an absolutely gorgeous ivory wrap sweater by Valentino. I also have on fur leg warmers, and then on my feet I've got faded converse sneakers. Claire wants me to stand on pointe, which is difficult; she obviously doesn't know the difference between pointe shoes and sneakers, but I make it work.

"More energy, Maya," Theo calls. "Don't just stand there like a doll. Show me intensity."

I knew it. He's not happy with me. He thinks I'm sluggish, weak, tired. I glide into every pose Theo asks of me, twirling on my toes, arching my back, raising my arms like swan's wings. Then Claire asks for poses that are more geometric, angular, and intense. I know what she means: more Martha Graham than George Balanchine, and I give her exactly what she wants.

My next shot is a long, full gauze skirt like something Tchaikovsky's Sleeping Beauty would wear, paired with a tight cropped silk top. I wear it barefoot, and I flow through a series of poses where I raise my legs and point my toes in every possible manner to show the skirt to its best advantage. Then Claire asks me if I can do a split in the air. She means a grand-jeté, a leap across the set with my legs extended into a split. Of course I can do a grand-jeté, but what Claire doesn't realize is that nobody does a grand-jeté without warming up their muscles thoroughly beforehand.

"Oh, I'm sure you're warmed up by now, aren't you?" Claire asks.

I'm not going to blow my chance to impress her. I break into a skip, then jump, pushing myself off the floor with my left leg, and stretch my right leg before me, my left leg back in mid-air and my arms extended. I land with my knees slightly bent to absorb the shock.

"Nice," says Theo. "Let's see that again."

This time I start a bit further back and when I jump I push off as high as I can. As soon as I extend my leg I feel a sharp twinge in my inner thigh. I gasp, and land, biting my lip. I clutch the inside of my thigh, certain that I've torn a muscle.

"Beautiful," cries Claire. "Really great!"

My thigh is searing with pain. I can't take a couple of pain tablets and wait for those to kick in; that will take too long. The only thing I can do is mask the pain. As I pause for a sip of water I slip another blue pill into my mouth and let it dissolve. Soon I feel my heartbeat accelerating, my energy increasing. The pain diminishes, and the fact that I have overcome it thrills me, it makes me feel stronger, faster, better than any of the other models who would be sniveling and complaining by now. I leap again, and again, and all the time Theo clicks away at the camera and Claire beams with approval. My heart is racing now, and whether it's from the pills or from all the leaping around I don't know, but it's pounding so hard now that it feels like it could burst out of my chest.

"Are you okay?" Henry asks me as he touches up my powder. "You're breathing really hard."

"Yeah, I'm fine," I say. "Just a little out of breath."

"Well, don't let them kill you," he jokes.

I run, turn around, jog back, turn around, and do it again, over and over. I show them that, whatever they want from me, I can deliver, I can exceed all their expectations.

"Her hair is coming loose," someone says, and I come to a

stop so Henry can fix it. I'm panting so much and my heart is beating so fast that I lean forward, propping my hands on my knees.

"I can't do your hair if you're leaning forward," Henry says, and I stand up straight.

I must have lifted my head too fast because suddenly I feel terribly dizzy, and in a split second a dozen thoughts go through my mind: I'm an athlete, I know better, I need to keep moving until my blood pressure adjusts, heart rate's too fast because I didn't cool down, and then the ground tilts up toward me and THUNK, I fall down and the whole world is pitch black and silent.

"She's waking up," someone says.

For a minute I have no idea where I am or who these people are. Two EMTs in their navy blue uniforms peer into my face. One of them helps me lift my head, and slowly he raises me by my shoulders into a seated position.

"Hi, Maya. It's Maya, right? How are you feeling?"

I mumble something incoherent.

"If you feel dizzy, just put your head down again," he says.

The other EMT — John, according to the label on his uniform — holds my wrist and checks my pulse. He then shines a little flashlight into my eyes and wraps a blood pressure gauge on my arm.

"Your heart rate is very high. Have you ever been diagnosed with tachycardia, Maya?"

"No, I don't think so."

"It's a heart disorder in which your heart beats much faster than normal. In some cases it can be a sign of a serious condition. Other than that, your vitals seem okay. But you should take it really easy for the rest of the day."

"Wait," says Claire. "Do you mean she can't finish the shoot?"

"Not if you don't want her dead," says John. Claire makes an I-don't-believe-this gesture with her hands.

"When you're feeling better, make an appointment with your physician," John says to me. "Get this checked out, okay? Meanwhile you need to go home and lie down for the rest of the day."

He hands me a bottle of water and makes sure I get a few sips down. They have me sign something, and then they pack up their equipment and leave.

"Maya, are you sure you can't finish? We're nearly done," says Theo.

"I don't think I can stand up without falling over," I reply honestly.

"Alright. We'll get you a taxi," he sighs. I know he's disappointed, and that I've really blown it, but I feel so weak that I can't think of anything but getting home.

I arrive back at the house, still wobbly on my feet, and slowly climb the stairs to my room where I collapse on my bed. My phone rings. It's Suzanne.

"Maya, what happened?" She cries. "They said you passed out at your booking, and that you left before they were finished. This is *Vogue*! Nobody ever walks out of a *Vogue* booking."

"I don't know what happened," I answer, my voice shaking. "I fainted. I've never done that before."

"You'll have to explain it to Gigi, Maya. I should warn you, she's absolutely furious."

No kidding. When Gigi gets home the first thing she does is come barging into my room.

"You better be half dead, because there is no other reason in the world to leave a booking, especially one for *Vogue*," she snaps as she enters my room. "What is the matter with you?"

I know I deserve her anger. Even she doesn't know how much I deserve her anger.

"I'm sorry," I say.

"What did you eat today, Maya? Are you still losing weight? If you did this to yourself because you're not eating properly I will send you home. I'm serious. I don't need models killing themselves, not in my agency, not under my roof!" (Aw, how sweet. She's worried about me.)

"I'm not dieting, I promise," I say. "Please, I'll be more careful. I won't let it happen again."

"It better not, because I mean it," Gigi says. "I'll have Betty bring you a tray for dinner. Get some rest. I'm going to have Suzanne make you an appointment with a doctor."

As Gigi leaves, I fight back tears. I can't remember ever feeling so lonely, so desperate. I've ruined everything. Vogue will never hire me again, and when word gets out that I'm the kind of weakling who can't make it through a day of work without falling to pieces, then neither will anyone else. What will I tell Mom, when she asks me how my shoot went? What will she say when I tell her I left the booking in disgrace? She'll think exactly what everyone else will: that I'm a loser who blew her chance. I clutch my head with my hands, trying to force the spiraling thoughts of hopelessness to stop, but I know they won't, that there's only one thing I can do to redirect my pain to where I can control it. I reach for my nail scissors, and, pulling my T-shirt above my waist, press the steel tips into the flesh of my hip. I press hard and long, until the searing pain obscures every other sensation. As the warm blood trickles down my hip I feel a welcome wave of dizziness, blurring the world around me.

16

CAMPBELL

O *pportunity is not a bus. It doesn't arrive on schedule, so be prepared every moment of your life to seize it when it comes.* — *The Supermodel's Handbook* by Gigi Towers.

IN THE MORNING, after Gigi has gone to the agency, I go into her bathroom to weigh myself. My heart sinks as I find I've gained weight again. I'm now fifteen pounds over the maximum weight that Gigi said she'd allow. I can blame five pounds on my menstrual cycle or whatever, but this is out of control. I'm following Gigi's stupid diet, I stay away from carbs and sweets, I don't drink sodas or fruit juices, I get enough exercise, but my body just does whatever it wants to.

"I don't know what to do differently," I wail to Sophia. "I'm barely eating enough to stay alive. How do you stay so thin?"

"Exhaustion and drugs," Sophia answers. "Nah, you don't

need the drugs. Just don't eat anything and when you get light-headed you can pretend you're high. God, I'm kidding. I just have a different body type. Honestly, I'd kill for your curves."

"But I've got to lose the weight! I haven't had a paying job in weeks. The only reason Gigi hasn't thrown me out yet is that she's been too busy to notice me."

I have to do something drastic. I'm going to start a liquid fasting diet and drink nothing but vegetable juice and herbal tea for a month. Maybe I'll get liposuction, or do that thing where they freeze your fat off. Until I lose this weight I'm wearing nothing but baggy sweaters so Gigi won't notice what a cow I've become.

I get a phone call from Sarah later in the morning.

"Campbell, Gigi and Marilyn want to meet with you," she says. "Can you come by in half an hour?"

My heart drops into the pit of my stomach. Marilyn, as the head booker, is the second to last word when it comes to deter-mining whether a girl has a future as a model. When Catherine from Toronto was let go, it happened just like this. She met with Marilyn and Gigi and even though she knew things weren't going as well as she'd hoped, she was totally blindsided when they told her it wasn't working out. They just gave her back her photos that they had on file and told her that her contract was voided. Then Catherine came back to the house and Margo helped her pack her bags while Carol made her travel arrangements back to Toronto. And that was the end of Catherine.

I can't believe it's coming to this, that I can disappear just as easily. Maybe I can try a different agency, but even if another agency is willing to take me on they'll make me find my own place to live, and I can't afford to pay my own rent in New York. I can't go home. I have nowhere to go, no money to fall back on. I go through a list of people at home who I might be able to crash with until I can get a job, but honestly,

I can't think of any. My friend Maddie wants me dead and she turned all our friends against me, and anyway, my friends back home live with their parents, they're kids, they can't help me.

When I arrive at the agency I'm actually shaking. The place is a buzz of activity, and it's incredible to me that everything still moves along when the ground is about to fall out from under my life. Carol sends me into Gigi's office. Everything at the Towers Agency is modern and efficient — except for Gigi's office. Gigi's office is like Gigi: classical, elegant, and feminine. She sits behind a large Queen-or King-Somebody desk in a chair upholstered in dark ashy rose, and there is a huge photo of Gigi surrounded by her supermodels of the 1990s, when the supermodel phenomenon was at its peak. Gigi motions for me to sit down and I take a chair across from her desk, next to Marilyn.

I remember the first time I entered this office, three months ago. I sat in this exact same chair. Gigi sat across from me flipping through my portfolio which I'd brought from home, containing a series of pictures for which I'd paid $450 to a second-rate wedding photographer in suburban Atlanta. She looked at me over the portfolio, declared the pictures awful but my face expressive, and called Sarah in to set up a test shoot with one of the agency's photographers. Those pictures became the beginning of my new life. A life that's about to be snatched away.

"We need to talk about your future with this agency," Gigi says.

I stare dumbly and wait.

"Not everyone is cut out for modeling, dear," Gigi begins, and right away I know that I'm not going to keep it together. I can feel the lump forming in my throat.

"I had a strong feeling when I met you," she continues. "I was certain you were going to become one of my stars. But sometimes even I make mistakes. I don't think you're destined to model, Campbell…"

Here it comes. My eyes are already burning with tears.

"…I think your future may be in film."

For a second I can't process what she just said.

"What?" I ask.

"Alan Dvorak wants you to audition for his movie," Gigi says.

"Huh? Which movie?" I ask, stupid with disbelief.

"*The Siren of Greenwich Village.* He saw you at Silverstar with Sophia and he was very impressed. He'd like you to do a screen test for the role of Zoey. To audition properly, this time." Marion says.

"But that's Sophia's role."

"It isn't anybody's role until the contract is signed," Gigi says. "And Alan is seriously considering you now."

I'm beyond stunned.

"Here's the script. It was just delivered by messenger." Gigi hands me a sealed manila envelope with my name on it and CONFIDENTIAL stamped across the front in red letters. "I want you to meet with an acting coach tomorrow. Sarah will set it up and give you the details. Meanwhile, Tom Dillon in the TV and Film division is waiting to meet with you to explain your application for SAG-AFTRA union membership, which needs to be done right away."

The words "script," acting coach," "SAG-AFTRA" and "film" echo in my ears. I've got to be dreaming, but I take the envelope and it feels solid and real.

"I…I thought you called me in here to fire me."

"Not quite," Gigi says, briskly. "I still have a feeling about you and I don't like being wrong. Now, go and study your lines."

~

"A PROBLEM that so many actors encounter is that they think they need to 'show' an emotion. Unless you're actually feeling it, it's going to come across as fake," explains Dominic, my acting coach. "For this scene, try not to *act* like you're sad. Don't worry about what your face is doing. See if you can really *be* sad."

We're practicing a scene where Zoey is wallowing in remorse and loneliness after she has betrayed Griffin, and she's tracing the tip of a kitchen knife along her veins as she contemplates ridding the world of herself.

"What that means, Campbell, is you need to delve into a time when you were deeply unhappy. You have to thoroughly bum yourself out."

I close my eyes and concentrate for a couple of minutes. I think about Maddie, my best friend at school. We lived three blocks away from each other and we were inseparable until last fall when a guy she liked told everyone that I slept with him. I had a reputation with guys at school, and it was probably deserved, but this was one guy I never touched. Maddie didn't believe me, and she not only didn't speak to me anymore but she managed to turn every one of my friends against me. I remember feeling the loss of someone I loved all over again, and realizing that loving someone doesn't do a damn bit of good if they don't love you back.

"Not bad," Dominic says when I say my lines. "But I want you to go deeper."

As unhappy as this makes me, I push myself further. My thoughts of Maddie change to thoughts of my Dad. I think of how he smelled like the green gel after-shave lotion he used and how he never shaved on weekends so his face was bristly and rough and I complained of his scratchy kisses but I secretly loved them, and how he used to hold my hands while I climbed up the front of his body in my socks and then flip me by my hands so I'd land on my feet. I think of how he and I both loved dogs, and we'd talk about all the imaginary dogs we would one day have, their breeds and their names, but we both knew there would never be a dog in our house because Mom hates dogs. I think of how at this moment my dad is living in Florida with his second wife, Amanda, who for all I know may be a perfectly nice person, and their two-year-old son, my half-brother, Cameron, who doesn't even know I exist because I have been screwed out of a relationship with any of them. And the unhappiness swells inside me but I can tell it's not enough. I need to dig deeper, into the part that really hurts.

Then I think about why I didn't fight harder for him, and I think of Mom, beautiful, golden, radiant Mom, the sun around whom my world revolved, the only person whom I really cared about. It was always about the two of us, everyone else could go to hell, I loved her more than everyone else put together. And I remember her eyes narrowed in hatred at me, her hands cruelly clawing at me as she literally threw me out of the house. This time when I deliver Zoey's lines my voice breaks and my mouth quivers as I fight to keep back tears, and there's nothing fake about it.

～

I EXPECT my audition to be the same kind of thing as Sophia's so I am very surprised when I arrive and find that, in addition to Alan and the casting crew, a young man stands up to greet me and it's Lucas McAllister. Lucas is an actor who's been in a couple of movies, including a teen musical, but his main background is in theater. He just came off an eight-month stint on Broadway playing the role of Connor Murphy in *Dear Evan Hansen*.

"This is Lucas, and he'll be playing Griffin, the male lead. I'd like to have you read opposite each other," Alan explains. Lucas is cute and funny and perfect for the part, attractive but not in a cocky way. He has a shy smile that is almost unconsciously sexy. "I like to make sure my actors have chemistry with each other," Alan explains.

This shouldn't be a problem because I have yet to meet the guy that I can't ignite a spark of chemistry with. When we read our scene I focus on Lucas like he's the only person in the room. I don't just let him finish his line so I can deliver my own; I listen to his words as though it's the first time I hear them. I don't just recite, I speak to him like I've never spoken these words before. I pull away from him to draw him toward me. I lean in to push him back. Our scene is as physical as it is vocal, a dance of the eyes and voice.

Next I read scenes on my own, while Alan reads the opposite part.

"Very good," Alan says. I'm not sure what he really thinks. With Sophia, he was gushing with praise, but then he didn't offer her the part.

"How's your singing?" he asks.

"Pretty mediocre," I answer truthfully.

"I don't need you to sound good," he explains. "That's what voice-overs are for. I need you to *look* like you sound good."

The production assistant hands me a guitar. "It's not plugged in," he says. "If you don't know how to play you can just fake it."

I strap the guitar across my shoulders and fumble with the strings. I know a few chords, just enough to look like I know what I'm doing.

"Just have fun," Alan says. "Pretend I'm not here. Pretend it's just you and Lucas." Ha. Like that makes it less awkward. I glance at Lucas, feeling terribly self-conscious. Lucas gives me that little smile again, and I smile back.

The assistant cues up the music, and the opening notes play to Joan Jett's "I Love Rock 'n' Roll." I used to sing this song in the middle of my bedroom in my underwear. I belt out the song with unbridled abandon, not caring whether I'm off-key, just having fun. It's just me and the music, and I know just how Zoey feels and how and why she sings, as every sad, anxious feeling I've wrought to the surface melts away. I look right into Lucas' eyes and strut toward him like a cat before I turn away, flipping my hair over my shoulder. I feel sexy and wild and when the music finishes I'm panting, my hair falling in my face, and I'm smiling. Probably more fun than I should be having. Joan Jett isn't a smily, giddy type of performer, but I think Zoey is.

Alan is smiling too.

"I think we've found our Zoey," he says.

After that things start to happen very quickly. First, however, I have to get the dreaded conversation with Sophia out of the way. Neither of us have been home much in the past couple of days, so we haven't seen each other alone, but today an encounter is finally inevitable. As I come up the stairs I hear Brigitte, Maya and Sophia talking in Sophia's room.

"I'm sorry. It should have been you," Maya says. "Everybody knows that."

"She totally stole the part from you," says Brigitte. "And she calls herself your friend."

Sophia's murmured answer is unintelligible, but Brigitte's answer is not.

"Oh, come on. You know how she got that role, don't you? She probably slept with the director. Same way she did with Theo, a fat lot of good that did her."

"I didn't sleep with the director," I interrupt them from the doorway, startling them. "I've slept with worse, but the fact is I didn't sleep with Alan. Sophia knows I didn't. You can stop talking bullshit about me now."

Maya has the grace to look embarrassed, but Brigitte just sneers at me.

"Why? You sleep with everyone else," Brigitte says.

I'm not here to fight with Brigitte. "Sophia, can I speak with you alone?"

Maya gets up and leaves the room. Brigitte doesn't move.

"What makes you think she wants to speak to you?" Brigitte says.

"I'm talking to Sophia, not you." I retort. "Sophia, please?"

Sophia gives Brigitte a signal that it's okay, she can leave us, like Brigitte is her bodyguard or something, which would be funny if it wasn't so ludicrous because Brigitte doesn't give a damn about Sophia, she just gets off on taking sides against me. Brigitte gives me a filthy look as she leaves the room.

"Please don't be angry, Sophia," I say. "I only went to the audition with you because you asked me to. I never thought this would happen."

"I'm not angry," Sophia says with a little smile, gracious as a queen.

"Really?"

"Really. It's not your fault."

"Okay. I mean, I couldn't stand it if you were angry at me. I'm so sorry."

"You don't have to be sorry."

"You're my best friend, Sophia. You know I'd do anything for you."

Sophia looks at me and her eyes harden. I'm lying and she knows it; I wouldn't do anything. I wouldn't turn down the part, even though she's their second choice. In the end, we both want the same thing, and even though I love Sophia more than anyone in the world, I'm not giving it up.

"Campbell, forget it. I don't even have time for it. I'm fully booked for months."

That's nonsense, of course, and we both know it, because the agency would move, cancel or reschedule all her other bookings for a movie role.

"You sure?" I ask. "So we're okay then?"

"It's not that big a deal, alright? I didn't even really want the part. I was barely trying. " She stands up from the bed, ending the subject forever, but I catch just the tiniest, quickest glint in her eyes before she looks away. Forget about it, her look says. Forget you ever heard me say I want it. Do not ever let anyone know that it meant anything to me or I will destroy you.

17

JANE

I have a little plaque in my kitchen that reads, 'A good hostess is like a swan. Graceful on the surface, and paddling like mad underneath.' As a hostess, you should be prepared to handle minor setbacks - a drunk bartender, a kitchen fire, or a passed-out guest - with composure and humor and without a hair out of place. — Living a Model Life: Beauty and Style Tips from Gigi Towers by Gigi Towers.

ON THE AFTERNOON of the 23rd, everyone in the house is in a whirlwind of preening for Sophia's party at the Oleander Club. Margo and Betty both have the night off. The girls obsess with their clothes and makeup, since the party will be attended by every big name in the business. Sophia may be the guest of honor, but the whole event is essentially one big go-see for all of Gigi's girls, an opportunity to promote her agency and her models while wining and dining the clients.

I'm wearing a dress because Gigi told me to, an A-line thing that makes me look like a tent, but it really doesn't matter what I wear because I plan to ditch the Oleander club about fifteen seconds after we get there and come right back here and change before my own guests arrive. Gigi wants us all at the Oleander club from seven o'clock on even though the party won't really take off until about nine or ten, and it'll probably go on past midnight.

Walking into the Oleander Club is like being transported to a planet of black light and acrylic furniture, where we get waited on by skinny aliens in tight red dresses and fluorescent makeup who walk around with appetizers on silver trays while a giant aquarium full of aquatic night creatures swim overhead, staring down at us. I've never been in a club this cool before; hell, I've never been in any nightclub before. The other girls, of course, are trying to act like they've seen it all a hundred times before but they're obviously excited out of their minds. All the staff and models of the Towers Agency are there, and it's not hard for me to disappear among them. Nobody is paying any attention to me anyway.

I slip out about twenty minutes after I arrive, and take a taxi back to the house. I quickly change into the lime green tulle skirt, fishnet stockings, skull-covered tank top and high-top sneakers. I've ordered an Italian restaurant in the neighborhood to deliver a big pan of lasagna for my party because it's my favorite food, and because there probably hasn't been a big fat delicious gooey lasagna in this house since Gigi moved in. Niko and Jazz are bringing beverages, and Ashley is bringing some dips and appetizers. I bought about a hundred Hostess Twinkies which I stashed in my room, and now I unwrap them and construct my own version of a cupcake tower on the dining table: a Twinkie pyramid. By the time I finish and get the music playing in the living room, Ashley is already at the door, and Niko and Jazz are getting out of a cab right behind her.

Ashley looks adorable in a navy vintage tea-length dress with a white collar and white belt from the 1950s. "It's my grandmother's," she says. "Isn't it cute? I wish girls still dressed like this." She goes inside and starts rummaging through the kitchen to set up the appetizers.

Niko wears the same khaki pants and shoes as always but he has on a Hawaiian shirt with a tie. "Best I could do on short notice," he says.

"You look perfect," I answer.

Jazz has got on pajama pants and a black T-shirt emblazoned with FUR HURTS, and her face is made up with pale foundation, heavy black eyeshadow and black lipstick. Right behind them people continue to arrive. Connor shows up in full-on punk gear, with torn black jeans, combat boots and spiked hair. He has two other people with him.

"I brought my brother, Shane, and his girlfriend Amber. I hope you don't mind."

"Of course not," I say. Shane is even better looking than Connor, if such a thing is possible. Amber is pretty, in a hard, bleached-blond way, and she's dressed like a streetwalker in a tight spandex miniskirt and tube top. I'm not entirely certain if she's actually in costume. A junior girl named Taylor, who I never spoke to before, arrives with two guys, both seniors, dressed like tacky tourists with baseball caps and Bermuda shorts. They carry bags of vodka, beer and mixers, which is a bit of a surprise but what the hell, it's not like anyone is driving. Before long I realize this crowd is going to be a lot bigger than I anticipated.

The crowd mills around the downstairs and I find it a little hard to relax because I keep picking up drinks from polished wooden surfaces and shoving napkins under them before they leave water stains, and wiping crumbs off of upholstery, but then I remind myself this is my house, and I can have a damn party if I want to. I hope Niko is having a good time. I don't think he gets to go to parties a lot. He's in a group listening to Connor tell a story, staring at Connor and laughing at everything Connor says. My heart aches for Niko. I can feel how lonely he is, living with parents who secretly despise him, an outsider at school, burying everything he feels inside. At least he has Jazz. And me.

Pretty soon the food is gone, the drinks are finished, and the energy starts to lag.

"Hey man, this party blows," Shane says to Connor. "I thought you said there were going to be models."

Connor looks at me, embarrassed.

"I said there *might* be models," he says. "I said she lives with a bunch of models." Connor jerks his head in my direction.

"You know, we expected some of the Towers girls to be here too," Taylor pouts. "I thought you were roommates with Sophia Thompson."

"They're not home," I explain. "Sorry I didn't put them on display for you."

"I don't believe you even know Sophia Thompson," says Amber.

"I do too. She lives here. Her room is right upstairs."

"Really? Up there?" says Shane.

"Yes, but you can't go up there," I say, but it's too late, he and Amber are already heading up the stairs. "Connor, tell your brother they can't go in the models' rooms!"

"Which models' rooms?" Connor asks, following his brother.

"I said NOT UPSTAIRS, dammit!" I run after them, but this has the wrong effect, and something similar to a stampede erupts, with everyone following me. I elbow my way to the top floor, and at the top of the stairs I plant my hands on the bannisters. "Back downstairs. I mean it," I yell, pushing a grumbling cluster of teenagers back down.

On the third floor, I can't believe what I'm seeing. A crowd has invaded Brigitte's and Ling's room, perusing their portfolios, picking up their composite cards and even pocketing some as souvenirs.

"Stop that! Get out of here!" I snatch the pictures out of their hands, and it takes all my strength, with Jazz's help, to shove everyone out of the room. In Sophia's room things are even worse. Amber is actually going through Sophia's closet, handling her clothes and looking at labels. She holds a dress in front of herself.

"Shane, take my picture," she says. She makes what she thinks is a sexy pout as she poses with Sophia's dress and Shane snaps a picture with his phone.

"This is private property, you idiot!" I yank the dress from her hands. Good grief, it's a Chanel from the Spring prêt-à-porter collection. Amber may be a bitch but she knows her clothes.

"Let's go," Amber says to Shane, linking her arm through his. "This party sucks."

The consensus seems to be that Amber is right, because most of my guests prepare to leave. Niko glances at me with pity, and he makes a last attempt at breathing life into the party.

"Have you guys been out back yet? There's a garden that connects to five other houses. Emma Watson's house is one of them."

"Emma Watson the actress?" Ashley asks, her eyes wide.

The group pours outside. You can't tell from the street, but our house backs up to a courtyard shared by six houses. Each one has a private garden with a low stone wall, and then there's a path between the gardens that connects them all to a fountain in the center.

"That one's Emma's house," I say, pointing to the house two doors down from ours.

"Do you ever see her?" Connor asks.

"All the time," I lie. I have never seen Emma Watson in my life.

"I bet you could look right into her bedroom if you could get on that balcony," Taylor points out.

"You *could* get on that balcony," says Shane. "See, the roofs are connected. You could climb from this roof over the next one and onto hers and drop down."

"Ohmigod we should totally do it," says Amber. "Connor, do it!" She gives him a playful shove between the shoulder blades.

"YOU do it," says Connor.

"Do it, dude," says Shane. "I'll give you a hundred dollars if you do it." Shane reaches into his pocket. "Here. A hundred dollars. I'll give it to you right now, I'll put it right in your hand, if you climb onto Emma Watson's balcony and look in her window."

"No."

"He's scared," says Amber.

"I'm not scared, I'm just not stupid."

"He's not going to do it," Amber says. "C'mon, let's go."

They're going to leave. That'll be the end of my party. My famously sucking sixteenth birthday loser party.

"I'll do it," I say.

"Bullshit," says Amber.

"If you go with me," I tell Connor. "I'm not going alone. And you," I point to Shane, "you still have to pay your brother."

Shane thinks for a second. "Yeah, okay."

"How do we get up there?" Connor asks.

"There's a fire door to our roof from the attic."

Connor looks at me as though he's seeing me for the first

time. The corner of his mouth turns up in a crooked smile, and I feel a warm thrill in my stomach.

"Come on," I say to Connor, grabbing him by his arm. The others stay and watch from the garden, waiting for us to emerge on the roof.

"You're crazy, you know that, right?" Connor says as we run upstairs

"So are you," I say, opening the attic door. Inside the attic it's dark and musty and I fumble for the light. I open the small door to the roof and we step outside. We approach the edge so we can see the others down in the garden and wave to them.

Connor and I make our way to the roof next door. There's a low wall around our roof, which we have to climb over before we can make the five-foot drop onto the neighbor's roof. Connor goes first, landing soundlessly, and I follow. I stumble as I land, and Connor helps me to my feet.

"You okay?" He whispers, and I nod. I'm more than okay. I'm having fun. The wall we just came across is going to be harder to get back over than it was to drop down, I realize. The neighbor's house has a skylight, so we stay close to the edge and keep low.

"Nice place. Whose is it?" Connor asks.

"Some publisher, I think. I forgot their name."

At the far side of the roof, the side which borders Emma's house, we have a problem. Emma's roof is several feet higher than the one we're standing on, and, what's worse, the roofs aren't actually touching. There is a space two feet wide between the houses. Two feet doesn't sound like much, but when you're four stories above ground and climbing across a two-foot-wide crevice, it's huge. If we slip while we're climbing, we'll fall to our deaths. We both look down at the garden where our audience stands watching, waiting to see what we'll do.

"Shit. We don't have to do this, you know," Connor tells me.

I look back at the garden, and a dozen expectant faces stare up at me. He's wrong. I do have to do this. There's only so much contempt I can put up with at my own birthday party.

My skirt is going to get in the way, so I wiggle out of it and throw it over the side to the garden below. Howls of appreciation from our spectators as my skirt wafts to earth. I put one foot on the edge of the roof, then the other, and place my hands on the edge of the wall before me. Directly below me is the drop all the way to the ground. One misstep, one slip of my feet, and I'll fall.

"Jesus, be careful," Connor whispers.

As long as I don't look down, as long as I pretend I'm standing on level ground, I'll be okay, I tell myself, but my heart is pounding so hard I can almost hear it. I take a deep breath. With a jump I hoist my upper body onto the wall, clutching the edge. I almost clear the top, but my weight shifts me backward again, and my feet frantically scrape against the wall. I get just enough traction to lift me up the side of the wall. With a grunt, I throw myself over the top, onto the other side.

"Jane! Say something!" Connor calls.

For a second I lie on the roof, panting, looking at the sky.

"Something," I gasp. When I do stand up I look over the edge at Connor, and he is wide-eyed. He shakes his head. He's not going to come across the wall, and that's fine, but I'm almost there and I have to finish this. I creep to the edge overlooking the balcony. If I hang from the edge I can put my foot on the top of the window frame, then climb down holding on to the shutter. Piece of cake.

I make it to the balcony, and a cheer goes up from the others below. Now just to take a couple of pictures with my phone through the windows so that I have something to show for my trouble. There's not much to see; through the slim opening between the curtains I can spy a small section of a darkened bedroom, and through the next window a hallway leading to a stairwell, and the third room looks like it's a study or something.

Suddenly I hear a series of thumping sounds and Connor yelping in alarm. I glance up at the roof next door, and look straight into the barrel of a handgun pointing at me, clutched between the hands of a navy-blue uniform clad police officer.

"Freeze!" He yells. "Let me see your hands!"

I'm so startled I almost fall backward over the balcony. A second police officer appears and I see that he's got Connor and he's holding Connor's arms behind his back. The first cop holsters his gun, then climbs onto the Watson roof. Next he's clambered down to the balcony and grabs me by my upper arm.

"Ohmigodohmigodohmigod," I say. "We were just kidding. We were so totally just kidding."

What doesn't help is that the crowd below is eating this up, they've actually started cheering and applauding.

"I'm going to give you a leg up onto the roof, and if you do anything stupid like try to run away, my partner is going to take you down with his taser, do you hear me?" The cop says. He helps me back up, and when he joins me on the roof he dusts himself off and looks me up and down. "How the hell old are you, anyway?"

"Fif--sixteen," I answer, standing there in my fishnet tights and shaking like a leaf.

"Stupid damn kids," he mutters.

Scaling the roof back to Gigi's isn't going to be a problem, it turns out, because the police officers lead us downstairs through the publisher's house —he was the one who called them when he heard our footsteps on the roof — and out the back.

"Party's over," the others murmur when they see us led outside by the cops. Quickly and quietly, they all disappear into Gigi's house and out through the front.

"I'm still not paying you," Shane says to Connor. "You never did make it to the balcony."

∽

"STUPID, SELFISH, IRRESPONSIBLE, INCONSIDERATE, IMMATURE," are just some of the word Gigi hurls at me as she stands over me. I'm sitting in the living room, my arms folded across my chest, chewing my thumbnail. I have never seen her so angry, in fact I don't think I've ever seen *anyone* so angry, in my life.

"I had to leave Sophia's party early, after weeks of planning and preparation, because I get a call from a police officer who says he has my granddaughter in custody! I almost had a heart attack!" Gigi paces up and down, flailing her hands. I hear the models whispering from behind the half-open doorway. They must be enthralled; Gigi never loses her cool, ever, but tonight all her composure has gone out the window and it's a spectacle that none of them would miss for the world.

"Then I arrive home to learn that you were caught in the process of breaking and entering…"

"That's not exactly true," I interrupt, "since we neither broke nor entered anything."

"Quiet! Do you realize…" she pauses, only just noticing something. "WHERE are you skirt or trousers?"

"I think my skirt is lying in the garden next door."

"Do you realize you could have gotten yourself killed? You could have gotten your friend killed, and you could have gotten a police officer killed trying to chase you across the roof!"

I didn't think of that. "I'm sorry."

"And WHO in the world gave you permission to have a party? How dare you? What in the name of heaven made you decide to give a party?"

"It's customary, when you have a birthday."

"What?"

"My birthday. It's today."

Gigi rolls her eyes and throws her hands out to her sides. She looks at me and shakes her head. "You should have told me," she says.

"I shouldn't have had to."

"I don't know what to do with you, Jane, I really don't." She closes her eyes and pinches the bridge of her nose with her fingers. "I'm done for tonight. We'll continue this tomorrow. I want everyone to go to bed. GIRLS! GO TO BED!" she bellows, her first indication that she knew the girls were listening at the door all along. There's a squeal from behind the door, then a scrambling as they trip over each other to get upstairs before Gigi comes out.

Before I go to my room I stop by Sophia's. I figure I owe her an apology for dragging Gigi away from her party and ending the evening on a bad note.

"I'm sorry," I say. "I know this was your night. I didn't want to mess it up. I just wanted to do something with my friends instead. For what it's worth, my party was a complete disaster."

"Don't worry about it. At least your party was your own," Sophia says.

GIGI LOSING it last night was unpleasant, but Gigi cool and collected after a night to think about my transgressions is far worse.

"We need to talk about how things are going to be, going forward," she says after she calls me to her room.

"Okay," I answer. I'm glad, for a moment, that we're talking at all. We haven't had a real talk since I arrived and it's long overdue.

"I think you need more attention and supervision than I've been giving you."

I nod silently.

"Which is why I don't think this arrangement is going to work out."

Wait, what?

"I want you to finish out the school year at Egleston, and then go to Overbrook Academy, a boarding school in Vermont, in the fall. The headmaster is a friend of mine and he's assured me of a place for you. Meanwhile, during the summer, you can attend their summer camp."

"Wait…you're sending me away?"

"I can't have you running wild in New York unsupervised, Jane. It's not fair to either of us."

"But I haven't been running wild. I just had a few friends over!" It's not like I've been sneaking off to nightclubs like some of the other girls. "And I like Egleston!"

"Overbrook is an excellent school and they'll take good care of you. Trust me, Jane, it's the best thing for you."

"But I don't want to go to camp in the summer. I want to do the New York Film School program. I'm entering a film in their competition."

"That won't be possible. Besides, summer is when I have the most new girls coming, the ones who are still in school during the rest of the year. I could put two new girls in your room."

Now I get it. This isn't about what's best for me. It's about what's best for the Towers Agency.

"That's the real reason, isn't it?" I retort. "You need me out of the way so that you can take in more girls. I'm just taking up room from girls who could be bringing in money."

"Don't be silly, Jane."

"I'm being honest. I wish for once that you would be honest with me! You never wanted me here anyway."

"I'm not going to let you turn this into a melodrama. A girl your age needs supervision and structure, and I'm not in a position to provide that. I have no control over you, and I can't take that responsibility. Boarding school is a much more practical solution. It will be best for both of us, truly."

She really doesn't see anything in any terms other than practical ones. I wish I was as cold and calculating. Then nothing would hurt me.

18

CAMPBELL

W ow. I've never seen Gigi that mad. I have to give Jane credit, though...nobody ever stands up to Gigi the way she did. Now Gigi is in a horrible mood and she'll take it out on anyone who crosses her path, so we all spend the rest of the weekend lying low, trying to stay out of Gigi's way. I'm glad when Monday finally comes and I can get out of the house.

The table reading for the film is scheduled for nine o'clock on Monday morning. The object of the table reading is for the entire cast to read through the whole script, including the set directions, in one sitting so we can familiarize ourselves with the story and get an idea of the final production. Everyone — the director, producer and all of the cast — will be there and it will be the first time that I'll meet them all together. I've planned my outfit, washed my hair, re-read my script and double-checked to make sure I know where I'm supposed to be and how to get there. As I get into bed, Maya breaks the uncomfortable silence that has been wedged between us since I interrupted her and Brigitte with Sophia earlier.

"Campbell, I didn't mean what I said to Sophia. I was just trying to make her feel better. I'm happy for you, really."

She sounds rehearsed and uncomfortable, but it's better than nothing.

"Thanks," I reply. "I feel bad for Sophia, too, you know. But I can't pretend I'm not happy either. And I'm not going to let someone like Brigitte ruin it for me."

"Brigitte's just jealous," Maya says. "You're going to have to get used to people being jealous."

When my alarm wakes me in the morning Maya is already up. She walks into the room, sweaty from her early morning run. She runs every morning, even when she has an early shoot and it's still dark out.

"Do you mind if I shower first, or do you need to?" she asks me.

"Go ahead," I say, getting out of bed. "I'll shower after breakfast."

Ling and Brigitte are downstairs having breakfast. Jane has left for school, and Gigi is already at the agency. Brigitte is being ever so slightly nicer today, at least she's not being openly hateful. I'm too nervous to eat a big breakfast but I manage to get down some whole-grain toast with almond butter and sliced bananas. When I'm finished I hurry upstairs to shower.

In the shower I take deep, calming breaths. I imagine the steam filling my nose and lungs and cleaning my body as every negative, toxic feeling is washed away. After the shower I dry off, wrap myself in a towel and brush my teeth. When I'm finished I reach for the doorknob.

But the door won't budge. I rattle the knob and push, but it's locked. The key, which always stays on the inside of the door, is gone. Someone reached inside while I was showering, removed the key and locked the door from outside!

"Hey!" I shout, banging on the door. "Not funny, you guys!"

I wait a few seconds, but I don't hear anyone. I bang on the door again.

"Open the door! Maya! Somebody! I'm locked in!" I shout.

Are they kidding me? Are these bitches for real? Someone must still be in the house. Maya can't have left already, can she? Even if she's not on this floor anymore, she must hear me from downstairs. Surely Brigitte or Ling or Sophia are still around, after all, it's just a little after eight.

I listen, and sure enough, I hear footsteps. Someone is still in the house.

"BRIGITTE!" I scream. "LING! Open the door! I know you can hear me!" I scream so loud my throat hurts. Through the door I hear the soft creak of the stairs between the fourth and third floor. I bang on the door and call out again, but nobody responds. Incredibly, the footsteps continue past the bathroom and down the next flight of stairs. They're leaving me! Somebody is deliberately leaving me to rot.

"No!" I shout. "Please!" But all the way downstairs I hear the front door slam. I know from the agonizing silence that I am alone in the house.

I let loose a string of every curse word I know, and a few more that I make up. My phone is in my room, I can't call anyone for help. If I'm late to the reading, or don't show up at all, they could still cast someone else for this part. I've seen how easy it is to lose a job in this business.

I make up my mind to break down the door, and throw myself against it with all my weight and strength. But all I do is bruise my shoulder. I kick the door repeatedly, but my kicking does nothing to the heavy oak door. This can't be possible, I think. It's too ridiculous. I can't let a simple door stand literally and figuratively between me and my entire future. Crumpling to the floor, I dissolve into tears.

Gradually my sorrow is surpassed by fury and I stop crying, rubbing my eyes angrily. I will not let whoever is trying to ruin my life have the satisfaction of succeeding. I yank open the cabinet under the sink and start pulling out every item I can get my hands on. Toilet paper, shampoo bottles, lotions, tampons, curlers, a hairdryer, everything goes flying onto the floor. If I could maybe find a wire hanger or something like that, perhaps I could pick the lock. Of course I don't; there's no reason a wire hanger would be in the bathroom cabinet. I find some hairpins. I don't know the first thing about picking a lock but I've seen people pick locks with hairpins in movies, so I give it a try. But after jamming a hairpin into the keyhole and twisting it around, all I manage to do is push the key out of the hole and drop it on the floor outside, where it doesn't do me any good at all.

Or does it? There's a thin crack between the bottom of the door and the floor, and if I could reach the key with something, maybe I could slide it toward the crack and under the door. The only thing that comes close to being the right shape is the hairdryer cord, but the plastic plug is too big to pass under the door. I try to tear the plug off of the cord but I can't. Finally I jam the plug between the cabinet door and slam the cabinet shut hard, several times, until the plug cracks and I can break it away from the cord.

The cord fits under the door, and I think I see the shadow of the key when I press my face to the floor and peek through the crack. I push the cord in the direction of the key. From this angle it's hard to see if I'm reaching it, but maybe…

Suddenly there's a flurry of motion as something swipes at the cord. I see the pink velvety pads of Dovima's paws, her claws extended like tiny needles.

"No! Bad cat! Go away!" I say. But she thinks it's a game

and attacks the cord, clawing and biting at it. That stupid cat! She's the most stuck-up, useless creature in the world, and NOW she wants to play?

"I said GO AWAY!" I bang on the door, hard, and I think I scared her off because she disappears. By some miracle, however, Dovima has knocked the key a little closer, and I can bring the cord around the key. Gently, slowly, I edge the key closer to the door, terrified that it won't fit through the crack. When it slides under the crack I grasp it with my fingers and give a sob of relief.

I open the door, run to my room and throw on my clothes. A minute later I'm out the front door. I don't have time to call a car service and good luck getting a taxicab in Manhattan between eight and nine a.m., so I sprint for the subway. I jump through the doors of the train just as they're closing, gasping for breath.

When I arrive at the studio downtown it's a couple of minutes past nine, so I'm late but I'm not too late. Fortunately, I don't think anyone even notices. Slowly my heart rate decreases from total panic to merely terrified. I'm certain that I'm the only person in the room who's never been to a table reading, but I do my best to look like I know what I'm doing. To my surprise there's not even a table. Instead, we're all spread out on sofas and comfy chairs with our scripts in hand.

Alan welcomes us all on board, and all the actors introduce themselves. There's Lucas, of course. There's also Emily Helms who is in a British Regency period series on BBC but she can do a perfect American accent. She plays Zoey's best friend. There's Rory Hewitt, who, even though he's two years older than I, plays my younger brother Tim. Rory has had supporting roles in about a half dozen films, including one as a soldier in a Spielberg film. When I meet George Milton, who plays the middle-aged and very handsome Ian, I'm so star struck my hand is actually trembling as he shakes it. This is partly because George Milton is a legend in theater and film, the winner of an Academy Award and author of a best-selling memoir, and also because at some point I'm going to kiss him. Zoey kind of gets around. He's very kind, though. He can tell how nervous I am, and he gives my hand a gentle squeeze with both his hands.

After a brief introduction by Alan the reading begins. Fortunately, Zoey doesn't show up until several scenes into the script, so by the time I read my first line I'm a bit more relaxed and the group is warmed up. But wouldn't you know it, my first line, my VERY first, I flub and start coughing. I'm blushing like a beet, but Lucas, sitting beside me, puts his hand on my shoulder and gives me a gentle squeeze.

Alan and the scriptwriters give us some notes, as a few scenes are reworked. By the end of the day it feels as if we've all known each other for ages. God, Lucas is attractive, but he's also practically married to an actress in a series. Probably a good thing, since I don't know how actors go through all the physical motions without actually falling in love with each other, and if he's unavailable then at least we won't complicate things by getting involved offscreen.

THAT EVENING Gigi gives me more attention than she ever has before. "What did you think of George Milton?" she asks, all chatty as we sit in the living room before dinner. She drinks a glass of wine while I sip a small glass of diet coke. "I've met him before, when he was briefly engaged to one of my models in the 1990s. That was when he was playing Richard III on Broadway."

"I was scared to death of him at first, but he was really nice. He got up to get his own coffee during our break, even though there were people there to fetch us whatever we wanted, and he brought me a cup as well. Isn't that cool?"

"Yes, he's famously charming, but a terrible womanizer," Gigi says. Soon the other girls enter the living room: Sophia and Maya, followed by Ling and Brigitte, and lastly Jane, as we wait for Betty to call us in to dinner. I give each of them a cold stare. One of them knows what's behind my look.

"Campbell was just telling me about meeting George Milton and the rest of the film cast. Jane, how many times must I tell you not to sit on the armrest? Sit on the sofa properly," Gigi sighs.

"Yes, and he was super nice, and so are Lucas, and Emily, and all the rest, and everyone already gets along so well, you know? There was so much laughing and excitement today, I just can't wait until we actually begin shooting. Of course there's still lots to do. I have costume fittings, and hair and makeup tests, and publicity shots…" I know I sound like an unbearable showoff, but the person who tried to ruin everything for me this morning is sitting right in this room and I want her to know that she didn't get to me. I'm not going to say anything about it, not to anyone, because I know there's nothing more infuriating to the person who did it than having her scheme go completely unacknowledged.

"I think the others would be happier for you if you didn't brag about how much fun you're having," Maya says as she gets undressed for bed.

"I'm not bragging. I'm just making a point to a certain person."

"Which person?"

"I don't know. Somebody locked me in the bathroom this morning. I don't know who did it, but it wasn't an accident."

"You were locked in the bathroom?" Maya's eyebrows go up.

"Yes, and I almost didn't make it to my table reading." I

don't look at Maya as I put my clothes away, slamming drawers.

"Well, when did it happen? Who was home?"

"While I was showering, and for a while everyone was home. Conveniently none of you could hear me when I was calling for help."

"None of us? Campbell, you don't think I had anything to do with that, do you? I left the house right after I went downstairs."

"So you say."

"Oh, stop it. You know I'd never do that."

I just shrug. I don't know anything anymore.

From now on I make sure to lock the door from the inside when I shower. I used to leave it unlocked because everyone is always in such a hurry in the morning and people are constantly running in and out of the bathroom to fix their hair or brush their teeth, but not anymore.

Be fanatic about punctuality. It shows your client you are dependable, professional, and self-disciplined, and in a competitive business, why would a client accept anything less? — The Supermodel's Handbook by Gigi Towers.

My costume fitting is at nine o'clock a few days later. The address is somewhere in Brooklyn and it should take about twenty minutes to get there, but last night I ordered a car to pick me up at eight twenty this morning to give myself plenty of extra time because I can't risk anything going wrong. The costume designer, Sandra, works on tons of movies and she's not somebody that people keep waiting.

My car arrives and I settle in the back seat, relieved to

make it out of the house without any mishaps. It's nice to be able to sit quietly in the back seat and read my script. However, after half an hour I check the time and realize we're cutting it a little close. When I finally pay attention to where we are, I almost jump out of my seat.

"Wait…what are we doing near the airport? We're in Queens! I'm supposed to be in Brooklyn!" I cry.

The driver is puzzled. "This is the address I got. 225th Street, Queens."

I open the car service app on my phone. It's a shared app for Gigi's house that we can all use, so anyone can access it. I entered the correct address when I ordered the car last night, but some time between then and this morning someone went into the account and changed it to a completely bogus address miles out of the way.

"Dammit!" I shout. I find the correct address and give it to the driver, who starts griping about his next fare, and how he's going to have to charge me three times more, but I pay no attention at all because I'm on the phone with Tom at the agency, trying to explain what's happened, and he's pissed.

"I'll tell them you're on your way," he says. "But don't let this happen again. It's too early for you to be causing dramas."

"I didn't cause it!" I answer, but he's already hung up. Great. Now he's mad at me too. We hit the peak of morning rush hour into the city and I'm half an hour late to my fitting. I scramble out of the car, and as I run up the stairs of the build-ing, I trip, dropping my bag, my script, and scraping my hands and elbows. I'm a bloody mess when I announce myself at the reception.

Sandra's assistant meets me when I get out of the elevator. "You're late," she says, as though I don't already know. She brings me over to meet Sandra. I reach out to shake Sandra's hand and Sandra is about to take mine when she pulls back and looks at it in horror. No wonder. My hand is dripping blood onto the white carpet.

"Oh, gosh, I'm sorry," I say. "I fell. I had the wrong address, and I was late, and I was running, and..."

"Well," Sandra says. "You've had quite a morning." Her assistant approaches with a damp paper towel. "Let's patch you up. We don't want your blood staining the clothes." While not unkind, Sandra's voice is brisk and business-like. I can't imagine how I could have made a worse first impression.

Once rehearsals start we work long and hard days, but I love them because when I'm working I feel really good about myself. Alan gives us notes after every scene, and sometimes he's pleased with us and sometimes he's impatient, but I think he likes my work. He told me that, even though I'm working, I should continue to study with an acting coach. At first I was alarmed when he said that, but then Emily told me that she still studies regularly with a dialect coach, and Lucas says he practices with an improv group whenever he's not working. So I'm going to keep working with Dominic on Saturday mornings.

Every person's script has their name printed on the front. We're supposed to guard our scripts with our lives, because if a script falls into the wrong hands the entire film could be leaked onto the internet before its release date, which would be catastrophic. So when I can't find my script, which I know I left on my bedside table, after dinner one night when Gigi is out of town I go into an absolute panic. I tear through the house, digging through every pile of magazines, crawling under furniture and cushions, groping through drawers. Ling, Jane and Sophia help me look.

"Did you look in the TV room?" Ling asks. "I saw you reading it in there yesterday."

"I looked all over the TV room! Under the sofa cushions and the furniture and everywhere!"

"Maybe you left it on the subway."

"No. I had it after I came home. I was reading it in my room until just before dinner. Someone took it. I'm sure of it." And as I say it, I know I'm right. When I came down to dinner, Ling and Sophia were already seated. Brigitte came to the table after I did. Maya and Jane came down last. But I stopped in the bathroom to wash my hands before I came down, so it could have been any one of them.

"Why would anyone do that?" Ling asks.

"I don't know, Ling," I shout, full of sarcasm. "Why are people assholes?"

"Wow. Sorry you can't keep track of your things but that's no reason to yell at me."

Great. Now Ling hates me too.

"Aaagh!" I groan in frustration, grabbing my head.

"Okay, calm down," Jane says. "If you really think someone took it, what do you think they would have done with it?"

Good question. If someone really wanted to mess with me they wouldn't just hide my script. They would destroy it. I run downstairs into the kitchen and open the broom closet where the trash can stands. I yank off the lid of the trash and plunge my arms elbow deep into a pile of garbage, and shove aside chicken bones, vegetable peelings and dirty paper towels as I search the contents. No script. As I was my hands and arms in the sink, Jane checks the trash compactor under the sink.

"Nothing here either," she says.

Then I have an idea. I hurry downstairs to the basement and flick on the light. Next to the recycling bins stands a paper shredder. With a firm yank I pull open the basket, and among the illegible strips I recognize the cream-colored paper of the script, and the pale green highlight of my lines.

"Oh my God," I cry as I run up the stairs. "Who did this? What's wrong with you people?" I throw a handful of my shredded script at the others who have collected on the third-floor landing, summoned by my screams. Their reactions give me no clue who's responsible. All of them stare in open-mouthed surprise as the strips of paper flutter to the ground. Sophia looks horrified, Brigitte looks amused, Ling looks disbelieving.

"Campbell, it'll be alright," Ling says. "It can be replaced."

"No it can't. I had notes written in it," I sob. "I'll get in a lot of trouble. I'll look like an idiot. We're not supposed to let anything happen to our scripts."

"Well, I think it's awful," Sophia says. "Whoever did this should feel terrible about themselves."

"How do we know you didn't do it?" Jane asks.

"I beg your damn pardon?"

"I'm just saying. It could be anyone."

"How do we know it wasn't you?" Sophia retorts.

"You don't. Like I said, it could be anyone," Jane shrugs.

"It doesn't feel like something Sophia would do," Maya says. "Brigitte, are you sure it wasn't you?"

"Oh, stop sucking up," Brigitte retorts. "I bet it was you. You can't stand anyone getting more attention than you."

I push past them into my room and slam the door. The sound of the girls' fighting carries through the house. I hope they tear each other to pieces.

19

MAYA

D *o not reward yourself with food. You are not a dog.* — Anonymous.

WELL, the world has officially gone insane. Sophia has been dethroned by Campbell. *Campbell.* Which means my standing in the house has fallen even lower. In fact, at this moment I'm pretty much worthless, since Gigi said she won't let me take any more bookings until I get a clean bill of health by a doctor. So I have an appointment for a physical this afternoon. I know I'm going to be weighed, so I drink as much water as I can right before my appointment. That should add about two or three pounds to the scale, without ingesting a single calorie.

As I fill out the questionnaire in the waiting room of Dr. Noronha's office I let my pen hover over the space after "Have you ever been treated for mental illness or depression?" But I hesitate only a second. Medical confidentiality rules or not, Dr. Noronha is in Gigi's pocket. I fill in "No." Under weight, I fill in 120, which I know is a bit off.

I didn't expect it to be as far off as it is: 109, the scale says, and that's with my jeans and sweater on and a quart of water sloshing around in my stomach.

"I've seen a lot of girls like you," Dr. Noronha says sternly, "and I'm going to tell you the same thing I tell all of them, even though I know you're going to leave here and do exactly what you want. Your body-mass-index is less than fifteen, which means you're seriously underweight. If you keep losing weight, you'll be at risk for acidosis, pancreatitis, and gall bladder disease, just to name a few. Your body will start to consume your own muscle tissue just to stay alive. Eventually you could experience seizures and organ failure, and possibly even die. Is that what you want to do?"

I'm going to assume Dr. Noronha isn't famous for his cheerful bedside manner.

"No, of course not," I reply. "I'm not trying to lose weight. I'm hardly running at all anymore."

Dr. Noronha gives me a sheet of paper with a sample diet printed on it.

"You should make sure you're eating at least 1,800 calories per day. At *least*. This is a 2,000 calorie meal plan."

I look at the sheet. Breakfast includes things like pancakes and oatmeal and turkey bacon, with lunch suggestions of pasta with tomato sauce, cheeseburgers, and pizza. He must be crazy if he thinks I'm going to sit in front of Gigi and the girls shoving pancakes and pasta into my face.

"1,800 calories," I say. "Got it."

"At the very least. Your body can't handle the stress you're putting it through, Maya."

I could tell him that I've always been tall and thin, I'm an athlete, my body is used to a strict regimen, but he won't listen to me any more than I'm listening to him. When I leave the office I toss the sheet into the nearest trash can.

As I walk home from the subway Sophia meets me on the sidewalk outside Gigi's house.

"I didn't want anyone else to tell you," Sophia beams. "Guess what?"

"I have absolutely no idea," I reply.

"*Vogue* just booked the two of us for an editorial feature with Theo! Isn't that great?"

An editorial feature in *Vogue*! I almost sob with joy and relief. They do want me! I didn't blow my chance after all. I grab Sophia's hands because I almost fall, I'm so dizzy with excitement.

"Are you serious? Oh my God, Sophia!" We both start screaming with joy. This is everything I wanted. Me and Sophia, the next team of supermodels. We really are the luckiest girls in the world.

"And guess who's in town!" she cries. "Jason! He's playing at the Beacon Theater on Broadway tomorrow night. He wants me to come to a party after the concert with him, and he asked me to bring a friend. Will you come? Please say you'll come!"

For a moment she sounds just as excited and dorky as any other teenage girl. I have to laugh at the sight of one of the most celebrated beauties in the world so giddy over a boy, even if that boy is a rock star.

"Of course!" A couple of weeks ago she would have asked Campbell instead of me, but since Campbell got that movie role I don't think those two have spoken to each other. "Will Gigi let us? We have a curfew."

"Oh please, Gigi will let us do whatever we want to do, as long as it's good PR, and being seen on the arms of one of the biggest rock stars of our time is good PR. Trust me, she'll make sure our pictures are all over the media by Saturday morning, and that's good for Gigi *and* for us."

Sophia is right. Gigi is already way ahead of us, and has worked out with Jason Cooper's manager exactly when we'll be picked up and how we'll be conveyed into the theater, who will take us backstage and which members of the media will cover the photo ops. Per Gigi's instructions, Abby Bernstein sends us a selection of outfits in the morning. After trying everything on, Sophia finally chooses a black leather mini-dress decorated with tiny gold studs by Versace, and I opt for a cream-colored viscose dress by Balmain. Before we leave, Gigi cautions us against answering questions from reporters about Sophia's relationship with Jason.

"Always leave them wondering," she explains. "Once the media have their answers they'll stop asking, and they'll forget about you."

ON SATURDAY A LIMO picks us up at seven o'clock, and Sophia and I clamber in the back.

"Oh, hey, look — champagne!" Sophia exclaims as she grasps the bottle standing in an ice bucket on the console.

"What are these, chocolate-covered strawberries?" I reach for one as Sophia pops the cork off the bottle.

We take pictures of ourselves, mugging for the camera with our legs crossed over each other on the back seat, laughing. The ride to the Upper West Side ends far too quickly, and the car delivers us to the address where we meet one of Jason's security staff.

"Wear these, ladies, and whatever you do, don't lose them." He hands us lanyards with VIP passes which we put around our necks.

He leads us through an alley off of West 74th street and

into a side entrance, where a small crowd stands outside, hoping to catch a glimpse of the band. The three of us hurry through the door and into a hallway filled with black-clad sentries wearing telephone headsets, and everyone looks very serious and important and they all wear the same VIP passes that show that we are deep inside the inner sanctum. When we reach the backstage lounge, we have to show our passes to a very burly guard who examines them closely before he lets us in.

The lounge is entirely decorated in blue and black, and dimly lit, like a nightclub. Large glass display cases contain faceless mannequins wearing some of Jason's iconic costumes from previous shows, as well as a few of his autographed guitars. Platters of chicken tandoori skewers and hamburger sliders, stacks of cupcakes and bowls of M & M's and Jolly Ranchers fill the tables, while a fully-staffed bar occupies the corner. There are about thirty other people there, in a range of age and attire, and the crowd gets thicker toward the back of the room where it blocks our view from the group seated on an L-shaped sofa and armchairs. That's where Jason and his bandmates are. I start to walk toward the crowd, but Sophia stops me.

"Slow down. We don't go to them. Let them come to us." She leads me to the bar and we sit down and order drinks. I'm already a little buzzed from the champagne in the car, so I order a Diet Coke.

"Don't be a baby," Sophia hisses. "Get a grown-up drink."

Sophia orders a vodka tonic and I order the same, "heavy on the tonic and with lots of ice, please." The bartender gives me an amused look. I've seen Sophia put away more drinks than I could keep down and still keep her perfect poise, but I'm going to have to be careful.

"Whatever happens tonight, let's stay together, okay?

Promise we won't leave each other alone?" Sophia says, and I agree.

It takes about five minutes after we sit down for the room to start to shift in our direction. First a murmur goes through the edge of the crowd. "Is that Sophia Thompson? Oh my God, that's Sophia Thompson!" I even hear my name in the undertone. Sophia's willowy body is draped like a curvy siren as she sits with her legs crossed and her elbow propped on the bar. Her presence has a magnetic effect, destabilizing the whole room. It's as though the floor just tilted in our direction and everyone rolls like marbles toward us. Despite a big sign that says "No Photographs Backstage" people point their phones at us and snap pictures, risking being thrown out of the most exclusive room in the city.

Jason elbows his way through the crowd toward us. He looks like he's a combination of pleased and annoyed — after all, this little eighteen-year-old chick just stole his audience. He kisses her hello and she smiles at him as though he's the only person in the room.

"C'mon," he says, looping his arm around her waist and leading her away, and Sophia grabs me by my hand, pulling me off my bar stool through the crowd.

Jason introduces us to the other band members. There's Reid, who plays bass and sings backup. He's about thirty years old, has a light beard and blue eyes. Then there's Bobby, the drummer who also sings harmony vocals. He looks a little younger than Reid, and he has long hair and a fat belly. Jason, of course, is the lead vocalist and plays acoustic guitar. He's the band's front-man, photogenic and charismatic. He's also the youngest member of the group at twenty-three. Jason and Sophia sit together in an armchair, his arm around her. I sit next to Reid, who moves over to make room for me. Bobby sits across from me, with a bleached blonde girl wearing heavy black eyeliner sitting on the armrest of his chair whose name, believe it or not, is Bambi. There are a handful of other young women hovering about, but none of them have been invited to sit down, and they stare at us full of envy.

On my other side sits the band's manager, Cyrus. He's a lot younger than I expected. I think he's in his late twenties. He wears jeans, a T-shirt and a baseball cap, and he has one of those soft-featured faces that looks younger than its age, but when he beckons someone to do something, people move fast. Even Jason listens to him.

"This your first Viper concert?" Cyrus asks me.

"Yeah. I was supposed to see them when they played at Constitution Hall in DC, but I had to go to Milan to work. I gave my tickets to my sister."

"This'll be so much better. You're sitting in the VIP section with me. It'll spoil any future concerts for you."

He's not kidding. Our seats are smack in the middle of the third row of the orchestra level. Sophia and I sit between Cyrus and one of the executives of a soft-drink company that sponsors the group. The show is, as expected, terrific, especially because I've never had such good seats at a rock concert before. We spend most of the time on our feet, dancing. At the end of the show, Cyrus whisks us out of the crowd and backstage again.

The band members reappear to cheers and applause, and Jason, dripping with sweat, takes Sophia's face in his hands and kisses her. Soon the security staff part the crowd for Jason, and with Sophia and me beside him, we leave the room to a barrage of camera flashes and fans clamoring for autographs. It takes about twenty guards to hold everyone back, while we're bustled out of the building the same way we came in and into a waiting limo.

"Where's the party?" Sophia asks.

"At the hotel," Jason answers. "The others will meet us there. Wasn't that fun? How'd you like your seats?"

We arrive at the Pierre Hotel, and I try to appear as nonplussed as Sophia but man, this place is gorgeous, it's even more understatedly beautiful than the Plaza which is where Alexandra and I stayed with our parents when we first came to New York as kids.

The party, it turns out, is on the thirty-ninth floor. It's a huge suite with a corner view of Central Park, a living area decorated in gold and silver tones in an Indian fusion style, and two bedrooms. When we arrive, there are waiters putting the finishing touches on a table of food and drinks including stone crab claws and roast tenderloin and various bottles of whiskey, wine and vodka. Music is playing and everything is perfect, except for the fact that we're the only ones there.

"The others will be here soon," Jason says as he pours us drinks. "See? Here they are."

The door opens and Reid and Bobby walk in with Bambi from backstage giggling and hanging onto Bobby's neck, staggeringly drunk.

"Awright," Bobby cries. "Let's get this party started!"

"Wheee!!!" cries Bambi. She lets go of Bobby's neck and collapses to the floor.

"Oops-a-daisy," says Bobby, pulling her to her feet, and she gives a shrill laugh. Bobby plonks her onto a chair like a giant rag doll. The wait staff exits, shutting the door behind them. It becomes clear to me that we aren't expecting anyone else.

Three guys. Three girls. I'm not an idiot, I got A's in math, and I know what Bambi, Sophia and I are here for. But Sophia isn't in the least bit worried. She's letting Jason give her a tour of the suite, of the big porcelain bathtub, of the luxurious four-poster bed. Bobby leads the drunk rag-doll into the other bedroom and shuts the door. I want to tell Sophia that this is turning into a weird scene, so I go and look for her, but when I spot her and Jason in the bedroom I see that Sophia has the font of her dress unzipped to her belly-button and Jason is snorting a line of cocaine off of her breast, and I just really don't know the protocol about how to interrupt people when they're in the middle of that particular activity. So I turn around and walk away.

That leaves me with Reid, who sits beside me on the sofa, places down his drink and puts his arm around my shoulders. He's much too close to me and he smells of sweat and I don't want his arm on me. I don't want to make small talk. I don't want to look at the view. I want to leave. But then the door to Jason's bedroom closes behind him and Sophia, and I hear the lock click shut.

Damn Sophia. We promised each other we'd stay together, and I'm not leaving her behind, but now Reid is getting frisky as well. He leans in for a kiss, and next thing I know he's trying to shove his tongue down my throat.

"Wait, stop," I say. "That's not what I'm here for."

"What are you here for, then?"

"I'm here because Sophia doesn't want me to leave her alone."

"You sure about that?" Reid jerks his head toward the bedroom. "I don't think you and your friend are in synch."

"Well, we promised each other. Look, I don't want to make out, okay?" I scoot over to the side. "We can just talk, if you want to."

Reid rolls his eyes. "Yeah, okay, talk, whatever. Will you at least have a drink?"

"Sure," I say.

He gets up and brings me a drink. I take a small sip. Reid turns on the television, surfing channels for a while, but he keeps glancing at me sideways.

"What?" I ask. He shrugs and looks away.

I'm feeling awfully sleepy all of a sudden, which is strange. I must be terrible company, because I can't keep my eyes open. At one point I open my eyes halfway and Reid's face is right in front of mine. Something is wrong, but I'm having such trouble opening my eyes…

The realization what happened gives me the strength to force my eyes open. That sick son of a bitch put something in my drink. Reid is on top of me now, he has one hand on my breast and the other is in the waistband of my pants, and in another moment he'll have me undressed. I have to stop him but I'm too weak to move. There's only one thing I can think to do, and it takes every ounce of energy I have. I bring my finger to my mouth and jam it down my throat. With a lurch, I vomit, right onto Reid's chest.

"Jesus Christ!" he yells. He jumps away from me, groaning and swearing. "You disgusting whore." I lie in my own vomit, too weak to move, and hear him stomp out of the room. A flood of relief gives way to oblivion as I fall into a deep, dreamless sleep.

∾

"Maya! Oh, God, Maya, wake up!" Sophia shakes me. "What happened?"

"He drugged me," I croak. Outside the sky is just starting to take on the sheen of dawn.

"Oh, no," Sophia whimpers. "Maya, did he…did he hurt you?"

"No. I don't think so. No."

Sophia soaks a hand towel in the bar sink and tries to wipe my dress clean. I take the towel from her and try to do it myself, but I move like a zombie. Sophia looks like she's about to cry.

"I'm so sorry," she says.

"Where's Jason?"

"Asleep. Should I wake him? Tell him what happened?"

"Why? What difference will it make?" I answer. "Can we go now? Can we please, finally, fucking go?"

I stagger to my feet and we leave the hotel, Sophia holding me up like a sad, pathetic drunk. Fortunately it's four in the morning and there's nobody in the lobby except for one receptionist and a doorman. We take a taxi home, each of us scrunched against opposite sides of the cab, not saying a word.

20

CAMPBELL

Filming started last week! They've been working on Griffin's scenes at NYU, and even though I'm not in any of these scenes I got to hang out and watch. They closed down a section of one of the streets in the Village and they got a bunch of college students to work as extras. Jane has asked me if she can come and watch when I start filming my scenes. She's still working on that school film of hers. Emily told me, though, that I shouldn't be in Jane's film anymore. "It's an amateur film," she said, "and you're a professional now." But Jane is one of the few people in the house who has always been nice to me, so I'm going to let her come to the set one of these days.

A lot of the cast arrive at work in "street makeup," so they won't be caught outside looking anything less than perfect, and then when they arrive on set the makeup artists wipe it off and apply their film makeup. But I don't usually bother with street makeup. In the morning I just tie my hair in a ponytail, rub moisturizer on my face, put on a little lip gloss and a pair of sunglasses and I'm done. Well, today I was halfway to work when my face started itching. As soon as I scratched at my face I knew I was making it worse. By the time the train arrived at my stop the itching was unbearable, and my face felt like it was burning. There was a public bathroom at the station but no way am I going into one of those places, who knows what kind of people are lurking in there, so I couldn't wash my face until I got to the makeup artist's trailer at the set.

"Geez, what's up with your face?" Lola, the makeup artist, asks. "It's all blotchy."

"I don't know! It just started a few minutes ago."

"You think it's an allergy?"

"I can't think to what," I reply. "I'm not wearing anything other than the same moisturizer I've worn for years…"

"Your skin is a mess. I don't know how I'm going to cover that up."

Then I understand. My moisturizer. I keep it in my toiletries bag in the bathroom, in plain reach of anyone. Somebody put something in my moisturizer, something harmful. I knew they were capable of being mean, but this is sick. My eyes fill with tears. I splash water on my face, rub it with soap, and rinse, and repeat the process, but if anything the itching is getting worse.

"Does it hurt?" Lola asks, alarmed.

"No, but it itches," I answer. It's not the itching that's making me cry, nor the blotchiness. It's the thought that someone hates me enough to do something like this to me. "Does it look any better?"

"I wish I could say it does, but…" Lola cocks her head, frowning. "The blotches are getting darker."

"Dammit," I cry. "Damn them!"

"Who?" Lola asks, but I don't answer. Lola pulls out her

phone and steps out of the trailer as she makes her call. A minute later she returns with Alan.

"Let's have a look at what's going on here," Alan says. I lift my red-eyed, tear-stained, blotchy face to him, and he raises his eyebrows as he exhales with a whistle. "Whew. Are you sick? You look like you have the measles or something."

"No. No, I'm fine, it's an allergic reaction to my moisturizer, I'm positive," I assure him. "It's not serious."

But it is serious. The itching gets worse, even though I've washed every trace of product off of my face.

"I think it's spreading," Lola says.

She's right. I feel it spreading down my neck, and the spaces between my fingers are itching now, too.

"It'll go away in a little while. It's just a rash. I can still work," I say. "Please don't send me home."

Alan puts his hand on my hair and tilts my head to the side, examining my face. "Home?" he says. "I'm going to send you to the emergency room."

I bring my hand to my searing face, and gasp. The blotches have turned to patches of blisters, tiny fluid-filled pustules that burn like fire.

"Oh, God!" I cry. "What's happening?" I dissolve into panic. Locked doors, torn scripts, wrong directions are one thing, but this is my face, my fucking face, my livelihood! And as I watch, my face gets worse, the colors darkening to almost purple, the blisters growing and spreading. It has to be a nightmare, but it's not, the pain in my face proves it's not.

One of the production assistants, Russell, pulls up to the trailer in a car and Alan and Lola bustle me down the steps and into the car.

When we arrive at the hospital, Russell takes my health insurance card, my SAG membership card and my driver's license and signs me in at the reception desk while I run into the bathroom because the itching is excruciating. I want to layer wet paper towels on my skin to cool the burning. But when I see myself in the mirror I almost faint. I don't even recognize myself. My face is a dark-purple mass of blisters, and some of them are oozing.

A nurse brings me into a curtained enclosure and tells me the doctor is on her way. The speed at which a doctor will see me is both a relief and worrisome, because it means my face is alarming even to New York City emergency room staffers. Soon the doctor arrives. Dr. Hilton takes my temperature, checks my throat, my blood pressure and my lymph nodes.

"You're not sick, at least," she says. "You have a severe case of contact dermatitis. Have you put anything unusual on your skin?"

"No. Just the same moisturizer I've used for years." God, even my voice sounds funny, because with the swelling around my lips I can't move my mouth properly.

"What about plants? Have you come in contact with any plants recently?"

"No. Not at all."

"Not even accidentally? Brushed against a bouquet perhaps?'

"No, why?"

"Well, it's very strange, but this looks like the kind of reaction caused by urushiol oil."

"Uru...what?"

"It's the toxin in plants like poison oak and poison ivy. But I've never seen a reaction this severe. I'm going to give you an antihistamine injection and put you on prednisone right away. It's a steroid, and should help prevent any long-term scarring."

Scarring. This can't be my life. I close my eyes, praying I'll wake up from this nightmare when I open them, but I don't. I catch my reflection in the stainless steel of the cabinet on the wall and an unrecognizable monster freak looks back at me.

They keep me at the hospital for the whole day, to monitor

my condition. Once they start shooting me up with antihistamines and medicating me, the rash at least seems to stop spreading, but by now my hands are almost as badly blistered as my face. The itching is a little less severe, too. But even though it isn't getting worse, it's not getting better, either.

"You said something about scarring," I say to Dr. Hilton when she checks on me again. "Do you think that's likely?"

"It's hard to say. It depends on how much of the toxin has been absorbed by your skin. For most people it takes as little as twenty micrograms of plant oil, or less than a millionth of an ounce, to cause a reaction. But in your case it looks like you've been exposed to a lot more. Don't worry," Dr. Hilton says, petting my hand. "We'll see how you do on the medication. If it doesn't clear up in a couple of weeks we'll decide what our next steps should be."

A couple of weeks! I can't be out of work for a couple of weeks. The film is on a twelve-week filming schedule. There's no way they're going to wait a couple of weeks for me. I close my eyes, tears streaming down my face, and let my head fall back on my pillow. It's over. They've won.

21

JANE

"**D**id you hear about Campbell?" Ling asks when I come home from school. She and Sophia are in the kitchen, looking very serious.

"No, what about her?"

"Something happened to her face," Ling says.

"What do you mean, 'happened to her face?'" I ask.

"She broke out in a weird rash or something. She had to go to the ER."

"The ER? Because of a rash?" That doesn't make sense. These fools don't know what they're talking about.

"It was an allergic reaction," Sophia explains. "A really bad one."

"Jesus. I mean, her face! How does she look?"

"I don't know. Margo went to fetch her so we'll know soon."

When Margo and Campbell arrive, Gigi is already home, and so are Maya and Brigitte. Gigi meets them in the hall and

I see Gigi's face before I see Campbell's. Gigi's eyes go wide and she looks like she's trying to stay composed but doesn't know what to say. Margo looks very sad. When I see Campbell my heart aches for her. Because she looks awful, just awful.

"Oh, Campbell," Sophia gasps, and reaches out to put an arm over Campbell's shoulder, but Campbell recoils as though Sophia was a cobra, she jerks her hand up to stop her and gives her a look of such cold fierceness that none of the rest of us dare to approach her.

"I want to go to my room," she whispers. "Everyone leave me alone."

Campbell trudges up the stairs, and after a brief pause Gigi follows her. It's not just Campbell's face that I don't recognize, it's everything about her. Campbell has always been the upbeat one, even when she's going through a rough time with work or Gigi or one of the other girls, but now she sounds like she's broken inside. We're all stunned.

When Gigi returns downstairs and addresses us she is back in control.

"I have warned you girls before not to experiment with beauty products and treatments. Many of those so-called natural products are full of allergens."

"What product was it?" Brigitte asks.

"She doesn't know. Probably some naturopathic garbage. Now she may have ruined her face for good." Gigi shakes her head in anger and disappointment.

Gigi has never been a font of compassion, but I think it's a bit rough of her to blame Campbell for her condition when she doesn't really know what caused it. For all she knows Campbell could have leprosy, but Gigi would still find a way to be angry at her about it. Maya and I decide to go check on Campbell.

Maya knocks on the door, even though it's her room too.

"Hey," she says in a kind voice. "How are you? Can we get you anything?"

Campbell ignores us. "Listen, Campbell, it's going to be okay. It'll get better in a few days," I say as I sit on the bed beside her.

"What if it doesn't? My face might be scarred permanently."

"Naah. My dad's a doctor, remember?" Maya says. "He knows some of the most famous plastic surgeons in the world. I bet he can find you a doctor who can make you look perfect again."

"It's not just about my face," Campbell sobs. "Somebody did this to me on purpose."

"How?"

"I don't know. I think someone put something in my moisturizer, but I don't know what, or how, or even why. Who would hate me this much?"

"Campbell, are you sure? It seems a little extreme," Maya says.

"Forget it then. Forget I said anything."

"No, I mean…I just can't believe anyone would do that."

"I don't believe anything anymore. I don't even believe you right now," Campbell replies.

"Well, that's nice to hear," Maya says.

"I just want to be alone." Campbell turns away from us. Maya and I leave her and shut the door behind us.

I find Gigi in her bedroom. "Campbell thinks somebody did this to her on purpose, and I think she may be right," I say.

"That is the silliest, most melodramatic thing I've ever heard," Gigi snaps. "I hope she doesn't get it in her head to say the same thing to me. As if one of my girls could do such a thing."

"Why do you think they couldn't? Seriously, Gigi, what do you know?"

"I know that my girls don't behave like thugs. I don't take

just anybody into my home. I know these girls. I know them better than I know you."

"Well, that's easy to believe. But do you really know them? Gigi, look, Maya is starving herself, Campbell is being harassed half to death, and Sophia and the others work so hard they take stimulants just to keep up. If you care so much about them, then put a stop to it."

"Enough, Jane, I mean it. I know what happens in this business, I've been in the business longer than you have been alive. But you are way, way out of line right now. I don't want to talk about this. Not now, not ever."

"Right. Because if you admitted it, you'd have to actually do something about it." I stand up to leave the room.

"Did you get a chance to look at the Overbrook Academy catalog yet?" Gigi calls after me. "I left it on your bed."

She might as well have told me straight out that my days in this house are numbered.

～

IN THE MIDDLE of the night my phone buzzes me out of a deep sleep. I pick it up just after it stops, and, squinting through bleary eyes, I see Niko's name on the screen. That idiot. I'm sure he's lying awake worrying about something stupid, like which physics section we're supposed to read. As soon as I start to drift back to sleep he calls again.

"What?" I answer, not disguising my irritation.

"Can you let me in?" he says. His voice sounds weird and nasal. "I'm right outside your house."

"Right now? Are you crazy?"

"It's an emergency. Please, Jane." He hangs up.

I tiptoe down the stairs in the dark. When I open the front door Niko, wearing only a T-shirt, sweatpants and sneakers despite the cold, steps into the light of the portico, his face downcast. The moment he looks at me I gasp in shock.

One side of his face is bruised and swollen. His upper lip is split, oozing blood. He hugs his chest, shivering, as he limps inside.

"Holy shit, Niko, what happened? Were you mugged?"

Niko just shakes his head. We stumble to the kitchen where I help him into a chair, and then I dampen a kitchen towel and wrap it around a handful of crushed ice.

"Here, hold this on your lip."

Niko flinches, and takes the towel from me.

"What happened?" I ask again. He won't even look at me. Finally he answers so softly I lean in close to hear him.

"My father," he whispers.

"Your father?" At first I don't understand, but with growing horror, the unimaginable truth dawns. "You mean your father DID this to you?"

Niko nods mutely. It's not possible, I think. No one could do something like this to their own child. I knew his parents were crazy, but this is criminal. I put my arm around his shoulder to hug him, and Niko gives a soft yelp. When I look at his back I see why. Pink stripes seep through his shirt. That bastard wasn't content just to beat up Niko's face; he beat him with a belt too. I feel sick.

"He went through the browser history on my computer," Niko says softly. "He saw that I'd been on a support website for kids who are g…like me. It's my fault. I wasn't careful enough." Niko starts crying. "He came in my room and pulled all the drawers out of my desk, threw everything on the floor, and then he found my notebook and tore it apart and threw it in my face, and then he started hitting me and hitting me…" by now Niko is crying.

"Niko, we should call the police."

"You don't understand," Niko sobs. "My father's a diplomat. He can't be prosecuted the way other people can. If he commits a crime, he may be deported. But see, I'm here under his visa. I can't stay here on my own."

I don't have an answer for that. All I know is that, right now, Niko needs to be somewhere safe where he can rest. I help him up the stairs to my room. Wincing, Niko lies on my bed, drawing his knees to his chest like a small child. I draw the comforter over him and pull the trundle bed out from under my bed and lie on it. Soon Niko's breathing becomes deep and rhythmic, but it takes a long time before I fall asleep myself.

In the morning I'm startled awake by Gigi's shrill yell from the stairwell.

"JANE! Get up and come here this instant!"

The door to my room is open, and Ling and Brigitte, still in pajamas, peek in anxiously from the hall.

"Shit. Stay here," I say to Niko who opens his eyes groggily. I meet Gigi at the top of the stairs.

"Is what Margo tells me true?" Gigi bellows. "Do you have a BOY in your room? This is unacceptable, Jane! It's the last straw! You know the rules, how DARE you…" She's sputtering with fury.

"It's not like that," I interrupt. "It's Niko, my friend. You've met him. He's hurt, Gigi, he needs help."

"What are you talking about? What do you mean, hurt?"

"His dad beat him up. He has nowhere else to go."

Gigi pushes me out of the way and marches down the hall. When Niko emerges from my room, his eyes large and frightened, Gigi stops in her tracks.

Niko's bruises have deepened to dark blue and purple, with tinges of yellow. Gigi, her mouth open with shock, approaches him and gingerly touches his cheek.

"My God," she says.

Taking Niko gently by the arm, Gigi leads him downstairs to her bedroom. Niko sits on the edge of her bed. I watch from the doorway as Gigi, with a tenderness and patience I didn't know she was capable of, wipes the blood and tear stains off Niko's face with a wet washcloth. Very, very carefully she removes Niko's shirt. She opens a tube of ointment and squeezes out a dollop, then applies the ointment to the welts on Niko's back, her fingers as light and gentle as a butterfly's wings. Without a word I come inside, and I take the tube and together, silently, we work on Niko's back. None of us say anything.

Only when Niko's injuries are treated, when we're in the kitchen and he's finished the scrambled eggs I made (which is all his torn mouth can handle) does Gigi coax his story out of him. Niko tells her everything he told me. When he's done, Gigi's eyes have that fierce, steely look. She is seething with anger, but not at us.

"I promise you this," she says. "You are not going back to that house. Not while your father is there. I don't care whether he has diplomatic immunity or whatever he has."

Niko doesn't look convinced. But Gigi stands up with a wry smile.

"You realize who I am, don't you? I have a *team* of lawyers who specialize in juvenile law. Your parents are going to do whatever we tell them to, or I'll turn this into an international public relations nightmare for the entire Argentinian Consulate."

She'll do it, too. Niko's monstrous parents have no idea of the shitstorm that's about to hit them. Gigi picks up her phone and as she leaves us she's already giving Carol instructions. For the first time, I'm glowing with admiration for Gigi. Real admiration. Not just appreciation for the fact that other people admire her, but genuine pride that she's my grandmother.

～

I DON'T KNOW the details, but I know that between Child Protective Services and Gigi's lawyers, Niko is in no immediate danger of being reclaimed by his parents. The Aguilars are the type of detestable posers who don't mind being cruel, they just mind other people knowing that they're cruel, so they don't care what happens as long as it happens with a minimal amount of noise. Meanwhile Mr. Singh, the Headmaster of Egleston, is working on finding Niko a host family for the rest of the school year.

I don't think I've ever hated anyone as much as I hate Niko's parents, but something surprising happens the next day. I leave the house to run a quick errand to the drugstore, and a woman steps out of a navy blue Mercedes parked in front of the house. With a start I see it's Mrs. Aguilar, and I realize she's been parked there for a while, waiting for me. Her face is cold and expressionless. I almost turn around and run back inside, when she thrusts a duffel bag into my hands.

"Thank you for being kind to my son," is all she says. Then she gets back into the car and drives off without another glance my way. I look inside the bag, which is filled with some of Niko's clothes and his school books. I don't know what to think. I mean, I still think she's a witch and a coward and a horrible person, but somewhere inside there may be a tiny glimmer of maternal concern.

Regardless of Niko's sexual proclivities, however, the idea of him and me sharing my room is too much for Gigi's sense of propriety, so with Ling's help I drag the mattress from the trundle bed into Ling's and Brigitte's room, where I will bunk until a more permanent arrangement is found for Niko. For now, however, he is Gigi's guest. The other girls are all really kind to him and seem to enjoy the novelty of male company. Niko gets along particularly well with Campbell. It's like the two of them have a special sympathy for each other. I'm not sure why, but I think it has something to do with the fact that

Campbell doesn't have a great relationship with her parents either.

NIKO, Jazz and I are still working on our documentary. We spend a lot of our time after school in the media center, editing our film. Some of the most interesting material is the stuff I filmed when no one was watching, although we have creative differences about how much of it we're going to include.

"Wow, these girls are a lot less well behaved when they're out from under your grandmother's watch," Jazz says. "Holy shit…Is Sophia doing blow?"

"Yup. Hey, you're sure you can blur out their faces, right?" I ask.

"Yeah, no problem. No one will recognize them. Whoa…is that the photographer's hand on Maya's breast? Nice catch, Jane."

"Check this out," I say, forwarding the video to Theo and Campbell making out in the kitchen.

"Eww. How old is that guy?" asks Jazz.

"Ancient. Forty or something. Campbell, by the way, is eighteen."

"Well, at least he's not a felon."

"No, just a creep, and all these stupid girls are falling over themselves to impress him. Listen," I add, "I'm not really comfortable including all of this. I'm worried about how it will make the Towers Agency look, especially alongside Gigi's speech about being so protective of her girls."

"That's what makes it such an interesting story," says Jazz. "We want it to be interesting, don't we?"

"I don't want to include anything that will make Gigi look bad," says Niko, who has gone from merely admiring Gigi to full-scale hero worship ever since she rescued him from his parents.

"We're not saying she's aware of these things," says Jazz. "She's not in any of those scenes, so it's not like we're compromising her integrity. We don't even have to identify the girls in the film as Towers girls."

"With my name on the film I don't think it's going to be a huge leap for anyone to make the connection that they're Towers girls," I say.

"So what? It's not like the whole world is going to see it."

"If we enter it in the New York Film School competition then we don't know who will see it," Niko says. "It could end up all over the internet."

"Look, I don't know about you two, but I intend to get an A in this class," says Jazz. "This is some good stuff. Mr. Vogels said that documentary filmmakers have a responsibility to document the truth. Well, this *is* the truth."

"It's still going to piss Gigi off," I say.

"I thought she was already pissed off at you. I thought she was sending you to boarding school because she's so pissed off at you."

"Look, I'll think about it, okay? We don't have to decide everything right this second." We glare at each other until Niko suggests we table the subject, and we browse some of our extra footage.

"I like this scene," Niko says, looking at a segment of the girls playing charades in the kitchen.

"It's one of the few times the girls were all having fun together," I say. We rewind it a few times, focusing on the girls' gestures and laughter as Margo unpacks her groceries around them. Suddenly I see something and my eyes go wide.

"Holy shit," I say. "Go back. Let me see that again."

"What?" Niko says.

"Right there. Zoom in on that," I say, pointing.

"What? I don't see anything," says Jazz.

"I get it. I totally get it now." I jump up from my chair, my hand to my forehead.

"Where are you going, psycho?" Niko calls after me.

"I'll see you at home," I yell over my shoulder as I grab my backpack and rush out of the room.

I know who's been messing with Campbell.

As I run home, my mind races with everything that happened in the past couple of weeks and it all makes sense. Campbell was right. Someone has been deliberately tormenting her.

The crazy thing is, Gigi was right too.

I let myself in the house and run upstairs. Breathless, I knock on the bedroom door next to the attic.

Margo opens the door to her room.

"Jane," she says. "Is everything all right?"

"No," I say. "It's not."

"What's the matter?"

"I want to know why you did it. Why you tried to ruin Campbell."

Margo looks stunned, then angry.

"How dare you say such a rude, hateful thing to me! Get out of my room. How dare you! I'll tell your Grandmother," she stamps with outrage.

"Tell her. I think you'd better. I'm going to tell her anyway."

Margo looks at me with hurt disbelief. "Jane, how can you say such a horrible thing? I've been taking such good care of poor Campbell, the poor child, nobody has been kinder to her than I have."

"Yes, I noticed. Is it because you feel guilty?"

Again Margo's expression changes, and now she just looks mean. I swear, she should be the actor in the house.

"What makes you think I had anything to do with it?" She asks.

"The day you came back from your sister's house in the country," I explain. "You were carrying bags of vegetables and things. One was a clear plastic bag full of green leafy stuff. I didn't pay attention, none of us did, it looked like spinach or something. But it wasn't. It was poison ivy, wasn't it?"

Margo raises her eyebrows but doesn't reply.

"Never mind, you don't have to answer. I was filming that day, do you remember? I have it on film. I looked at it closely, and there's no question about it."

This time Margo's expression is one of fear. She sits down on the edge of her bed. "*Mon Dieu*," she murmurs. "*C'est fini*."

"Why, Margo? What did Campbell ever do to you?"

"It wasn't meant to be so bad. That girl, she must have some kind of sensitivity," she says, like it's Campbell's fault.

"Her face could be permanently scarred, did you know that?"

"I didn't know. I thought, if I squeeze the oil out of the leaves with a knife and scrape it into the moisturizer, it would cause a little rash…"

"But why?"

Margo looks at me and her eyes are wet. "You must understand. I have my favorites too, you know." She dabs at her eyes with the edge of her sleeve.

"Campbell, she's a pretty girl," she continues with a dismissive wave of her hand. "I have seen hundreds of pretty girls come through this house. All of them the same — spoiled, vain, rude. But Sophia is a true beauty, inside and out. That movie role should be Sophia's. It is an absurdity that a girl like Campbell, a girl of low-class like that, should have it."

So Sophia's spell has even enchanted Margo. A part of me understands. Sophia is the only one of us girls, myself included, who greets Margo with a smile every day, who thanks Margo for the many little things, and sometimes big things, that Margo does to keep the house running, and who speaks to her about her beloved native France. Sophia is the only one who hugs Margo and brings her gifts when she returns from her travels. It's no wonder Margo adores her.

"Does Sophia know what you did?"

"No! Sophia would never be a part of this. She is a sweet girl."

I believe her. None of this is Sophia's fault. She can't help it that people lose their minds when they're around her.

"You know I'm going to tell Gigi, Margo."

"Yes, I know. Of course. But not tonight, please. I will tell her in the morning. First thing."

It's not up to Margo, but Gigi is out until late tonight so I can't do anything at the moment. The next morning, however, Margo isn't in her room, nor is she in the kitchen or anywhere else in the house.

"Where is Margo?" Gigi says as she enters the dining room at breakfast. "She needs to pick up the dry cleaning and take Dovima to the groomer. Has anyone seen her?"

No, no-one has seen her. Gigi goes upstairs to Margo's room. A few minutes later Gigi hurries back downstairs. "It's the strangest thing. Her room is empty, and all her things are gone. Margo has left!"

The other girls are finally paying attention. Margo, gone? Margo has always been here, long before any of them arrived, as reliable as the walls.

"It's not possible! Does anyone know what's going on? Have any of you spoken to her today?"

But nobody has any idea. Nobody ever speaks to Margo, except for Sophia, and she doesn't know either. I'll tell Gigi myself, after I finish my breakfast.

～

"Incredible," Gigi says, stunned by the news. "Just incredible.

I'll have her arrested. She has done irreparable damage to the Towers Agency."

"The Towers Agency? What about to Campbell?"

"Yes, of course, Campbell too. But the *New York Post* just printed a story about Alan Dvorak recasting Campbell's part for the film —even though he hasn't, not yet, those liars — and the Towers Agency is mentioned. They're suggesting Campbell was harmed by another model, which of course I vehemently denied. But people will believe what they want to believe."

"But it wasn't another model. You could have them print a correction."

"It's the same problem. The Towers Agency has always been above this kind of scandal. What does it say about my agency if I can't even trust the employees under my own roof?"

Gigi drums her perfect nails on the armrest of her chair and rubs her brow. "And now I'm left without a housekeeper. How much worse is this day going to get?"

"*That's* the worst of your problems? Seriously?"

"Jane, for God's sake, I don't need your sarcasm now. Aren't you late for school?" She pulls out her phone and taps a number. "Carol, have you found me a replacement for Margo yet? How difficult can it possibly be? There must be hundreds of women who would kill for the job. If you can, find me one who speaks Portuguese. I could use an interpreter for some of the Brazilian models arriving this summer."

I stomp down the stairs where Niko waits impatiently by the door.

"We're putting it all in," I tell him as we hurry off to school. "Every sordid, scandalous second. If we're going to make a movie then let's make a good one."

The hell with what Gigi thinks. It's not like she cares what I think.

22

CAMPBELL

"Margo!" I exclaim when Gigi tells me. "Why? What did I ever do to her?"

"Dear, she was obviously a very unstable, unhappy woman. I'm so sorry that I never realized it. But she's gone now. She returned to France. She's probably afraid that I'll prosecute her if she ever comes back, which I intend to do."

"Gosh...of all people. I never considered her." That, I realize, may have something to do with it. None of us ever considered Margo. Maybe that's why she hated us.

"So you see, you have nothing to worry about. No-one under my roof has any reason to harm you."

It's been a week since my face incident, and during this time the Towers Agency people have gone to the table with Alan Dvorak's people about whether I can stay in the film. I don't even know who's on my side anymore. I thought it was the agency, but all they care about is that a Towers Agency girl stays on the film, and if it's not me it will probably be Sophia, so I bet they don't care what happens to me.

Surprisingly, the tables seem to be turned around. Alan is the one who wants to keep me on. It's Alan — not his personal assistant or a production assistant — who calls me to see how I'm doing.

"I still want you in this part," he says. "I'm changing the shooting schedule so that you won't have to be on camera for another week. As long as the swelling on your skin goes down, we can try to cover the discoloration with makeup. I won't make any decisions about recasting until we see what happens. In the meantime, you rest, take care of yourself and let your face heal."

Every couple of hours I check my face in the mirror, but there's not much change. The discoloration will probably last for several weeks, the doctor said, but if the blisters and swelling subside then I still have a chance at saving my job. I have a prescription medicated cortisone cream that I rub on my face several times a day, and I keep the jar in my bag and by my side everywhere I go. It's pitiful that I'm still so scared even though I know it was Margo who did all those mean things and she's gone, but I don't trust anyone anymore.

AT THE END of the week my face finally looks better. The spots aren't raised anymore, and the discoloration has faded a lot, so with makeup on I actually look normal again. Marilyn told me that *People* magazine wants to do an interview with me, as a "talent to watch" piece. She's my booker now, not Sarah, because Sarah mainly works to promote the new girls and Marilyn has the big names. I miss Sarah. We talked every day, and she's really funny, but Marilyn still kind of scares me. I wish I could tell Sophia, or Maya, about the interview but they'd think I was bragging again, so I don't tell anybody. Sophia walks past me now like we're strangers. I'd talk to Jane, but we never seem to be home at the same time. I wonder if she knows how lucky she is. She has real friends, not people who secretly want her to fail. Plus, she'll always be Gigi's no matter what she does or looks like. I thought I'd be so happy when I got everything I always wanted, but I feel so lonely. Lucas and the others in the cast are nice, but this film is just another job to them. I remember what it was like when I did plays in school. We'd all get so attached to each other, we'd spend every day for weeks working together, watching the production take shape, and after the last performance — poof, it was over, there'd be a cast party where people shed tears and hugged and vowed to stay friends forever, followed by such a feeling of letdown, and by the following week everyone had gone their separate ways. It'll be a hundred times worse this time. It may be the last time I ever work in a film. There are too many one-hit wonders, and I don't know yet where I'm going to end up. So I don't want to get too close to anyone. That's how you get really hurt.

"THERE'S some guy at the door for you," Brigitte barks at me from the hall.

"Who is it?" I ask as I emerge from my room. I'm not expecting anyone.

"How should I know? I'm not the doorman," Brigitte says and shuts the bathroom door in my face.

I hurry down the stairs. Probably someone from the film crew, I think, delivering a script revision or something. Or could it be Lucas? It would be so like Brigitte not to tell me it's Lucas. I run my fingers through my hair before I enter the foyer. I see his outline in the vestibule and open the door. When he turns to face me, I gasp.

Jack. My stepfather.

"Hi, baby," he says.

It takes me a second to find my voice.

"What are you doing here?"

"Aren't you going to invite me in?" He moves toward me as though he expects a hug.

"No." I take a step back. "That's close enough."

"Campbell, honey, I know we didn't leave things in a good way, but I really hope we can get past that. I think we all did some things we regret."

I don't want to hear anything from him. "Where's my mom?"

"Well, your mom still needs a little more time. But she misses you, sweetheart, she cares a lot about you."

I don't believe him. If that were true, she would be here, not Jack. Why the hell is he here, anyway?

"Why are you here, Jack?"

"Because I want us to get back to the way we ought to be. A family. Look, can't you let me in so we can talk?"

"No."

"I've come a long way to see you, Campbell. You're not going to make me leave without even talking to me, are you?"

"I don't want to talk to you."

"Just give me a few minutes. Just let me try to make things right. Please."

He gives me that smile that gets him everything he wants from women, that same smile that made my mom choose him over her own daughter. If anything, that smile steels me even more against him. I want him gone so badly that I decided the quickest way to get rid of him is to hear him out, if only for a few minutes.

"I'm not supposed to have male visitors," I say. "There's a diner around the corner. We can go there if you want to talk."

A short while later we sit across from one another in a booth at the diner.

"What'll you have?" he asks. "My treat."

"Nothing. I'm not eating." I order a diet coke. If he thinks we're going to have a nice long lazy lunch he's got another think coming. He looks disappointed, and orders an Irish coffee. I wait for him to talk.

"I bet you want to know how your mom's doing," he says. "She's doing just great. She got her real estate license, you know."

"That's nice."

"We're both real sorry we never hear from you."

"Bullshit. She heard from me every day for weeks after I got here. She never called me back."

"Really? I didn't know that."

"Yeah, I figured. I'm guessing she doesn't talk about me very much."

"Well, your mom's a complicated woman, honey." He tries to pat my hand but I pull away. He shifts in his seat and tries to change the subject.

"Hey, we read about you getting a part in a movie. That's great news, kiddo! Always knew you'd make a name for yourself. Congratulations!"

"Thanks," I mumble, twirling my straw in my coke.

"We're real proud of you. Your mom, too."

"She said that? That she's proud of me?"

"Hell yeah. She told all her friends, and she brags about you all the time."

I think about this for a moment. I don't remember, even at the best of times, my mom ever saying she was proud of me.

"Campbell, at the end of the day, we're your family. We're not perfect, but we love each other. I'm sorry for everything that went down. I never meant anything by it. You know that, don't you?"

I don't answer.

"It was an accident, that's all. I'm an affectionate person; so are you. It was just a hug that went a little overboard. But it shouldn't have happened. I see that now. I'm sorry."

I still can't look at him. Remembering that day in the kitchen is making my stomach hurt.

"I told your mom it was all my fault."

"Really?"

"Yeah, I did."

"What did she say?"

"Well, you gotta understand, it's been hard for her. She was real mad at me for a long time, but your mom and I love each other, Campbell, we didn't want to lose each other, and she forgave me. I wish you could forgive me too."

"If she knows it wasn't my fault, then why hasn't she called me?"

"Honestly? Between you and me, sweetheart, I think she's a little ashamed. She feels real bad for how she treated you. She's scared, you know. I think she's scared of reaching out to you and having you reject her." Jack leans back in his seat, takes a swig of his drink and wipes his mouth.

"That's why I'm here," he continues. "I was the cause for this whole mess, so I'm trying to make things right by paving the way for you and your mom to reconcile. Your mom loves you, Campbell. We both do. What do you think, Campbell? Can you give us another chance?"

I finally look him right in the eyes, which are clouded with regret and sorrow.

"Maybe," I whisper. After a moment I add, "I've missed her," and my voice breaks.

"She's missed you too. She wants to see you. She was afraid

to come, but she won't be now, once she knows you've forgiven her. It's all going to be okay."

"Okay," I sniffle.

"I'm only here for a day, but your mom and I will come back together, soon, and it'll be just like we're on vacation, just the three of us. You can show us around, introduce us to your friends, we'll go see a show, all that fun stuff."

I nod.

"This kind of a life is hard enough for someone your age, Campbell, without trying to navigate it alone. We're your family, your mom and me. Not these people here in New York. They don't care about you, not the way we do. These people — your agency, your movie people — they just care about you while you're making money for them. But your family is forever. We will always, *always* be on your side."

"I know."

"You gotta be careful, a young kid like you. There's always going to be people who pretend they care about you because you're a success. You need to know who to trust."

"Yeah, I know."

"Now, your family, we'll always have your best interest in mind."

"Uh huh."

"For example, when you start making serious money, you want to make sure it's being taken care of by people who put your interests first."

"I know. Gigi made me meet with a financial advisor. He suggested I open a 401K and put the rest in a money market, for starters, and then, next year if I've doubled my earnings…"

"A financial advisor isn't family, sweetheart. You're paying the financial advisor what, a chunk of money to tell you what to do? I bet Gigi gets a cut of that too, if she's referring her girls to him."

"Well, what would you do?"

"There are a lot of things you need to consider," Jack leans back and rubs his chin. "Risk factors, time horizon, that kind of thing. I've had some very good results with mutual funds and ETFs. I can definitely help you make the right choices."

"Yeah?"

"If you let me handle it I could take care of everything for you. And I wouldn't charge you a fee, either. You're eighteen now, so the easiest way would be if you signed something called a Power of Attorney form. It just takes all the hassle and stress out of your hands and puts it in mine."

"I know what power of attorney means."

"But I bet you don't know how simple it is. In fact, I have a form with me." He reaches into his breast pocket. "Have a look at it. All you need to do is fill in your name and information, and sign it." He hands me the form.

He came all the way from Georgia and just happened to have a power of attorney form in his pocket? He gives the form a little thrust toward me until I take it.

"I'll think about it," I say, putting the folded document on the table beside me.

"Well, now, like I said, I'm only here for the day, honey, and we'll have to go get it notarized, so it would really help if you did it now. Like we talked about, you want to start protecting yourself right away from people who might want to take advantage of you."

I open the form and spread it out beside me.

"Take a moment to look it over," he says. "I'm going to hit the bathroom." As he stands up he gives me a smile.

Maybe it's that smile that jolts me into reality. That smile that charms every woman he sees into doing whatever he wants.

Whatever. He. Damn. Wants.

How long did it take him to plan this meeting once they heard about my movie role? How soon before he realized that I was about to make some real money, and that there might be something in it for him? I'm still a little stunned as I stare at the form when his phone, which he left on the table, gives a ding. On the screen a text pops up. A text from Alicia. My mother.

"Signed yet?" it reads.

I'm not even surprised. The only thing I'm surprised at, is that I allowed myself to believe for one instant that they were reaching out to me because they care about me. I tear the Power of Attorney form in half, leave it on the table and get up. I walk out the door and I'm gone before Jack even gets back from the bathroom.

23

———

MAYA

T*oo much time under the spotlight isn't good for anyone. It wreaks havoc on the complexion. — The Supermodel's Handbook* by Gigi Towers.

SOPHIA and I haven't talked about the night of Jason's concert, which is awkward because it seems everybody else has been. After Sophia posted pictures of us in the limo and backstage to social media, tagging me in each of them, my number of followers skyrocketed to over 200,000. There's a picture of Sophia, Jason and me in *Us Weekly* and *OK!* magazine, and the *New York Post* is hinting that Sophia and Jason are practically engaged. But I think Sophia knows Jason is a dangerous subject to bring up to me, because I don't find out that she has another date with Jason until I hear about it from Ling. Not just any date, mind you. This one's for front-row seats at a Lakers game.

In Los Angeles! I thought she was going to LA for a booking, but Jason had her flown over just for their date.

"You didn't know?" Ling asks. "It was even on E!online."

I'm not letting some limp-dick little punk-rock creep drive a wedge between me and Sophia, so I shoot Sophia a text. "Have fun at the Lakers game! So excited for *Vogue* tomorrow!" followed by a bunch of peppy emojis. Sophia sends me back a selfie making a kissy face at the Staples Center arena, sandwiched in between Jason and, on her other side, Olivia Knightley. Even more disturbing to me than the news that she is in Los Angeles with Jason is the fact that she's hanging out with Olivia. If there's any model the media is as excited about photographing as Sophia, it's Olivia, and I have no doubt that if Olivia were based in New York instead of LA, she and Sophia would be inseparable. Before the end of the night, the same picture is posted all over Olivia's social media as well. A surge of fear comes over me as I realize how easily my role as Sophia's best friend can be filled by someone else.

Once again that terrifying sensation of becoming invisible, of being consumed by a huge black maw of nothingness, looms over me. I'm sitting in miserable silence in the TV room while Ling and Brigitte chatter like bluejays, oblivious that I'm quietly disintegrating, and I feel a terrible urgency to root myself back in reality before I disappear for good. I pick up a pencil from the bureau beside me in the TV room and press the tip into my thigh. Slowly but steadily I press harder until the pain takes over my thoughts, pushing away the darkness. There's only pain now, but it's a manageable pain, a controllable one, and once again I am present, back from the brink of nonexistence. The small dark red stain of blood on my thigh proves that I'm still here.

～

SOPHIA RETURNS to New York the following afternoon. Since Theo wants to recreate the feel of the pictures we did in the Hamptons by sunset, our booking is in the evening. If I were Sophia I would want to crash for a couple of hours, but she's wide awake and bouncing around the house.

"I don't need to sleep, I'm too excited," she says. "I haven't slept in two days. We went to the most amazing party last night after the game at the house of this music producer, and Jason and I watched the sun come up, and then he put me on a private jet. I should have slept on the plane but I've never flown on a private plane, it was so cool and I didn't want to sleep through any of it. There was a whole breakfast with champagne and orange juice…" She's so excited she waves her hands as she's talking and knocks over the bottles on my dresser.

"Careful! That's a $200 perfume you just spilled," I exclaim. "Are you in love with him?"

"Well, you have to admit, he's absolutely perfect," Sophia smiles.

I don't have to admit anything of the sort because I couldn't agree less. He's a real asshole, and he treats people like garbage, and he enables his rapist friends. But Sophia babbles on.

"He's a huge star, he just won the MTV Music award, and the Teen Choice music award, and he's worth a hundred million dollars. And we look great together."

If those are her criteria, then sure, he's the whole package. But it doesn't sound like love to me. However, if she's airborne with happiness then I'm not going to be the one to pull her back to earth.

We meet Theo and the *Vogue* crew on a rooftop in Battery Park overlooking the harbor. This is one of the first warm days of spring, which is lucky because we're shooting summer fashions. I can't help worrying about my body. I've put on three pounds since my meeting with Dr. Noronha, only because I don't want to give Gigi a reason to send me home. But Theo isn't Dr. Noronha. He doesn't want me three pounds fatter, he wants me as light as a thistle.

"Gigi'd never send you home, silly," Sophia says as we change into our first outfit under a canvas tent set up to serve as a changing room. "You're one of her favorites."

"Maybe, but Dr. Noronha scared the shit out of me. He made it sound like I'm about to drop dead of a heart attack any second."

"Oh, baloney. I've heard the same thing from doctors all my life. They don't know anything about what's normal for us."

She's probably right. She's even thinner than I am and she's got more energy than anyone I know. Although today I have a pretty good idea where that energy comes from. I can tell she's hopped up on something. She's antsy and she can't keep her eyes focused anywhere for more than a few seconds.

"What did you take?" I whisper. "You're acting weird."

"What do you mean? I'm just excited." She gives a sniff and rubs her nose.

"Are you on coke again? You are, aren't you?"

"Give it a rest, will you?" she retorts. "I've been working non-stop for weeks, and I haven't slept in days, so pardon me if I need a little help getting through this shoot."

"Okay, I'm sorry. I'm just worried about you."

"Well, stop it."

We both finish getting dressed in silence. Then Sophia softens. "I don't need you to mother me, okay? I just need you to be my friend."

"Okay. Whatever you want."

"I want you to have fun. You're allowed to have fun, Maya. It's a beautiful day, it's Vogue, we're the luckiest people in the world! Why don't you do some too? It'll get you out of this funk you're in."

"No thanks."

Sophia makes a sound of irritation as she exits the tent, and my heart aches with the knowledge that she's angry with me, she thinks I'm a bore, she's tired of me. I watch as Sophia spins around the set radiating youthful energy, and Theo, delighted to be working with his favorite model, indulges her bouncing around like a young gazelle until he finally calls us to get in position. He arranges us in a pose on the balcony, over-looking the southern tip of Manhattan. A reflector to our right bounces the light from the setting sun onto us. When Theo begins to shoot, I try to flow into each subsequent pose in synch with Sophia, but she's being so fidgety that I can't figure out what she's doing.

"Sophia, slow it down," Theo calls. "I've got very low light. Don't move so fast."

A few minutes later Theo calls out again. "Focus, Sophia. Relax your face. Quit twitching like that."

Sophia never needs this kind of direction. I wonder if anyone else can tell how wired she is. Theo finishes the shot, but he doesn't look happy. When he releases us Sophia jumps up, as though she's been coiled like a spring the whole time. She almost skips back into the changing tent.

The next shot is a single of Sophia, and because the light is dropping, Theo wants us both ready. I stand a few feet out of the frame watching Sophia as she works this shot, waiting for my turn. Sophia, wearing a long white dress, stands in front of a low wall at the edge of the roof, her hair loose and blowing in the wind. She looks like an angel against the skyline of down-town Manhattan, but she can't stand still, and paws impatiently at her hair as it gets in her eyes.

"If you can't concentrate I'm putting the dress on Maya," Theo barks. I've heard him yell at crew members plenty of times, but it's the first time I've ever seen him lose patience with Sophia.

"Okay, man, chill out," she says. ""God, everyone's so crabby today." She raises her arms over her head, bent at the elbows, and turns to a three-quarter angle as she gazes at the camera. She touches the side of her face, parts her lips, and flips her hair over her shoulder.

"Better," says Theo. "Give me more."

Sophia obeys. She rises on her toes and does a beautiful twirl, and as Theo clicks away Sophia's face is almost beatifically happy. She looks deep in her own reverie, bathed in pinkish-gold sunlight, and as she flows from one pose into another it looks like she's found her groove, but I am the only one who knows that she's high as a damn kite and the knowledge makes me scared.

"That's it, Sophia, more," Theo calls, the camera clicking furiously, and Sophia keeps moving. She arches her back as she extends her arms to the sky.

Exactly what happens in the next moment no-one can agree on, even though it will remain branded in my mind for the rest of my life, haunting my days and waking me screaming from my sleep. It lasts mere seconds, but it feels like time is at a complete standstill. Theo would later say Sophia tripped over the hem of her dress. His assistant would say she stumbled backward over the wall. What everyone agreed on was that, in one instant Sophia was there, and the next she was gone. She landed twelve stories below us. Of all the covers Sophia graced, her most famous cover photo of all was the one that both the *New York Post* and the *Daily News* featured on the front page, of Sophia sprawled on the sidewalk, the white dress spread around her, with not a mark on her face, as beautiful in death as she was in life.

Me, I remember it differently. I remember freezing in terror as I saw her smile and spread her arms and reach toward the sky and arch back, back, back…and then she was gone without a sound. Yes, I'm certain of that part. She didn't scream when she fell. No one else can vouch for that, perhaps because they were all screaming themselves. But I was close enough to her to be sure. Perhaps, under the influence of whatever she was on, she really did think, just for a moment, that she could fly.

24

JANE

hen the police cars leave, when the reporters outside the door give up on anyone from the house showing their faces, when the curious crowds have thinned, the house is silent. The other girls huddle upstairs like victims of a natural disaster, clinging to each other, sobbing. But no sound carries as much raw pain as the primal wailing that comes from Gigi's room.

Her bedroom door is closed and no one will go near it, but I push it open. Gigi sits on the floor beside her bed, her skirt crumpled like a linen handkerchief, her hair disheveled, head in hands, and her face sticky with tears and snot. I sit beside her, and she clings to me like a person drowning, sobbing as though all the tears that she hasn't shed in her life are bursting through a broken levy. Her body, usually so austere and intimidating to me, is frail and light in my arms.

"I'm sorry, I'm so sorry," she says, which doesn't make any sense.

"It's okay," I say, even though I have no idea what she's talking about. "It's going to be okay." Such an idiotic thing to say, but what else is there?

Then the large, familiar figure of Betty appears in the doorway. She crouches down beside us and murmurs in her Irish brogue, "There, now, hush dear, I canna stan' to see you hurtin'." Betty helps Gigi to her feet and onto the bed. Together we remove Gigi's shoes and pull the covers over her. Gigi won't let go of my hand, so I lie beside her, holding her head in my arms against my chest. We lie like this for what seems like hours, until I feel Gigi breathing rhythmically against me and know that she's cried herself to sleep. Careful not to wake her I slip out of the bed and go downstairs. I missed dinner so I'm hungry. To my surprise Betty is still here. She usually goes home right after she serves dinner.

"You hungry, child? There's some fish soup if you'd like it." She opens the refrigerator and reaches inside. "I'll heat up a… oh, to the devil with the fish soup. I know you hate it. How about a lovely grilled ham and cheese sandwich?"

"I'd like that very much. Thank you."

While Betty prepares my sandwich I sit perched on a stool in the kitchen, my knees pulled up to my chin and my arms wrapped around my legs.

"How is she doing, then, our Gigi?" Betty asks.

"She's sleeping," I reply.

"Good. Sleep is good for 'er, the poor thing. I've never seen 'er so distraught, not since your ma Victoria passed away."

"Really?"

"T'be sure. T'is a terrible thing to lose a child, even if they haven't spoken to one another in years. Maybe t'is even worse then."

This is the first time I've really spent time with Betty. I think there may be a lot more I can learn from her, both about Gigi and about my mom. But not tonight. We don't need to talk about another death while we're all coping with Sophia's.

"You know, this is a really excellent sandwich," I say, my mouth full. "I mean, you may not have a lot of occasions to make sandwiches, what with these girls and all their crazy food hangups, but if you ever feel like making another one of these" — I point to the sandwich — "I'm here for you."

Betty laughs. When I finish she takes my plate from me and I go upstairs. After I brush my teeth I go back to Gigi's room. She's still asleep. I get in bed with her. I don't want her to be alone when she wakes up.

GIGI HASN'T BREATHED a word while watching the film that Jazz, Niko and I completed, and when it ends, I switch off my laptop.

"That's everything, then. That's the finished version," I say.

Still Gigi is silent.

"We're not going to enter it in the New York Film School competition, of course. Niko and Jazz agree with me. It would be like we were taking advantage of Sophia's death and we'd never do that."

"Too bad, really. You and your friends made a good job of it. I'm quite impressed."

"I thought you'd hate it. It doesn't put the agency in a very positive light."

"No, you're right, it doesn't. But if you set out to show the truth, then you succeeded." Gigi presses her fingertips to her eyebrows. "The truth was always there, of course. If I knew about Sophia…no, that's a lie. If I had to *admit* that I knew about Sophia's drug use, maybe she'd be alive today."

"Or maybe not. Sophia was always going to do whatever she wanted to do."

"I could have threatened her with expulsion from the agency. But then she would have just gone to another agency. Everyone wanted her."

"Gigi — maybe, if you actually follow through on what you always said — refuse to book your girls with photographers like Theo, people who sexually assault girls or pressure them for sexual favors or push drugs, no matter how important they are — then maybe other agencies will follow suit."

"If I did that I would have to refuse some of the most influential people in the business. I would lose a lot of clients, and many of the models. I could lose the agency," she says. "But I'm not sure I care anymore."

"Maybe at first. But a lot of people would support you, and if enough people sided with you, you could bring about real change."

Gigi sighs. She doesn't look convinced.

"Jane, all those reporters out there, they're dying to blame somebody for Sophia's death. They're going to try their best to lay open everything that's wrong with the industry. And I'm at the top of the industry. They're going to crucify me."

"Unless..." I suggest, "unless you lay it open first. I mean they can't expose anything about you if you've already shared it."

Gigi is quiet for a moment. I see a trace of the savvy, intelligent woman that I know emerging through the fog of sorrow.

"My teacher said that documentary films need to advocate for something," I continue. "You could use this film to advocate for health standards in the fashion industry, to illustrate the pressure the girls face and the kind of changes that need to happen. It could be your platform, Gigi. What if you started a whole social movement?"

Gigi thinks for a while.

"It could work," she murmurs, half to herself. "Let's see…*Dateline* has been after us for a story. But then Anderson Cooper is an old friend. Yes, CNN would do very well."

I see my chance and I lunge for it. "Gigi, please let me help. I want to stay in New York with you. I don't want to go to boarding school. Please, Gigi. Don't send me away. I'll stay out of trouble. I'll keep out of the way, you and the models won't even know I'm here."

Gigi sighs. "Is that what you think? That you're in the way? It isn't about that, Jane. I'm not a nurturing person. I wasn't good at it with your mother — she told me her whole life what a rotten mother I was — and I'm not good at it with you."

"But if you can take care of half a dozen girls that you're not even related to, then why not me?"

"Because I'm not afraid to fail with them. At the end of the day, I don't care about them, not really. Oh, I care about their careers because it's *my* career, I care about their success because it's *my* success, but I don't love them. If I lose someone to another agency or if she doesn't make it in this business then there'll always be another pretty girl. But with you, Jane, it's different."

Did she just say she loves me? She didn't, but she came close.

"Vicky hated me for making the models my priority. She and I weren't even on speaking terms when she died," Gigi continues. "She was my greatest failure, and my biggest heartbreak. I'm afraid of making the same mistakes all over again. I don't think I can stand that."

"I'm not Vicky," I say. "I spent a lot of time looking after myself when dad was alive. I don't expect to be your only priority."

"Jane, I'm a terrible guardian. I spend half my time traveling, and when I am here I'm fussing over the models and the agency and I hardly have a moment to give to you. I have no idea what I'm doing. It wouldn't be fair to you."

"I don't need you to be a perfect grandmother. I haven't been a perfect granddaughter either. Maybe we should stop expecting perfection from each other."

We're both silent for a while. Then Gigi takes my hand and squeezes it.

"Alright," she says. "I'm willing to try if you are. Perhaps we both need a fresh start."

I'm so relieved I could cry. I'd hug her, but I think that would be pushing it. So instead we shake hands, like we've just closed a deal. It feels silly, but not in a bad way; like we know our oddball relationship has its own practices, and that those just might work for us.

25

CAMPBELL

I don't know how long it will take before it stops hurting. Sometimes I black out the fact that she's gone for a moment and it becomes bearable for a few seconds, and then it hits me again like a mule kick to the chest. I never knew how really physical the pain of grief is. I feel it deep in my limbs, as though someone is scraping the blade of a red-hot knife across my raw bones. It hurts like hell and I can't stop shaking.

The media can't get enough of Sophia. Suddenly everyone "knew" her, everyone has a tale to tell, every tabloid has her photo on the front page and all the papers in the city have sold out, unable to satisfy the public's ravenous hunger for more details about the Tragedy of Sophia Thompson. The city is swept up in a bandwagon of mourning, with hundreds of people leaving bouquets of flowers, teddy bears and home-made cards on the ground outside the Towers Agency. The pile of gifts gets so big that it spills over the edge of the sidewalk and the bookers have to dig a pathway to get to the front door. Some of the flowers and gifts get delivered to hospitals, but eventually the sanitation department just hauls it all away. Still the flowers keep coming.

I remember very little of the memorial service, which was at St. Patrick's Cathedral. I sat behind Gigi and Jane, but even though the church was packed with the entire who's who of the fashion world, all of them parading their most elegant black couture, I didn't bother looking around me and just stared at the ground. Ling later told me that Anna Wintour was sitting two seats to my left. According to the photos that ran in *The New York Times*, Gigi wore a black knee-length Oscar de la Renta, Ling wore Issey Miyake, and Maya wore Giorgio Armani but I have no idea what I wore. Something that Maya and Jane pulled together for me. After the service I got undressed and got in bed, and spoke to no one for two days.

Lots of collective sniffling out there. The other girls think they'll feel better if they sit around sharing Sophia stories, like the Von Trapp children singing through a thunderstorm.

"Remember when Sophia didn't have any cash to give to a homeless woman so she took off her gold bracelet and gave it to her?"

"Remember when she climbed on the roof to smoke a joint and she almost started a fire in the leaves in the gutter?"

"Remember when she hid Betty's disgusting fish mousse in the Tiffany's flower vase and then Dovima knocked it over?"

But I get no comfort from sharing my grief with anyone, because none of them have any idea how I feel. How dare they hijack my grief and make it theirs? How dare they pretend their sorrow even comes close to the pain I feel? Everyone who knew Sophia adored her, but I loved her. I really did, more than I've ever loved anyone in my life. I can't imagine ever feeling about someone the way I did about her. I miss her so much. I missed her already before she died. I missed her from the moment I was offered the part in the movie. I knew things were never going to be the same between us, but I would have spent the rest of my life trying to repair our friendship.

The only place where I feel somewhat whole is on the set of *Siren*, because when I'm filming then I'm out of my own head and inside Zoey's. In between takes I hang out mostly with Rory, because he likes to talk so much that he doesn't notice that I don't. Lucas is always on the phone with his girl-friend, and Emily is already reading script treatments for her next role, so, fortunately, nobody feels the need to talk about Sophia. Alan checks on me regularly to make sure I'm okay. I've finally started losing weight because I haven't been able to eat anything since Sophia died, I mean I've barely been able to get out of bed, but Alan isn't having that. After my first day back at work he takes me out to dinner at Minetta Tavern, where I pick at a cheeseburger.

"I need you to take care of yourself," he says. "I know you're hurting, but I can't let you waste away."

"I thought it was a good thing that I was losing weight," I answer glumly.

"Why?" Alan asks, raising his eyebrows. "Your weight is fine."

"My weight has been an issue ever since I joined the Towers Agency."

"Well, screw them, you're an actor. You're playing a healthy, beautiful young girl, and that's what you are."

I could fall madly in love with Alan if I let myself. Yes, I know…he's much too old for me, I'm confusing my fucked-up daddy-issues with love, I'm aware of the twisted psychology of it all. That's why I'm careful to keep my feelings in check. For the first time, I'm not using my sexuality to influence a man. I've seen that go wrong too often to risk having the same thing happen with Alan. I want him to be blown away by my talent, to admire my work ethic, to like me as a person, and that means I need to focus on what I bring to my role. Alan has warned me that some of the scenes are going to be emotionally rough. I know that it's going to hurt, but I also know that I can use everything that has happened to me to deliver the best performance he could ask for.

The Towers Agency wants me to go to Los Angeles for a couple of weeks after the movie wraps, so I can meet some of the casting directors there. I've never been to LA before. Alan thinks it'll be good for me to get away from New York for a while.

"Personally, I can't stand LA," Alan confides, "but I bet you'll love it. I have no doubt that they'll love you. You may even decide to stay."

I doubt that. As hard as these past few months have been, New York hasn't got the better of me yet. Ling and I have already agreed to get an apartment together when I get back. We've even found a place. It's a two-bedroom walkup on Thompson Street, and it has a fire escape that we're going to fill with tomato plants and flower pots. If it's okay with Ling, I want to get a cat.

Will I be inundated with offers for acting jobs, or will I be old news by then, waiting tables for tips at the Oleander Club? I wish it depended on how much I want to succeed, although in the end it'll come down just as much to luck. But you know, I have a good feeling about my luck. It's taken a long, long time, but I think it's finally improving.

26

MAYA

There is no amount of hurt I can inflict on myself, no amount of bleeding, that can numb this pain, not unless I bleed to death. I'm teetering at the edge of a cold black abyss, a hair's breadth from falling headlong into it, and madness beckons from its depth. I have no appetite at all and I can't even remember the last thing I ate. Every time I close my eyes I see Sophia fall, so I don't sleep anymore. I lie awake, afraid of where my thoughts go in the darkness, haunted by regret that I didn't slap the drugs out of her hands, tell Gigi she was using, turn away from her until she promised to quit. I did nothing because I needed her. I was riding on her high right alongside her. I killed her. We all did. Gigi, Theo, Jason, all her clients, everyone who wanted a piece of her. She was a star burning too fast and too bright and we all knew it, but we didn't care because we basked in her brilliance, and now we're standing, dazed, in the smoldering debris that remained when she burned herself out like a supernova.

There's another thought, even darker than the rest, that haunts me, one that I am afraid to articulate even to myself. None of us knew what was going on in Sophia's mind. All we knew was what she showed the world, a thousand pictures of perfection. When I remember the silent smile on Sophia's face the moment she fell, I wonder…was it really an accident? No one will ever know the answer, so I don't ask it out loud, not to anyone. The fact that she had enough drugs in her system to totally scramble her mind seemed to satisfy everyone that her fall was accidental, but I'll never stop wondering. And if it wasn't an accident, if she was cracking up under the pressure, why did I not notice? What kind of a shitty, self-absorbed friend was I? Campbell would have noticed, I bet, if I hadn't shoved her aside and taken her place.

Incredibly, the fashion world keeps turning. But the mere thought of getting in front of a camera again makes me want to vomit. I turn down bookings, don't go to castings, and don't answer Suzanne's daily calls checking up on me. Gigi, herself broken into a thousand pieces, doesn't even know who's coming or going.

There's one person who won't let me ignore her. Alexandra calls me after Sophia's accident makes the news, and I let her go to voicemail.

"Did you know that I had to hear from my *roommate* that you were with that model who died? That's some crazy shit, Maya. Call me back!"

I don't answer, and the next day she calls again.

"Me again. I just read about you and your friend's last photoshoot in the *New York Post* — and by the way you're the only reason I've ever read a word of the *New York Post* in my life — and are you okay? I mean I can't even imagine what you're dealing with! Call me!"

I ignore that one too because I'm ignoring everything.

"Okay, you're not going to believe this," goes her message a day later, "…or maybe you are. I just talked to Mom and first of all she had *no* idea about any of this because, as she said, she 'doesn't pay attention to entertainment news.' And then I said I was worried about you — which I am you twat, why don't you call me back?— and Mom goes, 'Oh, I'm sure she's fine, it wasn't Maya who fell off the roof.' Can you *believe* what a straight-up bitch she is sometimes? Call me back!"

Then, a couple of days later, there's another message.

"Okay you, joke's over. If you don't call me back right now I'm coming over there, and I'm going to be in a really bad mood about it because I've got tons of stuff going on but you're starting to freak me out so call me back. I'm serious, Maya!"

The message is several hours old and I really should call her, but she'll inevitably want to rehash everything that's happened and I am so very, very sick of talking about it. Instead I have a shower, letting the water run as hot as I can stand it, as though I can purify myself of the haunting guilt by steaming it out of me. I get out of the shower, my skin glowing, and put on my robe. It turns out I don't have to call Alexandra after all because as I sit on my bed combing my hair there's a knock at my bedroom door, and, true to her word, there stands my sister looking extremely put out.

"Hey Al, what are you doing here?" I ask vaguely.

"I told you I'd come if you didn't return my calls, which you didn't, so here I am. It's a big pain in the ass, I have a paper due tomorrow, and…damn, Maya, what have you been doing to yourself?"

"What are you talking about?"

"I know you just lost your friend, but my God! Look at you!"

"I don't need to look at myself. All I ever do is look at myself. I'm sick of looking at myself."

"Well let me look at you then. Jesus. What is this shit?" Al grabs my forearm and pulls back the sleeve of my robe, exposing the cuts in my skin and the bruises from my fingernails.

"Stop it!" I yank my arm free. "Go away!"

"I will not. What are you doing, you idiot? Are you trying to kill yourself?"

"Mind your own damn business!" How dare she strut her smug Ivy League ass into my room and boss me around when she NO IDEA what I've been through, no idea how hard I've struggled. "You don't get to judge me, Al. You live in a cocoon! You live in fucking Disneyland! You don't know anything about me!"

"I know you're hurting yourself," she retorts. "I've seen cadavers in better shape than you!"

"Oh, go back to school. Nobody invited you here. Go play doctor with your friends!"

But as though to remind me that she's my older sister and she's never taken orders from me, Al grabs me and pulls me off the bed. My robe falls open, and her eyes widen at the sight of my nearly naked body. I shove her away but she grabs my wrists and, holding my arms behind me, tries to drag me in front of the mirror.

"Let go of me, you psycho!" I yell.

I curse and kick at her but Al is done messing around. She holds my arms tightly against my side and turns me to face the mirror.

"Maya, stop it! Stop! Look, Maya, just look!"

I squirm in rage but I am no match for her strength, and panting, look at myself in the mirror.

"Don't you see?" Al asks. "I don't even recognize you

anymore. This isn't beautiful, Maya! This is what sick people look like."

"Fuck off, I'm not sick."

"You're not healthy. You're weak as a dishrag. Try breaking my grip. Here, I'll use one hand." She pins my forearms together, spanning them with a single hand. I struggle to break free but I can't and it's infuriating. We've always been pretty well matched in a fight but now I'm as feeble as a child and, like a child I dissolve into tears. Finally I go limp and I crumple to the floor. Al sits beside me.

"You need help, Maya," Al says, and I don't argue. I'm too tired.

Alexandra calls Dad from Sophia's room so she can talk in private. He's almost impossible to get on the phone, because we're not supposed to use his emergency number and he lets all his other calls go straight to his answering service, so we usually call Mom to get through to Dad, but Al isn't bothering with Mom anymore. I overhear words like physiological and mental evaluation, nutritional therapy, and treatment plan. I should probably be more interested in what they're saying but it all seems oddly irrelevant, as though they're talking about someone else. They can say whatever they want, but I don't see how any of those things can fit into my life. I have other stuff to think about, like how to reply to Suzanne, who's been dangling bookings in front of me like shiny lures. In just the past hour I got two new voice messages from her. I play them back while I wait for Alexandra to get off the phone.

"I know you needed some time off," Suzanne's latest message says, "but you're hotter now than you've ever been. You're at almost a million followers! *Vogue* wants to book you again! Isn't that great? And Saks Fifth Avenue wants to book you, and so does Ralph Lauren, and Revlon has you on hold. Time to get back on track, Maya. When will you be ready to work?"

I look at the bleary-eyed, shadow-faced mess of my reflection, and for the first time, instead of appraising every inch for perfection, I focus on the faded bruises where I've dug my fingernails into my arms, the scars that are becoming increasingly difficult to hide, the protruding ribs and hip bones that reveal months of deprivation and exhaustion. This is the body that I thought was so powerful, that I thought could take me anywhere I wanted to go, and just look how frail it has become.

My answer comes as clear as a bell: Never.

I'm done. Finished. And with that realization, a crushing weight suddenly lifts from my soul. I feel as though the sun has emerged after months of darkness, and I give a short, almost hysterical laugh. I've been driving myself to the brink of insanity trying to run a race that I now realize has no finish line. I thought I was in total control as long as I could manipulate my body by working it, hurting it, and starving it. But I forgot that I can't control what isn't mine, and my body isn't mine, it belongs to the Towers Agency. Alexandra is right. It's time to take ownership of my body back. And this time I'm going to be a little kinder to it.

"I WISH I could change your mind," Gigi sighs a few days later as we wait for the car that will take me to the airport.

"I hope you won't try," I answer.

"You would have been one of my really big stars, you know," Gigi says. "Millions of girls would kill to be in your shoes, and you're throwing it all away. You belong at the very top, Maya, you're so close already."

But I've seen that there's only one direction to go from the top. I want to move forward, and I see a new trajectory taking shape. It will begin with getting healthy. Dad told me he pulled a lot of strings to get me in an intensive outpatient program at the top eating disorder clinic in DC, and in return I promised I'll give it my best effort. I meant it, too. Not because I owe it to him, but because I owe it to me.

"I really am grateful for everything, Gigi. I hope we can stay friends," I say.

Gigi tilts her head and reaches out to embrace me.

"Of course we're friends. I wish you good luck in everything, Maya. And if you ever change your mind, don't hesitate to come back, do you hear me? The Towers Agency will always have a place for you."

She still thinks there's a chance she can have me, poor woman. But I am done with being had.

I wish I'd said goodbye to Campbell, but she's filming, and she won't be home until tonight. Campbell hasn't spoken much to anyone, least of all to me, since Sophia died. There are some things I wanted to tell Campbell but I never found the right time. I want to tell her that the friendship that I had with Sophia was never as real as what she and Sophia shared. I want to tell her that I was jealous of her, because Sophia truly loved her. I want to tell her I'm sorry — sorry that I wedged myself between them, and sorry that I wasn't able to save Sophia.

Campbell may not know it yet, but she's going to be alright. I'm certain of it. She may be the most gifted, the most talented, the luckiest of all of us. And the other girls? Brigitte is going to Paris in the beginning of May. Ling just landed a big campaign for L'Oreal, and she's getting enough work now to afford her own place. By the summer, Gigi's house will be full of a whole crop of new girls.

Jane helps me take my bags to the car.

"Call me and let me know how your college visits go, okay?" She says.

I've scheduled some college interviews over the coming weeks for January admission, and Jane has been really interested in the whole process. Probably because after next year she'll be going through the same thing herself. I think I might want to study Psychology. According to Alexandra all the Psychology students are halfway crazy themselves, or at least that's what the pre-med students think. Perfect, I told her. I'll fit right in.

"I will, I promise. You take care of yourself. And take care of Gigi too, will you? She needs you more than you know," I say as I hug Jane. "And hey, give my congrats to Niko and Jazz for your film being shown on CNN! That's a pretty huge achievement for a bunch of scruffy high schoolers!"

As the taxi pulls away I take one last look at Gigi's house, and at Jane waving on the front steps. I wave back, waiting for the pang of sorrow I expect to feel at leaving that world behind me, but it doesn't come, and I turn around, settle in my seat and face the direction I'm going.

THE END

ABOUT THE AUTHOR

Nathalie van Walsum Fuson was born in Bucharest to Dutch diplomat parents, and grew up in Romania, Switzerland, Brazil, New York and Washington DC. She speaks Dutch, English, Portuguese and French. As a teenager and in her twenties she modeled with the Ford Models agency in New York, and for several months lived with various other young models in the house of legendary agent Eileen Ford, an experience upon which *The Luckiest Girls* is loosely based. She studied Fine Arts at New York University and received a MA from Columbia University in Cultural Anthropology. After modeling, Nathalie worked in the field of international relief and development for several years before focusing on her fiction writing. Her short stories have appeared in *Cicada* and *The MacGuffin*. Currently Nathalie lives in Atlanta, Georgia with her husband and two teenage daughters. *The Luckiest Girls* is her debut novel.

You can follow Nathalie on Twitter at @NathalieFuson, or visit her website www.nathalievanwalsumfuson.com for news about *The Luckiest Girls* and information about upcoming works.

Made in the USA
Columbia, SC
14 November 2019

83267013R00148